Harry helped he_____
that led to his bed, and jumped up
himself to sit on the edge, beside her.

He brushed a lock of hair off her face and kissed her, and
it was a pleasant surprise, for other than one brief kiss
when he had proposed, and another in the chapel after the
wedding, he had offered no displays of affection. But this
was different. He rested his lips against hers for a moment,
moving back and forth, and then parting them with his
tongue.

The longer he kissed her, the more she was convinced
that she could feel the kiss in other parts of her body,
where his lips had not touched. And when she remarked
on it, he offered to kiss her there as well, and his lips slid to
her chin, her throat and then to her breast. It was wonderful
and strange, for it made the feelings even more intense,
and he seemed to understand, for his lips followed the
sensation lower....

* * *

The Mistletoe Wager
Harlequin® Historical #925—December 2008

Author Note

When I set out to write about Christmas in the Regency, I had to unlearn a lot of our current Christmas traditions. Much of what we do now to celebrate the season did not become popular until Victorian times. No Christmas cards or Santa, of course. And Christmas trees were still quite a novelty in the early nineteenth century.

With no television or radio to entertain them, people passed the time eating and drinking holiday foods, and playing parlor games. As I was doing the research for this story, I came across a game that didn't make it into this book. A player must answer every question asked of him with the word "sausage." When he laughs, he loses his turn.

A week later, my sons returned from summer camp. They had been surviving without electricity for a week, and had learned to play "Sausage" to pass the time.

So although the showier aspects of the Christmas season were years away, people had already found ways to amuse themselves that are still able to tame bored teenagers in the twenty-first century. Very impressive!

Merry Christmas and Happy Reading.

CHRISTINE MERRILL

The Mistletoe Wager

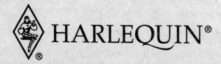

HARLEQUIN®

TORONTO • NEW YORK • LONDON
AMSTERDAM • PARIS • SYDNEY • HAMBURG
STOCKHOLM • ATHENS • TOKYO • MILAN • MADRID
PRAGUE • WARSAW • BUDAPEST • AUCKLAND

Recycling programs
for this product may
not exist in your area.

ISBN-13: 978-0-373-29525-8
ISBN-10:   0-373-29525-1

THE MISTLETOE WAGER

Copyright © 2008 by Christine Merrill

First North American publication 2008

www.eHarlequin.com

Printed in U.S.A.

man, his appearance was at the bottom. But it was on the list all the same.

The room was nearly empty, but Harry could feel the shift in attention among the few others present as though there had been a change in the wind. Men looked up from their cards and reading, watching his progress towards Tremaine. They were curious to see what would happen when the two notorious rivals met.

Very well, then. He would give them the show they hoped for. 'Tremaine!' He said it too loudly and with much good cheer.

His quarry gave a start and almost spilled his brandy. He had recognised the voice at once, and his eyes darted around the room, seeking escape. But none was to be had, for Harry stood between him and the door. Harry could see the faint light of irritation in the other man's eyes when he realised that he would have no choice but to acknowledge the greeting. 'Hello, Anneslea.' Then he returned his gaze to the paper he had been reading, showing no desire for further conversation.

How unfortunate for him. 'How goes it for you, old man, in this most blessed of holiday seasons?'

The only response was a nod, followed by a vague grunt that could have indicated satisfaction or annoyance.

Harry smiled and took a chair opposite the fire, facing Tremaine. He took a sip from the brandy that a servant had rushed to bring him. He examined the liquid in the glass, holding it out to catch the firelight. 'A good drink warms the blood on a day like this. There is a chill in the air. I've been tramping up and down Bond Street all morning. Shopping for Christmas gifts. Tailors, jewellers, whatnot. And the fixings for the celebration, of course. What's not to be had in the country must be brought back with me from town.' He waved his hand at the foolishness of it. 'I do not normally take it upon myself. But now that I am alone…' He could almost feel the ears of the others in the room, pricking to catch what he would say next.

Tremaine noticed as well, and gave a small flinch. It was most gratifying.

Harry looked up from his drink into Tremaine's startled face. 'And, by the by, how is Elise?' It was a bold conversational gambit, and he was rewarded with a slight choke from his opponent.

The other man turned to him and sat up straight, his indolence disappearing. His eyes glittered with suppressed rage. 'She is well, I think. If you care, you should go and ask her yourself. She would be glad of the call.'

She would be no such thing. As he remembered their last conversation, Elise had made it plain that if she never saw Harry again it would be too soon. 'Perhaps I will,' he answered, and smiled as though they were having a pleasant discussion about an old friend and nothing more.

It must have disappointed their audience to see the two men behaving as adults on this most delicate of subjects. But their moderate behaviour had not quelled the undercurrent of anticipation. He could see from the corner of his eye that the room had begun to fill with observers. They were reading newspapers, engaging in subdued chat, and gazing out of the bay window while sipping drinks. But every man present was taking care to be uninterested in a most focused fashion, waiting for the cross word that would set the two of them to brawling like schoolboys.

If only it were so easily settled. If Harry could have been sure of a win, he would have met his opponent on the field of honour long before now. The temptation existed to hand his jacket to the nearest servant, roll up his sleeves, raise his fists and lay the bastard out on the hearth rug. But physically, they were evenly matched. A fight would impress no one, should he lose it. And Elise would think even less of him than she did now if he was bested in public by Nicholas Tremaine.

He would have to strike where his rival could least defend himself. In the intellect.

Tremaine eased back in his chair, relaxing in the quiet, perhaps thinking that he had silenced Harry with his indifference. Poor fool. Harry set down his empty glass, made a great show of placing his hands on his knees, gave a contented sigh and continued the conversation as though there were nothing strange about it. 'Any plans for the holiday?'

'Has Elise made plans?' There was a faint reproof in the man's voice, as though he had a right to take Harry to task on that subject. Harry ignored it.

'You, I mean. Do you have plans? For Christmas?' He smiled to show all the world Elise's plans were no concern of his.

Tremaine glared. 'I am most pleased to have no plans. I intend to treat the day much as any other.'

'Really. May I offer you a bit of advice, Tremaine?'

He looked positively pained at the idea. 'If you must.'

'Try to drum up some enthusiasm towards Christmas—for her sake, at least.'

In response, Tremaine snorted in disgust. 'I do not see why I should. People make far too big a fuss over the whole season. What is it good for, other than a chance to experience diminished sunlight and foul weather while in close proximity to one's fellow man? I find the experience most unpleasant. If others choose to celebrate, I wish them well. But I do not wish to bother others with my bad mood, and I would prefer that they not bother me.' He stared directly at Harry, so there could be no doubt as to his meaning.

Perfect. Harry's smile turned sympathetic. 'Then I wonder if you will be any better suited to Elise than I was. She adores this season. She cannot help it, I suppose. It's in her blood. She waits all year in anticipation of the special foods, the mulled wine, the singing and games. When we were together she was constantly dragging trees where they were never intended to be, and then lighting candles in them until I was quite sure she meant to burn the house down for Twelfth Night. I doubt she will wish to give that up just to please you. There is no changing her when she has an idea in her head. I know from experience. It is you who must alter—to suit her.'

A variety of emotions were playing across

Tremaine's face, fighting for supremacy. Harry watched in secret enjoyment as thoughts formed and were discarded. Should he tell Anneslea what to do with his advice? It had been offered innocently enough. Accuse him of ill treatment in some way? Not possible. Should they argue, Tremaine would gain nothing, for society would find him totally in the wrong. Harry's only offence was his irrational good humour. And Tremaine was at a loss as to how to combat it.

At last he chose to reject the advice, and to ignore the mention of Elise. 'I am adamant on the subject. I have nothing against the holiday itself, but I have no patience for the folderol that accompanies it. Nor am I likely to change my mind on the subject to please another.'

'That is what I thought once.' Harry grinned. 'And now look at me.' He held out his arms, as if to prove his honest intentions. 'I'm positively overflowing with good will towards my fellow men. Of course, once you have experienced Christmas as we celebrate it at Anneslea Manor…' He paused and then snapped his fingers. 'That's it, man. Just the thing. You must come out to the house and see how the feast is properly done. That will put you to rights.'

Tremaine stared at him as though he'd gone mad. 'I will do no such thing.'

The other men in the room were listening with obvious interest now. Harry could hear chuckles and whispers of approval.

'No, I insist. You will see how the season should be shared, and it will melt your heart on the subject. I doubt there is a better gift that I could offer to Elise than to teach you the meaning of Christmas. Come to Lincoln-shire, Tremaine. We are practically family, after all.'

There was definitely a laugh from somewhere in the room, although it was quickly stifled. And then the room fell silent, waiting for the response.

If it had been a matter of fashion, or some caustic wit-ticism he was directing at another, Tremaine would have loved being the centre of attention. But today he hated the idea that he was the butt of a joke, rather than Harry. There was a redness creeping from under Tremaine's collar as his anger sought an outlet. At last he burst out, 'Not in a million years.'

'Oh, come now.' Harry pulled a face. 'We can make a bet of it. What shall it be?' He pretended to consider. 'Gentlemen, bring the book. I am willing to bet twenty pounds to Tremaine, and any takers, that he shall wish me a Merry Christmas by Twelfth Night.'

Someone ran for the betting book, and there was a rustling of hands in pockets for banknotes, pens scratch-ing IOUs, and offers to hold the stakes. It was all ac-companied by a murmur of agreement that hell would freeze before Tremaine wished anyone a Merry Christ-mas, so well known was his contempt for the season. And the chance that anything might induce him to say those particular words to Harry Pennyngton were equal to the devil going to Bond Street to buy ice skates.

But while the room was raised in chaos, the object of the wager stared steadfastly into the fire, refusing to acknowledge what was occurring.

Harry said, loud enough for all to hear over the din, 'It does not matter if you do not wish to bet, Tremaine, for the others still wish to see me try. But it will be easier to settle the thing if you will co-operate.' Then he addressed the room, 'Come out to my house in the country, all of you.' He gestured to include everyone. 'Bring your families, if you wish. There is more than enough space. Then, when Tremaine's resolve weakens, you will all be there to witness it.' He stared at the other man. 'And if it does not, if you are so sure of your position, then a wager on it will be the easiest money you could make.'

The mention of finances brought Tremaine to speech—just as Harry had known it would. 'I no longer need to make a quick twenty pounds by entering into foolish wagers. Especially not with you, Anneslea. A visit to your house at Christmas would be two weeks of tedious company to prove something I already know. It would be an attempt to change my character in a way I do not wish. It is utter nonsense.'

Harry grinned. 'You would not find it so if the wager were over something you truly desired. Now that you have received your full inheritance, I suppose twenty quid is nothing to you. I have no real desire to spend a fortnight in your company either, Tremaine. For I swear you are one of the most disagreeable fops in Christendom. But I do care for Elise's happiness. And if she means to have you, then you must become a better man than you are.' He touched a finger to his chin, pretending to think. 'I have but to find the thing you want, and you will take the wager, right enough.' Then he reached into his pocket and pulled the carefully worded letter from his breast pocket. 'Perhaps this will change your mind.'

He offered it to Tremaine and watched the colour drain from the man's face as he read the words. Others in the room leaned forward to catch a glimpse of the paper, but Harry stepped in to block their view.

'For Tremaine's eyes only, please. This is a matter between gentlemen.' For a moment he gave vent to his true feelings and let the words drip with the irony he felt at having to pretend good fellowship for the bastard in the seat in front of him. Then he turned back to the crowd. 'The side bet will in no way affect our fun. And it will be just the thing to convince our victim of the need to take a holiday trip to Anneslea.'

Or so he hoped. Tremaine was still staring at his offer, face frozen in surprise. When he looked up at Harry their eyes locked in challenge. And it was Tremaine who looked away first. But he said nothing, merely folded the paper and tucked it into his own pocket before exiting the room.

Harry smiled to himself, oblivious of the chaos around him.

And now he had but to wait.

Chapter Two

Elise Pennyngton straightened her skirt, smoothed her hair, and arranged herself on the divan in her London sitting room so that she could appear startled when the door to the room opened. Her guest was in the hall, just outside, and it would be careless of her to let him find her in true disarray. With a little effort she could give the impression that she awaited him eagerly, without appearing to be desperate for his company.

As he paused in the open doorway, awaiting her permission to enter, she looked at Nicholas Tremaine and steeled her nerves. Taking a lover was the first item on her list, if she truly wished to be emancipated from her husband. And if she must have male companionship, Nick was the logical choice. In her mind, he had been filed under 'unfinished business' for far too long. He was as elegantly handsome as he had been when he'd first proposed to her.

And she'd turned him away and chosen Harry.

But, since Harry did not want her any more, she was right back to where she had started.

'Nicholas.' She pushed the annoying thoughts of Harry from her mind, and held out her hands to the dashing gentleman before her.

He stepped forward and took them, raising her fingers to his mouth and giving them a brief touch of his lips. 'Elise.' His eyes were still the same soul-searching blue, and his hair just as dark as the day they'd met, although it had been more than five years.

There was no grey in her hair, either. And she took special care that when they met she looked as fresh and willing as she had at eighteen. Her coiffure was impeccable and her manner welcoming. And her dress was dotted with sprigs of flowers that perfectly matched the blue of her eyes.

Or so Harry had always claimed.

She gave a little shake of her head to clear away that troublesome memory, and gazed soulfully at the man still holding her hands. She was not the naïve young girl he had courted. But surely the passage of time on her face had not been harsh?

If he noticed the change the years had made in her, he gave no reason to think it bothered him. He returned her gaze in the same absently devoted way he always had, and she could see by his smile of approval that he found her attractive.

'Come, sit with me.' In turn, she took his hands in hers, and pulled him down to sit on the divan beside her. He took a place exactly the right distance away from her body—close enough to feel intimate, but far enough away not to incite comment should someone walk in on them together.

She hoped that she had not misunderstood his interest. For it would be very embarrassing if he were resistant to the idea, when she had raised sufficient courage to suggest that they take their relationship to a deeper level. But she had begun to suspect that the event would not happen until she had announced herself ready. It would be so much easier if he were to make the first move. But he had made it clear that he would not rush her into intimacy until she was sure, in her heart, that she would not regret her actions.

For a well-known rake, he was annoyingly protective of her honour.

'Are you not glad to see me?' She gave a hopeful pout.

'Of course, darling.' And after a moment he leaned forward to kiss her on the lips.

There was nothing wrong with the few kisses they had exchanged thus far. Nicholas clearly knew how to give a kiss. There was no awkwardness when their mouths met, no bumping of noses or shuffling of feet. His hands held her body with just the right level of strength, hinting at the ability to command passion without taking unwelcome liberties. His lips were firm on hers, neither too wet nor too dry, his breath was fresh, his cheek was smooth.

When he held her she was soft in his arms, languid but not overly forward, giving no sign that he need proceed faster, but neither did she signal him to desist immediately.

The whole presentation smacked of a game of chess. Each move was well planned. They could both see the action several turns ahead. Checkmate was inevitable.

Of course if it all seemed to lack a certain passion, and felt ever so slightly calculated, who was she to complain of it? She had thought about Nicholas in the darkest hours of her unhappy marriage and wondered how different it might be had she chosen otherwise. Soon she would know.

And if it would ever be possible to gain a true divorce from Harry she must accept the fact that at some point she would need to take a lover, whether she wanted one or not. Her confirmed infidelity was the only thing she was sure the courts might recognise as grounds. But even then, whether she could persuade her husband to make the effort to cast her off was quite another matter.

The matter was simple enough, after all. Harry must have an heir. Since she had been unable to provide one for him, he would be better off free of her while he was still young enough to try with another. But she had grown to see a possible divorce as one more thing in her marriage for which she would need to do the lion's share of the work, if she wished the task accomplished. The last five years had proved that Harry Pennyngton could not be bothered with serious matters, no matter how she might try to gain his attention.

And now Nicholas had pulled away from her, as though he could not manage to continue the charade.

She frowned, and he shook his head in embarrassment. 'I'm sorry if I seem distracted. But the most extraordinary thing happened at White's just now, and we must speak of it. I received an invitation to Christmas.'

She stared at him with a barely raised eyebrow. 'Hardly extraordinary, darling. Christmas is less than two weeks away. It is a bit late, I suppose. You should have made plans by now.'

'Certainly not.' Nicholas, had he had feathers, would have ruffled them. 'I do not make it a habit of celebrating the holiday. It is much better to use the time productively, in reading or some other quiet pursuit, and to avoid gatherings all together. With so many others running about country drawing rooms like idiots, hiding slippers and bluffing blind men, it makes for an excellent time of peaceful reflection.'

Nicholas Tremaine's aversion to Christmas was well known and marked upon. She had commented on it herself. And then she had placed it on the list of things that she would change about him, should their relationship grow to permanence. 'You are most unreasonable on the subject, Nicholas. If someone has chosen to call you on it, it can hardly be a surprise.'

'But the invitation came from a most unlikely source.' He paused. 'Harry. He's asked me up to the house 'til Twelfth Night, and has bet twenty quid to all takers that he can imbue me with the spirit of the season. He says the celebration at Anneslea Manor is always top drawer, and that I cannot fail to bend. And he invited all within earshot to come as well.' He paused. 'I just thought it rather odd. He's obviously not keeping bachelor's hall if he thinks to hold a house party.' He paused again, as though afraid of her reaction. 'And to induce me to yield he gave me this.' He removed a folded sheet of paper from his pocket and handed it to her.

She read it.

I, Harry Pennyngton, swear upon my honour that if I cannot succeed in making Nicholas Tremaine wish me a Merry Christmas in my home, by January the fifth of next year, I shall make every attempt to give my estranged wife, Elise Pennyngton, the divorce that she craves, and will do nothing to stand in the way of her marriage to Nicholas Tremaine or any other man.

It was signed 'Anneslea', in her husband's finest hand, and dated yesterday.

She threw it to the floor at her feet. Damn Harry and his twisted sense of humour. The whole thing had been prepared before he'd even entered into the bet. He had gone to the club with the intent of trapping Nicholas into one of his stupid little jokes, and he had used her to bait the hook. How dared he make light of something that was so important? Turn the end of their marriage into some drawing room wager and, worse yet, make no mention of it to her? Without thinking, she reverted to her mother tongue and gave vent to her frustrations over marriage, divorce, men in general, and her husband in particular.

Nicholas cleared his throat. 'Really, Elise, if you must go on so, please limit yourself to English. You know I have no understanding of German.'

She narrowed her eyes. 'It is a good thing that you do not. For you would take me to task for my language, and give me another tiresome lecture in what is or is not proper for a British lady. And, Nicholas, I am in no mood for it.'

'Well, foul language is not proper for an English gentleman, either. Nor is that letter. If you understood the process, Elise… He is offering something that he cannot give. Only the courts can decide if you are granted a divorce, and the answer will often be no.'

'We will not know until we have tried,' she insisted.

'But he has done nothing to harm you, has he?' Nick's face darkened for a moment. 'For if he has treated you cruelly then it is an entirely different matter. I will call the man out and we will finish this quickly, once and for all, in a way that need not involve the courts.'

'No. No. There is no reason to resort to violence,' she said hurriedly. 'He has not hurt me.' She sighed. 'Not physically.'

Nicholas expelled an irritated sigh in response. 'Then not at all, in the eyes of the court. Hurt feelings are no reason to end a marriage.'

'The marriage should not have taken place at all,' she argued. 'There were no feelings at all between us when we married. And as far as I can tell it has not changed in all these years.' *On his part, at least.*

'It is a natural thing for ardour to cool with time. But he must have felt something back then,' Nicholas argued. 'Or he would not have made the offer.'

Elise shook her head and tried not to show the pain that

the statement brought her. For she had flattered herself into believing much the same thing when she had accepted Harry's offer. 'When he decided to take a wife it was no different for him than buying an estate, or a horse, or any other thing. He did not so much marry me as collect me. And now he has forgotten why he wanted me in the first place. I doubt he even notices that I am gone.'

Nicholas added, in an offhand manner, 'He enquired after you, by the way. I told him you were well.'

'Did you, now?' Elise could feel the temper rising in her. If Harry cared at all for her welfare, he should enquire in person, not make her the subject of talk at his club. 'Thank you so much for relaying the information.'

Nick looked alarmed as he realised that he had mis-gauged her response to his innocent comment. 'I had to say something, Elise. It does not do to ignore the man if he wishes to be civil about this. If you truly want your freedom, is it not better that he is being co-operative?'

'Co-operative? I am sure that is the last thing on his mind, no matter how this appears. He is up to something.' She narrowed her eyes. 'And how did you respond to his invitation?'

Tremaine laughed. 'I did not dignify it with a response. It is one thing, Elise, for us to pretend that there is nothing unusual between us when we meet by accident in the club. But I hardly think it's proper for me to go to the man's home for the holiday.'

She shook her head. 'You do not seriously think that there was anything accidental in your meeting with my husband, Nicholas? He wished to let me know that he is celebrating in my absence. And to make me wonder who he has for hostess.' She furrowed her brow. 'Not his sister, certainly.' She ran down a list in her head of women who might be eager to step into her place.

'Harry has a sister?' Nicholas asked, surprised.

'A half-sister, in Shropshire. A vicar's daughter. Far too proper to give herself over to merriment and run off to Anneslea Manor for a house party.'

Nicholas frowned. 'You would be surprised what vicar's daughters can get up to when allowed to roam free. Especially at Christmas.'

Elise shook her head. 'I doubt it is her. More likely my husband is trying to make me jealous by sending the hint that he has replaced me.' And it annoyed her to find that he was succeeding.

'It matters not to me, in any case,' Nicholas replied. 'A tiresome sister is but one more reason for me to avoid Anneslea—the Manor and the man.'

If Nick refused the invitation then she would never know the truth. A lack of response, an unwillingness to play his silly game, would be proper punishment for Harry, and might dissuade him from tormenting her, but it would do nothing to settle her mind about her husband's reason for the jest.

And then a thought occurred to her. 'If we are doing nothing wrong, Nicholas, then there can be no harm in a visit, surely?' Perhaps if she could persuade him to go she would discover what Harry really intended by extending the offer.

Nick was looking at her as though she were no more

trustworthy than her husband. 'I see no good in it, either. Harry is all "Hail fellow, well met," when we meet in the club, darling. He is being excessively reasonable about the whole thing. Which is proof that he is not the least bit reasonable on the subject. He wants you to come home, and is trying to throw me out of counte-nance with his good humour. And he is succeeding. I would rather walk into a lion's den than take myself off to his home for the holiday. God knows what will happen to me once he has me alone.'

'Do not be ridiculous, darling. It is all decided between Harry and me. There was nothing for us to do but face the facts: we do not suit.' She put on her bravest smile. 'We are living separately now, and he is quite content with it. I suspect we will end as better friends apart than we were together. And, while I do not doubt that he has an ulterior motive, I am sure he means you no real harm by this offer.'

'Ha!' Tremaine's laugh was of triumph, and he pointed to her. 'You do it as well. No truly content couple would work so hard to show happiness over their separation. It is a façade, Elise. Nothing more. If I go to Harry's little party in Lincolnshire, I suspect we will be at each other's throats before the week is out. The situation is fraught with danger. One too many cups of wassail, and he will be marching me up a snowy hillside for pistols at dawn.'

'Harry challenge you over me?' She laughed at the idea. 'That is utter nonsense, Nicholas, and you know it.'

'I know no such thing.'

'If Harry were the sort to issue challenges, then it is far more likely that I would be there still, celebrating at his side. But he has given no evidence of caring at all, Nicholas, over what I say or do.' She tried to keep the pain from her voice, for she had promised herself to stop hurting over that subject long ago. 'It is possible that his invitation was nothing more than it sounded. I know the man better than anyone alive, and I can find many defects in him, but I do not fault his generous spirit.'

He had certainly been generous enough to her. After a two-month separation he was still paying all her bills, no matter the size. If he truly cared he would be storming into her apartments, throwing her extravagances back in her face, and demanding that she remove from London and return home immediately. She gritted her teeth.

'But his sense of humour leaves much to be desired. Inviting you for the holiday could be nothing more serious than one of his little pranks. It is a foolish attempt to be diverting at Christmas.'

Tremaine nodded. 'As you will. I will thank him for the generosity of his offer, which has no ulterior motive. And if what you say is true he will be equally polite when I decline it.'

'You will do no such thing. Accept him at once.'

He stared at her without speaking, until she began to fear that she had overstepped the bounds of even such a warm friendship as theirs.

'I only meant,' she added sweetly, 'that you will never know what his true intentions are until you test them. And if we are to continue together, the issue will come up, again and again. If he is mistaking where I mean to make my future, the sooner Harry learns to see you as a part of my life, the better for all concerned. And you need to see that he can do you no harm once he has accepted the truth.'

'But Christmas is not the best time to establish this,' Tremaine warned. 'In my experience, it is the season most likely to make fools of rational men and maniacs of fools. There is a reason I have avoided celebrations such as this before now. Too many situations begin with one party announcing that "we are all civilised adults" and end with two adults rolling on the rug, trading either blows or kisses.'

'I had no idea you were so frightened of my husband.' She hoped her sarcasm would coax him to her side.

'I am not afraid, darling. But neither do I wish to tempt fate.'

She smiled. 'If it helps to calm your nerves, I will accompany you.'

He started at the idea. 'I doubt he meant to invite you, Elise.'

'Nonsense again, Nicholas. It does not matter what he meant to do. I do not need an invitation to visit my own home.' And it would serve Harry right if she chose to put in an appearance without warning him. 'It is not as if we need to go for the duration of the party, after all. A day or two…'

'All three of us? Under the same roof?' Tremaine shuddered. 'Thank you, no. Your idea is even worse than his. But if you wish to visit Harry, you are free to go without me.'

'If I visit Harry alone, then people will have the wrong impression,' she insisted.

'That you have seen the error of your ways and are returning to your husband?'

'Exactly. But if we visit as a couple then it will be understood. And we will not go for the holiday. We need stay only a few hours at most.'

He covered his brow with his hand. 'You would have me traipsing halfway across England for a visit of a few hours? We would spend days on the road, Elise. It simply is not practical.'

'All right, then. We will stay long enough to win Harry's silly bet and gain his promise that he will seek a divorce.' She tapped the letter with her hand. 'Although he probably meant the offer in jest, he has put it in writing. And he would never be so base as to go back on his word if you win.'

If Harry was willing to lose without a fight, then she had been right all along: their marriage was of no value to him, and he wanted release as much as she wished to set him free. But she would never know the truth if she could not persuade Nicholas to play along.

Then a thought struck her, and she gathered her courage along with her momentum. 'And afterwards we will return to London, and I will give you your Christmas present.'

'I have given you my opinion of the holidays, Elise. It will not be necessary to exchange gifts, for I do not mean to get you anything in any case.'

'I was thinking,' she said, 'of a more physical token of gratitude.' She hoped that the breathiness in her tone would be taken for seduction, and not absolute terror at making the final move that would separate her permanently from the man she loved. But if her love was not returned, and there were no children to care for, then there was no reason to turn back. She ignored her rioting feelings and gave Nicholas a slow smile.

Nicholas stared at her, beginning to comprehend. 'If we visit your husband for Christmas? You cannot mean…'

'Oh, yes, darling. I do.' She swallowed and gave an emphatic nod. 'I think it is time to prove that my marriage is every bit as dead as I claim. If you are convinced that Harry carries a torch for me, or that I still long for his attention, then see us together. I will prove to you that your ideas are false. And if it is true that he wants me back, your presence will prove to him that it is hopeless. We will come away from Lincolnshire with everything sorted. And afterwards we will go somewhere we can celebrate in private. I will be most enthusiastically grateful to have the matter settled.' And she leaned forward and kissed him.

There was none of the careful planning in this kiss that had been in the others, for she had taken him unawares. She took advantage of his lack of preparation to see to it that, when their lips parted from each other, his defences were destroyed and he was quite willing to see her side of the argument.

When he reached for her again, she pulled out of his grasp. 'After,' she said firmly. 'We cannot continue as we

Chapter Three

Harry crossed the threshold of Anneslea Manor with his usual bonhomie. It had always been his way to treat everyone, from prince to stablehand, as though he were happy to be in their presence and wished them to be happy as well. If Rosalind Morley had not been in such a temper with him, she could not have helped but greet him warmly. She could feel her anger slipping away, for it was hard not to be cheerful in his presence.

Although his wife had managed it well enough.

'Dear sister!' He held out open arms to her, smiling.

She crossed hers in front of her chest and stood blocking his entrance, in no mood to be charmed. 'Half-sister, Harry.'

'But no less dear for it.' He was not the least bit dissuaded, and hugged her despite her closed arms, leaning down to plant a kiss on the top of her head. 'Did you receive my letter?'

'I most certainly did. And a very brief missive it was.

It arrived three days ago, missing all of the important details, and strangely late in the season. I wish to know what you are about, sending such a thing at such a time.'

He tipped his head to the side. 'Sending plans for Christmas? I should think this would be the most logical time to send them. It is nearing the day, after all.'

'Aha!' She poked him in the chest with a finger. 'You know it, then? You have not forgotten the date?'

'December twentieth,' he answered, unperturbed.

'Then you do not deny that in the next forty-eight hours a horde will descend upon us?'

'Hardly a horde, Rosalind. I invited a few people for Christmas, that is all.'

'It will seem like a horde,' she snapped, 'once they are treated to what is in the larder. You said to expect guests. But you cannot tell me who, or when, or even exactly how many.'

'It was a spur-of-the-moment invitation, to the gentlemen at the club,' he said, and his gaze seemed to dart from hers. 'I am not sure how many will respond to it.'

'And what am I to give them when they arrive? Napoleon had more food in Russia than we have here.'

'No food?' He seemed genuinely surprised by the idea that planning might be necessary before throwing a two-week party. If this was his normal behaviour, then Rosalind began to understand why his wife had been cross enough to leave him.

'With Elise gone, Harry, the house has been all but shut up. The servants are airing the guest rooms, and I have set the cook to scrambling for what is left in the village, but you cannot expect me to demand some poor villager to give us his goose from the ovens at the baker. We must manage with whatever is left. It will be thin fare.'

'I am sure the guests will be content with what they have. We have a fine cellar.'

'Good drink and no food is a recipe for disaster,' she warned, trying not to think of how she had learned that particular lesson.

'Do not worry so, little one. I'm sure it will be fine. Once they see the tree they will forget all about dinner.'

'What tree?' She glanced out of the window.

'The Christmas tree, of course.'

'This is some custom of Elise's, is it?'

'Well, of course.' He smiled as though lost in memory. 'She decorates a pine with paper stars, candles and gingerbread. That sort of thing. I have grown quite used to it.'

'Very well for you, Harry. But this is not anything that I am accustomed to. Father allows only the most minimal celebration. I attend church, of course. And he writes a new sermon every Advent. But he does not hold with such wild abandon when celebrating the Lord's birth.'

Harry rolled his eyes at her, obviously amused by her lack of spirit. 'It is rather pagan, I suppose. Not in your father's line at all. But perfectly harmless. And very much fun—as is the Yule Log. You will see.'

'Will I?' She put her hands on her hips. 'I doubt I shall have time to enjoy it if I am responsible for bringing it about. Because, Harry, someone must find this tree and have it brought to the house. And there is still the question of finding a second goose, or perhaps a turkey. If I am to feed a large group, one bird will not be enough.'

'And you must organise games. Do not forget the games.' He held up his fingers, ticking things off an imaginary list. 'And see to the decorations in the rest of the house.'

She raised her hands in supplication. 'What decorations?'

'Pine boughs, mistletoe, holly, ivy. Elise has a little something in each room.' He sighed happily. 'No matter where you went, you could not forget the season.'

'Oh, it is doubtful that I shall be able to forget the season, no matter how much I might try.'

He reached out to her and enveloped her in another brotherly hug. 'It will be all right, darling. You needn't worry so. Whatever you can manage at such short notice will be fine. Before I left London I filled the carriage with more than enough vagaries and sweetmeats. And on the way, I stopped so that the servants might gather greenery. When they unload it all you will find you are not so poorly supplied as you might think.'

Rosalind took a deep breath to calm herself, and tried to explain the situation again, hoping that he would understand. 'A gathering of this size will still be a challenge. The servants obey me sullenly, if at all. They do not wish a new mistress, Harry. They want Elise back.'

His face clouded for a moment, before he smiled again. 'We will see what can be done on that front soon enough. But for now, you must do the best you can. And look on this as an opportunity, not an obstacle. It will give my friends a chance to meet you. They do wonder, you know, that you are never seen in London. I think some of them doubt that I have any family at all. They think that I have imagined the wonderful sister I describe.'

'Really, Harry. You make me sound terribly antisocial. It is not by choice that I avoid your friends. Father needs me at home.'

He was looking down at her with a frown of concern. 'I worry about you, sequestered in Shropshire alone with your father. He is a fine man, but an elderly vicar cannot be much company for a spirited girl.'

It was perfectly true, but she smiled back in denial. 'It is not as if I have no friends in the country.'

He waved a hand. 'I am sure they are fine people. But the young gentlemen of your acquaintance must be a bit thick in the head if they have not seen you for the beauty you are. I would have thought by now that there would be men lined up to ask your father for your hand.'

'I am no longer, as you put it, "a spirited girl", Harry. I do not need you to act as matchmaker—nor Father's permission should any young men come calling.' And she had seen that they hadn't, for she had turned them all away. The last thing she needed was Harry pointing out the illogicality of her refusals. 'I am of age, and content to remain unmarried.'

He sighed. 'So you keep telling me. But I mean to see you settled. And if I can find someone to throw in your path…'

'Then I shall walk politely around him and continue on my way.'

'With you so far from home, you could at least pretend to need a chaperon,' he said. 'Your father made me promise to take the role, and to prevent you from any mis-alliances. I was quite looking forward to failing at it.'

Her father would have done so, since he did not trust her in the slightest. But she could hardly fault Harry for his concern, so she curtseyed to him. 'Very well. I will send you any serious contenders for my hand. Although I assure you there will be no such men, nor does it bother me. I am quite content to stay as I am.'

He looked at her critically, and for a change he was serious. 'I do not believe you. I do not know what happened before your father sent you to rusticate, or why it set you so totally off the masculine gender, but I wish it could be otherwise.'

'I have nothing against the masculine gender,' she argued. In fact, she had found one in particular to be most to her liking. 'I could think of little else for the brief time I was in London, before Father showed me the error of my behaviour and sent me home.'

'You are too hard on yourself, darling. To have been obsessed with love and marriage made you no different from other girls of your age.'

'I was still an ill-mannered child, and my rash be-haviour gave many a distaste of me.' She had heard the words from his lips so many times that she sounded almost like her father as she said them. 'I am sure that the men of London breathed a hearty sigh of relief when

I was removed from their numbers before the season even began.' At least that was true. At least one of them had been more than glad to see the last of her.

'But it has been years, Rosalind. Whatever it was that proved the last straw to your father, it has been forgotten by everyone else. I think you would find, if you gave them a chance, that there are many men worthy of your affection and eager to meet you. There are a dozen in my set alone who would do fine for you. But if you insist on avoiding London, then I must bring London to you.'

'Harry,' she said, with sudden alarm, 'tell me you have not done what I suspect you have.'

'And whatever is that, sister dear?'

'You have not used the Christmas holiday as an opportunity to fill this house with unattached men in an attempt to make a match where none is desired.'

He glanced away and smiled. 'Not fill the house, precisely.'

And suddenly she knew why he had been so cagey with the guest list, giving her rough numbers but no names. 'It is all ruined,' she moaned.

'I fail to see how,' he answered, being wilfully oblivious again.

'There should be a harmonious balance in the genders if a party is to be successful. And it sounds as though you have not invited a single family with a marriageable daughter, nor any young ladies at all. Tell me I will not be the lone partner to a pack of gentleman from your club.'

He laughed. 'You make them sound like a Barbarian invasion, Rosalind. You are being far too dramatic.'

She shook her finger at him. 'You will see the way of things when we stand up for a dance and there is only me on the ladies' side.'

He ignored her distress. 'I do not care—not if you are presented to best advantage, dear one. This party will give you a chance to shine like the jewel you are.'

'I will appear if anyone notices me at all, to be a desperate spinster.'

'Wrong again. You assure me you are not desperate, and you are hardly old enough to be a spinster.' He held her by the hands and admired her. 'At least you certainly do not look old enough.'

'That has been the problem all along,' she said. 'When I came of age I looked too young to consider.'

'Many women long for your problem, dear. When you are too old, I expect they will hate you for your youth. It is something to look forward to.'

'Small comfort.'

'And you needn't worry. You will not be the only female, and I have not filled the house to the roof with prospective suitors. I believe you will find the company quite well balanced.' He smiled as though he knew a secret. 'But should you find someone present who is to your liking, and if he should like you as well, then I will be the happiest man in England. And to that end, I wish you to play hostess to my friends and to try to take some joy in it for yourself, even though it means a great deal of work.' He was looking at her with such obvious pride and hope for her own welfare that she felt churlish for denying him his party.

'Very well, Harry. Consider my good behaviour to be a Christmas gift to you. Let us hope, by the end of the festivities, that the only cooked geese are in the kitchen.'

For the next two days, Rosalind found herself buffeted along with the increasing speed of events. Harry's carriage was unpacked, and servants were set to preparations. But they seemed to have no idea how to proceed without continual supervision, or would insist that they knew exactly what was to be done and then do the tasks in a manner that was obviously wrong. It was just as it had been since the moment she had stepped over the threshold and into Elise's shoes. At least she'd managed to gain partial co-operation, by begging them to do things as Elise would have wanted them done, as proof of their loyalty to her and in honour of her memory.

It sounded to all the world as if the woman had died, and she'd been left to write her eulogy instead of run her house. But the servants had responded better to her moving speech then they had to anything she could offer in the way of instruction. At some point, she would have to make her brother stir himself sufficiently to retrieve his wife from London. For Rosalind was not welcome in the role of mistress here, nor did she desire it. But it must wait until after the holidays, for she had made Harry a promise to help him for Christmas and she meant to stick to it, until the bitter end.

At last the house was in some semblance of readiness, and the guests began to come—first in a trickle and then a flood. Arrivals were so frequent that the front door was propped open, despite the brisk wind that had arisen. A steady fall of snow had begun in the late afternoon and followed people across the stone floor in eddies and swirls. She busied herself with providing direction to servants, and praying that everyone would manage to find their way to the same room as their baggage.

Couples and families were talking loudly, shaking the snow from their coats and wraps and remarking in laughing tones about the deteriorating condition of the roads and the need for mulled wine, hot tea, and a warm fire. It seemed that Rosalind was continually shouting words of welcome into an ever-changing crowd, promising comfort and seasonal joy once they were properly inside, making themselves at home. Just to the left, the library had been prepared to receive the guests, for the sitting room would be packed solid with bodies should she try to fit all the people together in that room. The great oak reading tables had been pushed to the edges of the room and heaped with plates of sandwiches and sweets, along with steaming pots of tea, carafes of wine and a big bowl of punch.

There were sounds of gratitude and happiness in response, and for a moment she quite forgot the trouble of the last week's preparation. And although at times she silently cursed her brother for causing the mess, she noticed that he was behaving strangely as he moved through the hubbub, making many restless journeys up and down the stairs. It was as if he was anticipating something or someone in particular, and his pleasure at each new face seemed to diminish, rather than increase, when he did not see the person he expected.

And then the last couple stepped through the open doorway.

'Rosalind!' Elise threw her arms wide and encompassed her in an embrace that was tight to the point of discomfort. 'So you are the one Harry's found to take the reins.'

'Elise?' The name came out of her as a phlegm-choked moan. 'I had no idea that Harry had invited you.'

'Neither does Harry,' Elise whispered with a conspiratorial grin. 'But how can he mind? This was my house for so long that I think I should still be welcome in it, for a few days at least. And since he made such a kind point of inviting my special friend, he must have meant to include me. Otherwise he would have left me quite alone in London for the holidays. That cannot have been his intention.'

'Special friend?' Elise could not mean what she was implying. And even if she did, Rosalind prayed she would not have been so bold as to bring him here. If Elise had taken a lover, Rosalind suspected that it was very much Harry's intention to split the two up.

'Have you met? I doubt it. Here, Nicholas—meet little Rosalind, my husband's half-sister. She is to be our hostess.'

When she saw him, Rosalind felt her smile freeze as solid as the ice on the windowpanes. Nicholas Tremaine was as fine as she remembered him, his hair dark, his face a patrician mask, with a detached smile. It held none of the innocent mirth of their first meeting but all of the world-weariness she had seen in him even then. And, as it had five years before, her heart stopped and then gave an unaccustomed leap as she waited for him to notice her. 'How do you do, Mr…?'

But it was too much to hope that he had forgotten her. 'I believe we've met,' he said, and then his jaw clenched so hard that his lips went white. He had paused on the doorstep, one boot on the threshold, snow falling on his broad shoulders, the flakes bouncing off them to melt at his feet. His clothing was still immaculate and in the first stare of fashion. But now it was of a better cut, and from more expensive cloth than it had been. It hardly mattered. For when she had first seen him, Nicholas Tremaine had been the sort of man to make poverty appear elegant.

If his change in tailor was an indication, his fortunes had improved, and wealth suited him even better. In any other man, she would have thought that pause in the doorway a vain attempt to add drama to his entrance, while allowing the audience to admire his coat. But she suspected that now Tremaine had seen her he was trying to decide whether it would be better to enter the house or run back towards London—on foot, if necessary.

The pause continued as he struggled to find the correct mood. Apparently he'd decided on benign courtesy, for he smiled, although a trifle coldly, and said, 'We met in London. It was several years ago, although I cannot remember the exact circumstances.'

Liar. She was sure that he remembered the whole

incident in excruciating detail. As did she. She hoped her face did not grow crimson at the recollection.

'But I had no idea,' he continued, 'that you were Harry's mysterious sister.'

Was she the only one who heard the silent words, *Or I would never have agreed to come?* But he was willing to pretend ignorance, possibly because the truth reflected no better on him than it had on her, so she must play the game as well.

'I am his half-sister. Mother married my father when Harry was just a boy. He is a vicar.' She paused. 'My father, that is. Because of course Harry is not…' She was so nervous that she was rambling, and she stopped herself suddenly, which made for an embarrassing gap in the conversation.

'So I've been told.'

'I had no idea that you would be a guest here.' *Please*, she willed, *believe I had no part in this.*

If the others in the room noticed the awkwardness between them, they gave no indication. Elise's welcome was as warm as if there had been nothing wrong. 'How strange that I've never introduced you. Rosalind was in London for a time the year we…the year I married Harry.' She stumbled over her own words for a moment, as though discovering a problem, and Rosalind held her breath, fearing that Elise had noticed the coincidence. But then the moment passed, and Elise took Tremaine's arm possessively. 'I am sure we will all be close friends now. I have not had much chance to know you, Rosalind, since you never leave home. I hope that we can change that. Perhaps now that you are old enough, your father will allow you to come to London and visit?'

'Of course,' she replied, fighting the temptation to remind Elise that Rosalind was her senior by almost two months. Her age did not signify, for her father would never let her travel, and certainly not to visit her brother's wife. If Elise meant to carry on a public affair, no decent lady could associate with her. And the identity of the gentleman involved made an embarrassing situation into a mortifying one.

Elise continued to act as if nothing was wrong. 'I am glad that you have come to stay with Harry. He needs a keeper if he has taken to engaging in daft wagers for Christmas. And this party will be an excellent opportunity for you to widen your social circle.'

'Wagers?' She looked at her sister-in-law with helpless confusion. And then she asked, 'What has Harry done now?'

Elise laughed. 'Has he forgotten to tell you, little one, of the reason for this party? How typical of him. He's bet the men at the club that he can make Mr Tremaine wish him a Merry Christmas. But Nick is most adamant in his plan to avoid merriment. I have had no impact on him, and you know my feelings on the subject of Christmas fun. It will be interesting to see if you can move him, now that you are in charge of the entertainments here.'

'Oh.' This was news, thought Rosalind. For at one time Nicholas Tremaine had been of quite a different opinion about the holiday, much to their mutual regret.

But there was no reason to mention it, for Tremaine seemed overly focused on his Garrick and his hat, as though wishing to look anywhere than at his hostess.

Now Elise was unbuttoning her cloak, and calling for a servant, treating this very much as if it was still her home. It was even more annoying to see the servants responding with such speed, when they would drag their feet for her. It was clear that Elise was mistress here, not her. Rosalind's stomach gave a sick lurch. Let her find her own way to her room, and take her lover as well. She signalled to the servants to help Tremaine, and turned to make an escape.

And then she saw Harry, at the head of the stairs. The couple in the doorway had not noticed him as yet, but Rosalind could see his expression as he observed them. He saw Tremaine first, and there was a narrowing of the eyes, a slight smile, and a set to the chin that hinted of a battle to come. But then he looked past his adversary to the woman behind him.

Resolution dissolved into misery. The look of pain on his face was plain to see, should any observe him. Then he closed his eyes and took a gathering breath. When he opened them again he was his usual carefree self. He started down the stairs, showing to all the world that there was not a thing out of the ordinary in entertaining one's wife and her lover as Christmas guests.

'Tremaine, you have decided to take up my offer after all.' He reached out to clasp the gentleman's hand, and gave him a hearty pat on the back that belied his look of a moment earlier. 'We shall get you out of the blue funk you inhabit in this jolly time.'

Tremaine looked, by turns, alarmed and suspicious. 'I seriously doubt it.'

'But I consider it my duty,' Harry argued. 'For how could I entrust my wife to the keeping of a man who cannot keep this holiday in his heart? She adores it, sir. Simply adores it.' There was the faintest emphasis on the word 'wife', as though he meant to remind Tremaine of the facts in their relationship.

'Really, Harry. You have not "entrusted" me to anyone. You speak as though I were part of the entail.' Pique only served to make Elise more beautiful, and Rosalind wondered if it was a trick that could be learned, or if it must be bred in.

'And Elise.' Harry turned to her, putting a hand on each shoulder and leaning forward to kiss her.

She turned a cold cheek to him, and he stopped his lips just short of it, kissing the air by her face before releasing her to take her wrap. 'This is most unexpected. I assumed, when you said that you never wished to set foot over my threshold again…' he leaned back to stare into her eyes '…that you would leave me alone.'

Elise's smile was as brilliant as the frost glittering from the trees, and as brittle. 'When I heard that you wished to extend your hospitality to Nicholas, I assumed that you were inviting me as well. We are together now, you know.' There was a barb in the last sentence, but Harry gave no indication that he had been wounded by it.

'Of course. And if it will truly make you happy, then I wish you well in it. Come in, come in. You will take your death, standing in the cold hall like this.' He looked out into the yard. 'The weather is beastly, I must say. All the better to be inside, before a warm fire.'

Tremaine cast a longing glance over his shoulder, at the road away from the house, before Harry shut the door behind him. 'Come, the servants will show you to your rooms.'

'Where have you put us?' Elise asked. 'I was thinking the blue rooms in the east wing would be perfect.'

Rosalind swallowed, unsure of how she was expected to answer such a bold request. Although Harry might say aloud that he wished for his wife to have whatever made her happy, she doubted that it would extend to offering her the best guest rooms in the house, so that she could go to her lover through the connecting door between them.

Before she could answer, Harry cut in. 'I am so sorry, darling. Had I but known you were coming I'd have set them aside for you. But since I thought Tremaine was arriving alone, if at all, I had Rosalind put him in the room at the end of that hall.'

'The smallest one?' Elise said bluntly.

'Of course. He does not need much space—do you, old man?' Harry stared at him, daring him to respond in the negative.

'Of—of course not,' Tremaine stuttered.

Harry turned back to Elise. 'And I am afraid you will have to take the room you have always occupied. The place beside me. Although we are full to the rafters, I told Rosalind to leave it empty. I will never fill the space that is rightly yours.'

The last words had a flicker of meaning that Elise chose to ignore. 'That is utterly impossible, Harry. I have no wish to return to it.'

His voice was soft, but firm. 'I am afraid, darling, that you must make do with what is available. And if that is the best room in the house then so be it.' He turned and walked away from her, up the stairs.

Elise hurried after him, and Rosalind could hear the faint hiss of whispered conversation. Nicholas Tremaine followed after, his retreating back stiff.

Chapter Four

By the time they reached the door to her bedroom, Nicholas had made a discreet exit. And for the first time in two months, Elise was alone with her infuriatingly reasonable husband.

'But, my dear, I cannot give you another room, even if I might wish to. On my honour, they are all full.'

Harry was smiling at her again, and she searched his face for any sign that he had missed her, and had orchestrated the situation just to have her near. But in his eyes she saw not love, nor frustrated passion, nor even smug satisfaction at having duped her to return. He was showing her the same warmth he might show to a stranger. He held a hand out to her again, but made no attempt to touch her.

'I am offering you the best I have, just as I have always done. And you will be more comfortable, you know, sleeping in your own bed and not in a guest room.'

He was being sensible again, damn him. And it was

likely to drive her mad. 'It is not my own bed any longer, Harry. For, in case you have forgotten, I have left you.' She said it with emphasis, and smiled in a self-satisfied way that would push any man to anger if he cared at all for his wife or his pride.

Harry responded with another understanding smile. 'I realise that. Although it is good to see you home again, even if it is only for a visit.'

'If you were so eager to see me you could have come to London,' she said in exasperation. 'You were there only last week.'

Harry looked confused. 'I was supposed to visit you? If you desired my company, then you would not have left.' He said it as though it were the most logical thing in the world, instead of an attempt to provoke her to anger.

'You tricked Nicholas into coming here for Christmas with that silly letter.'

'And he brought you as well.' Harry beamed at her. 'I would hardly call my invitation to Tremaine a trick. I promise, I meant no harm by it. Nor by the arrangement of the rooms. Can you not take it in the way it is offered? I wish Tremaine to have a merry Christmas. And I wish you to feel at home. I would want no less for any of my guests.' If he had a motive beyond that she could find no trace of it—in his expression or his tone.

'But you do not expect the other female guests to share a connecting door with your bedroom, do you?' She had hoped to sound annoyed by the inconvenience. But her response sounded more like jealous curiosity than irritation.

He laughed as though he had just remembered the threshold he had been crossing regularly for five years. 'Oh, that.'

'Yes. That, Harry.'

'But it will not matter in the least, for I have no intention of using it. I know where I am not welcome.' As he spoke, his cordial expression never wavered. It was as though being shut from his wife's bedroom made not the slightest difference in his mood or his future.

And with that knowledge frustration got the better of her, and she turned from him and slammed the door in his face.

Nick made it as far as the top of the stairs before his anger got the better of *him*. In front of him Harry and Elise were still carrying on a *sotto voce* argument about the sleeping arrangements. In truth, Elise was arguing while her husband remained even-tempered but implacable. In any case, Nick wanted no part of it. And he suspected it would be the first of many such discussions he would be a party to if he did not find a way back to London in short order.

But not until he gave the girl at the foot of the stairs a piece of his mind. Rosalind Morley was standing alone in the entryway, fussing with the swag of pine bows that decorated the banister of the main stairs. She was much as he remembered her—diminutive in stature, barely five feet tall. Her short dark curls bobbed against her face as she rearranged the branches. Her small, sweet mouth puckered in a look of profound irritation.

It irritated him as well that even after five years he fancied he could remember the taste of those lips when they had met his. It was most unfair. A mistake of that magnitude should have the decency to fade out of memory, not come running back to the fore when one had troubles enough on one's hands. But he doubted she was there by accident any more than he was. And she deserved to know the extent of his displeasure at being tricked by her again, before he departed and left Elise to her husband. He started down the stairs.

She was picking at the boughs now, frowning in disapproval and rearranging the nuts and berries into a semblance of harmony. But her efforts seemed to make things worse and not better. As he started down towards her, the wire that held the thing in place came free and he could see a cascade of needles falling onto the slate floor at her feet, along with a shower of fruit.

'Damn,' she whispered to herself, sneaking a curse where she thought no one could hear her.

'You!' His voice startled her, and she glanced up at him, dropped the apple she had been holding, and stared fixedly at it as it rolled across the floor to land against the bottom step.

'Yes?' She was trying to sound distant and slightly curious, as though she were talking to a stranger. But it was too late to pretend that she had no idea what he meant by the exclamation, for he had seen the panic in her eyes before she looked away.

'Do not try to fool me. I know who you are.'

'I did not intend to hide the fact from you. And I had no idea that you would be among Harry's guests.'

'And I did not know, until this moment, that you were Harry's sister, or I'd never have agreed to this farce.'

'Half-sister,' she corrected.

He waved a hand. 'It hardly matters. You were more than half-loyal to him the day you ruined me.'

'I ruined you?' She laughed, but he could hear the guilt in it.

'As I recollect it, yes. You stood there under the mistletoe, in the refreshment room at the Granvilles' ball. And when you saw me you held your arms out in welcome, even though we'd met just moments before. What was I to think of the offer?'

'That I was a foolish girl who had drunk too much punch?'

He held up a finger. 'Perhaps that is exactly what I thought, and I meant to caution you about your behaviour. But when I stepped close to you, you threw your arms around my neck and kissed me, most ardently.'

Rosalind flinched. 'You did not have to come near to reprimand me, or to reciprocate so enthusiastically when I kissed you.' She stared down at the floor and scuffed at the fallen pine needles with her slipper, looking for all the world like a guilty child.

He shook his head, trying to dislodge the memory. 'Believe me, I regret my reaction, no matter how natural it was. That little incident has taught me well the dangers of too much wine and too much celebration.'

'So you blame me, personally, for ruining Christmas for you?'

'And my chances with my intended, Elise. For when she got wind of what had occurred she left me and married another.'

Nicholas was surprised to see the girl start, as though she was just now realising the extent of her guilt and the chaos her foolish actions had caused. 'You were engaged to Elise? The woman who was in the entry with us just now? My sister-in-law?' Rosalind shook her head, as though she were misunderstanding him in some way.

'The woman who married your brother after you so conveniently dishonoured yourself and me.'

She gave a helpless little shrug. 'But I had no idea, at the time, what I was doing.'

'Because you were inebriated.' He held up a second finger, ticking off another point in his argument. 'And on spirits that I did not give you. So do not try to tell me I lured you to disaster. Although you appeared fine to the casual observer, you must have been drunk as a lord.' He puzzled over it for a moment. 'If that is even a possible state for a girl. I do not think there is a corresponding female term for the condition you were in.'

She winced again. 'I was sorry. I still am. And I paid dearly for it, as you remember.'

'You were sick in the entry hall before your father could get you home.'

If possible, the girl looked even more mortified, as though she had forgotten this portion of the evening in question. 'I meant when I was sent off to rusticate. I never had the come-out that my father had promised, because he said he could not trust me. I am unmarried to this day.'

'You are unmarried,' he said through gritted teeth, 'because your father could not persuade me that it was in my best interests to attach myself for life to a spoiled child.'

'I never expected that you would marry me,' she assured him. 'And I had no wish to marry you. We had known each other for moments when the incident occurred. It would have done no good to pile folly upon folly trying to save my reputation.'

He smiled in triumph. 'Miss Morley, I think I know very well what you expected. For now that I have come to this house the picture is suddenly clear to me. You expected Elise would get word of it and that she would choose your brother over me. And that is just what occurred.'

'Half-brother,' she corrected. 'And I did no such thing. To the best of my knowledge, Harry knows nothing of the happenings of that night. Father kept the whole a secret, and does not speak of it to this day. Harry does not enjoy the company of my father, and seldom visited his mother. We had only just arrived in London, and I did not get a chance to call on him before my behaviour forced the family to leave again. Even now, all my brother knows of that visit is that I did something so despicable that I was sent from London in shame, and that the family is forbidden to speak of it. We could not have the thing fall from memory if it was a continual topic of conversation.'

'You expect me to believe that you were not in col-
lusion with Harry to ruin my engagement to Elise?' He
arched an eyebrow at her and glared, waiting for her
resolve to break under his displeasure.

She raised her chin in defiance. 'Do you honestly
think that my brother would destroy my reputation so
casually in an effort to defeat you?'

'Half-brother,' he corrected.

'Even so,' she allowed. 'You may not like him, but
do you think Harry is the sort of person who would
behave in such an underhanded fashion as to get me
foxed and throw me at you? It is not as if he does not
care for me at all. He would have no wish to hurt me.'

He paused and considered the situation, trying to
imagine Harry Pennyngton as the mastermind of his destruction. While he could imagine Harry viewing an
affair of the heart with the same shrewdness he brought
to his business dealings, he would never have orchestrated the disaster with Rosalind Morley. More likely,
when he had discovered that Elise was free, he had
simply capitalised on an opportunity, just as she assumed.

At last, he admitted, 'Harry has always been the most
even-handed and honourable of fellows. Elise comments on it frequently.'

'See?' Rosalind poked him smartly in the chest with
a holly branch she had pulled from the decorations
during her agitated repairs, and a leaf stuck in the fabric
of his jacket. 'If he'd had wind of it at the time it is far
more likely that he'd have called you out for it, or helped
to cover the whole thing up, just as my father wished to

do. And he'd have never invited you here while I was hostess, even after all this time. If Elise had learned anything about it she would not have greeted me as warmly as she did just now. I doubt that either of them has a clue as to what happened.' She blinked at him, suddenly worried, and whispered, 'And I would prefer that it stay that way. Which will be difficult, if you insist on arguing about it in a public room.'

Nick took this information in and held it for a while, examining it from all sides before speaking. If it was in any way possible that the girl told the truth, then he must give her the benefit of the doubt. Revelation of the story at this point would turn a delicate situation into a volatile one. He said, 'I have no desire to unbury any secrets during this visit, if it is true that we have managed to keep them hidden. What's done is done. We cannot change the past.'

'This meeting was none of my doing, I swear to you,' she said earnestly, before he could speak, again. 'I would never have agreed to any of it had I known…' He could see the obvious distress in her eyes, and she twisted the holly in her hands until the leaves scratched her fingers and the berries had been crushed. 'I never meant to hurt you or anyone else by my actions. Or to help anyone, for that matter. I simply did not think.' She looked down at the destruction, dropped the twig, and hurriedly wiped her hands on her skirt. She held them out in appeal. 'I am afraid I am prone to not thinking things through. But I have worked hard to improve my character, and the messes I make are not so severe as they once were.'

He nodded, though her unexpected presence still filled him with unease. 'I understand. I am beginning to suspect we are both here for reasons that have little to do with our preference in the matter and everything to do with the wishes of others.'

She said, 'I think Harry hoped that I would have the opportunity to impress eligible male guests with my ability as a hostess. I doubt that will be the case, since my skills are nothing to write home about. In any case, the single gentlemen he promised have failed to materialise. There is you, of course, but if you are with Elise…' She trailed off in embarrassment, as she realised that her babbling had sounded like an invitation to court her.

He watched her for a time, allowing her to suffer a bit, for it would not do for the girl to think he was interested. Whatever Harry had planned for him this weekend, he doubted it would include courting his sister. Rosalind could not tell by looking at him what his real feelings might be for Elise, and he had no wish to inform her of them. But if Elise learned the truth before he could escape, there would be hell to pay.

He said, 'It is very awkward for everyone concerned. Elise wished to come and speak with Harry, and she did not want to come alone. Now that my job as escort has been done, I mean to stay no more than tonight—whatever Harry's plans might be. I suspect I will be gone shortly after breakfast, and I will trouble you no more.'

Rosalind glanced out of the window at the fast-falling snow. 'You do not know how treacherous the local roads can be after a storm such as this. You may find travel to be impossible for quite some time. And you are welcome until Twelfth Night in any case.'

But she looked as though she hoped he would not stay, and he did not blame her. 'Thank you for your hospitality. I trust you will not find it strange if I avoid your company at breakfast?'

She nodded again. 'I will not think it the least bit odd. As a matter of fact, it is probably for the best.' She hesitated. 'Although I do wish to apologise, one last time, for what happened when we first met.'

'It is not necessary.'

'But I cannot seem to stop. For I truly regret it.'

He gave a curt bow. 'I understand that. Do not concern yourself with it. We will chalk it up to the folly of youth.' And how could he fault her for that? For he had been guilty of folly as well, and was paying for it to this day.

'Thank you for understanding.'

'Then let us hear no more apologies on the matter. Consider yourself absolved.'

But, while he might be able to forgive, he doubted he would ever forget her.

Chapter Five

Elise glared through the wood of her bedroom door at the man in the hall. She had not thought when she made this trip that she would end up back in her own room. She would be alone with her memories, and scant feet from her husband, while Nicholas was stowed in the remotest corner of the guest wing like so much discarded baggage. Though he showed no sign of it, she was sure that Harry had anticipated her appearance and sought an opportunity to separate them.

But if he did not want her, then why would he bother? So Harry did not mean to come and take her in the night? Fine. It was just as she'd feared. She meant nothing to him any more. And telling her the truth, with that annoying little smile of his, had removed all hope that he had been harbouring a growing and unfulfilled passion since her precipitate retreat from his house. If he cared for her, an absence of two months would have been sufficient to make him drag her back to his bed the first chance he got, so that he might slake his lust. But to announce that he meant to leave her in peace for a fortnight while she slept only a room away…

She balled her fists in fury. The man had not left her alone for a fortnight in the whole time they had lived together. But apparently his visits had been just as she'd feared: out of convenience rather than an uncontrollable desire for her and her alone. Now that she was not here he must be finding someone else to meet his needs.

The thought raised a lump in her throat. Perhaps he had finally taken a mistress, just as she'd always feared he would. It had been some consolation during the time that they had been together to know that he was either faithful or incredibly discreet in his infidelities. For, while she frequently heard rumours about the husbands of her friends, she had never heard a word about Harry.

And to have taken a lover would have required equally miraculous stamina, for even after five years he had been most enthusiastic and regular in his bedroom visits, right up to the moment she had walked out the door. Then, his interest in her body had evaporated.

If they had not married in haste, things might have been different between them. She should never have accepted Harry Pennyngton's offer when she had still been so angry with Nicholas. She had been almost beyond reason, and had hardly had time to think before she had dispensed with one man and taken another.

But Harry's assurances had been so reasonable, so comforting, that they had been hard to resist. He had said he was of a mind to take a wife. And he had heard that she was in desperate straits. That her parents were returning to Bavaria, and she must marry someone quickly if she wished to remain in England. If so, why could it not be him? He had described the house to her, the grounds and the attached properties, and told her of his income and the title. If she refused him he would understand, of course. For they were little better than strangers. But if she chose to accept everything he had would be hers, and he would do all in his power to assure that she did not regret the decision.

He had laid it all out before her like some sort of business deal. And although he had not stated the fact outright, she had suspected that she would not get a better offer, and would end up settling for less should she refuse.

That should have been her first warning that the marriage would not be what she'd hoped. For where Nicholas had been full of fine words of love and big dreams of the future, Harry had been reason itself about what she could expect should she choose to marry him.

It had been quite soothing, in retrospect, to be free of grand passion for a moment, and to give her broken heart a chance to mend. Harry had been willing to give without question, and had asked for nothing in return but her acceptance.

They had been wed as soon as he'd been able to get a licence. And if she'd had any delusions that he wished a meeting of hearts before a meeting of bodies, he had dispelled them on the first night.

Elise had thought that Harry might give her time to

adjust to her new surroundings, and wished that she'd had the nerve to request it. For intimacy had hardly seemed appropriate so soon. They had barely spoken. She hadn't even learned how he liked his tea, or his eggs. And to learn how he liked other things before they had even had breakfast? It had all happened too fast. Surely he would give her a few days to get to know her new husband?

But as she had prepared for bed on her wedding night, she had reached for her nightrail only to have the maid pull it aside. 'Lord Anneslea says you will not be needing it this evening, ma'am.'

'Really?' She felt the first thrill of foreboding.

'Just the dressing gown.' And the maid wrapped her bare body in silk and exited the room.

What was she to do now? For clearly the staff had more instruction than she had over what was to occur. And it was not likely to be a suggestion that they live as brother and sister until familiarity had been gained.

There was a knock at the connecting door between his bedroom and hers. 'Elise? May I come in?'

She gave him a hesitant yes.

He opened the door but did not enter. Instead he stood framed in the doorway, staring at her. 'I thought tonight, perhaps, you would join me in my room.' He stepped to the side and held a hand out to her.

When she reached to take it, his fingers closed over hers, and he led her over the threshold to his room.

It was surprisingly warm for a winter's night, and she could see that the fire was built to blazing in the fireplace. 'I did not want you to take a chill,' he offered, by way of explanation.

'Oh.'

Then he helped her up the short step that led to his bed, and jumped up himself to sit on the edge beside her. He brushed a lock of hair off her face, and asked, 'What have you been told about what will happen tonight?'

'That it will go much faster if I lie still and do not speak.'

His face paled. 'I imagine it will. But expediency is not always the object with these things. If you wish to move at any time, for any reason, then you must certainly do it. And by all means speak, if you have anything to say. If I am causing you discomfort I will only know if you tell me. And if something gives you pleasure?' He smiled hopefully. 'Then I wish to know that as well.'

'Oh.'

'Are you ready to begin?'

'I think so, yes.' She was still unsure what it was that they were beginning. But how else was she to find out?

He kissed her, and it was a pleasant surprise, for other than one brief kiss when he had proposed, and another in the chapel after the wedding, he had offered no displays of affection. But this was different. He rested his lips against hers for a moment, moving back and forth, and then parting them with his tongue.

It was an interesting sensation. Especially since the longer he kissed her the more she was convinced that she could feel the kiss in other parts of her body, where his lips had not touched. When she remarked on it, he offered to kiss her there as well, and his lips slid to her chin, her throat, and then to her breast.

It was wonderful, and strange, for it made the feelings even more intense, and he seemed to understand for his lips followed the sensation lower.

She scrambled away from him, up onto the pillows on the other side of the bed. Because she understood what it was he meant to do, and it was very shocking. It was then that she realised her robe had come totally undone and he was staring at her naked body. The feeling of his eyes on her felt very much like the intimate kiss she was avoiding, so she wrapped the gown tightly about her and shook her head.

'I have frightened you.' He dragged his gaze back to her face and looked truly contrite. 'Here, let us start again.'

He climbed past her on the bed, and reached for a pot of oil that rested on the night stand. It was scented with a rich perfume, and he took a dab of the stuff, stroking it onto the palm of his hand.

'Let me touch you.'

She tensed in anticipation of his caress. But he sat behind her this time. He slipped his hands beneath the neck of the robe to stroke her shoulders, kissing her neck before rubbing the ointment into the muscles there.

'See? There is nothing to be afraid of. I only mean to give you pleasure.'

And there certainly did not seem to be anything to fear. It was very relaxing to feel his hands sliding over her body, and she found it almost impossible to resist as he pushed the fabric of her robe lower, until he could reach the small of her back.

She was bare to the waist now. And even though he was behind her, and could not see them, she kept her hands folded across her breasts. But soon she relaxed her arms and dropped them to her sides. When he reached around her to touch her ribs, the underside of her breasts and her nipples, she did not fight him. It felt good. And then she leaned back against him and allowed him to play.

When he heard her breathing quicken he put his lips to her ear and kissed her once, before beginning to whisper, in great detail, just what it was he meant to do next.

For a moment her eyes opened wide in alarm, but his hands slipped down, massaging her belly, as his voice assured her that it would be all right. He nuzzled her neck. One hand still toyed with a breast, while the other slid between her legs and teased until her knees parted. The sensation was new, and intense, but he seemed to know just how to touch her until she moaned and twisted against him.

He explained again how wonderful it would feel to be inside her, and demonstrated with his hand, his fingers sliding over her body, inside and out again, over and over, until her head lolled back against him and her back arched in a rush of sensation.

He released her and turned her in his arms, so that he could kiss her again. And then he laid her down on the pillows. And she could see what it was that had been pressing against her so insistently as he had stroked her. She enquired after it.

He explained the differences in their bodies, but assured her that he would enjoy her touch just as she had enjoyed his. Then he kissed her again, and lay down beside her, guiding her hand to touch him.

It gave her a chance to observe him as she had not done before marriage. His own dressing gown had fallen away, and he was naked beside her on the bed. His body was lean and well muscled, although he had never given her the impression of being a sportsman or athlete. His eyes were half closed, and a knowing smile curled at the corners of his lips. He was a handsome man, although she had not thought to notice when he had made his offer to her. His hair was so light a brown as to be almost blond, and he had a smooth brow. His strong chin hinted at power of will, although his ready smile made him appear an amiable companion. There was no cruelty in his green-grey eyes, but a sly twinkle as he reached for her and, with a few simple touches, rendered her helpless with pleasure all over again.

Then he draped his hand over her hip and pulled her close, so her breasts pressed against his chest. His other hand slipped back between her legs, readying her. Her hand was still upon him, stroking gently, and she helped him to find his way to her, then closed her eyes.

He kissed her, and it was almost apologetic as he came into her and she felt the pain of it. But then she felt him moving in her, and against her, and his strength dissolved into need. Finally there was something that she could give to him, an explanation for his generosity. And it all made sense. So she ignored the pain and found the pleasure again, kissed him back as he shuddered in release.

He held her afterwards, and she slept in his arms. The next morning he was cautious and polite, just as he had been before they had married. She remembered the intimacy of the previous night and found it strange that he was still so shy. But she assumed that over time the distance between them would fade.

Instead it was as though the divide between them grew with each rising of the sun. He was friendly and courteous. He made her laugh, and was never cross with her over small things, as her own family had been. He did not raise his voice even when she was sure he must be angry with her.

But he never revealed any more of his innermost thoughts than were absolutely necessary. If he ever had need of a confidante he must have sought elsewhere, for he certainly did not trouble his wife with his doubts or fears.

In truth there was nothing about their relationship that would lead her to believe she was especially close to him in any way but the physical. At first, she thought that he had chosen her because he could find no other willing to have him. He had been too quick to offer, and with such minimal affection. Perhaps his heart was broken, just as hers had been, and he had sought oblivion in the nearest source?

But as time passed he spoke of no previous alliances, and showed no interest in the other women of the ton, either married or single. She had frequent opportunity to see that he could have married elsewhere, had he so chosen. And the compliments of the other girls, when they'd heard that she was to marry him, had held a certain wistful envy. Although he had offered for her, he had treated them all with the utmost courtesy and generosity, and they would have welcomed further interest had any been expressed.

They had done well enough together, Elise supposed. But he had never given her an indication, in the five years they had been together, that he would not have done equally well with any other young woman of the ton, or that his marriage to her had been motivated by anything other than the fortuitous timing of his need for a wife when she had desperately been in need of a husband.

When night came, there had been no question of why he had married her—for his passion had only increased, as had hers. It had been easy to see what he wanted, and to know that she pleased him, and he had taken great pains to see that she was satisfied as well. To lie in his arms each night had been like a taste of paradise, after days that were amiable but strangely empty. Even now she could not help but remember how it had felt to lie with him: cherished. Adored.

Loved.

It was all she could do to keep from throwing open the door between them right now and begging him to hold her again, to ease the ache of loneliness that she had felt since the moment she had left him.

But what good would that do in the long run? She would be happy at night, when he thought only of her.

But at all other times she would not be sure what he thought of her, or if he thought of her at all.

He would be pleasant to her, of course. He would be the picture of good manners and casual affection—as he was with everyone, from shopkeepers to strangers. But he did not seem to share many interests with his wife. While he had always accompanied her to social gatherings, she did not think he'd taken much pleasure in them, and he'd seemed faintly relieved to stay at home, even if it had meant that she was accompanied by other gentlemen. He had showed no indication of jealousy, although she was certain that her continued friendship with Nicholas must have given him cause. Her husband had treated Tremaine with a suspicious level of good humour, although they should be bitter rivals after what had gone before.

In time, Nicholas had forgiven her for her hasty parting with him, and his level of flirtation had increased over the years, overlaying a deep and abiding friendship. She'd enjoyed his attention, but it had worried her terribly that she might be a better friend to another man than she was to her husband.

But if Harry had been bothered by it she hadn't been able to tell. He'd either seen no harm in it, or simply had not cared enough about her to stop it.

Most important, if their lack of children had weighed on his mind, as it had hers, she had found no indication of it. In fact, he'd flatly refused to speak of it. The extent to which he'd appeared not to blame her for the problem had left her sure that he secretly thought she was at fault. Her own father had always said that girl children were a burden compared to sons. She dreaded to think what he would have said had his wife provided no children at all.

It had been hard to avoid the truth. She had failed at the one thing she was born to do. She had proved herself to be as useless as her family thought her. Harry must regret marrying her at all.

And on the day that she had been angry enough to leave she had shouted that she would return to her old love, for he at least was able to give her an honest answer if she asked him a direct question about his feelings on things that truly mattered.

Harry had blinked at her. There had been no trace of his usual absent smile, but no anger, either. And he had said, 'As you wish, my dear. If, after all this time, you do not mean to stay, I cannot hold you here against your will.'

Elise had wanted to argue that of course he could. That a real man would have barred the door and forbidden her from talking nonsense. Or called out Nicholas long ago for his excessively close friendship to another man's wife. Then he would have thrown her over his shoulder and marched to the bedroom, to show her in no uncertain terms the advantages of remaining just where she was.

But when one was in a paroxysm of rage it made no sense to pause and give the object of that rage a second chance to answer the question more appropriately. Nor should she have had to explain the correct response he must give to her anger. For if she must tell him how to behave, it hardly mattered that he was willing to act just as she wished.

So she had stormed out of the house and taken the carriage to London, and had informed a slightly alarmed Nicholas that there was nothing to stand between them and a much closer relationship than they had previously enjoyed.

And if she had secretly hoped that her husband would be along at any time to bring her back, even if it meant an argument that would raise the roof on their London townhouse? Then it was positive proof of her foolishness.

Chapter Six

After a fitful night's rest, Nick Tremaine sought out his host to say a hasty farewell. He found Anneslea at the bottom of the stairs, staring out of the window at the yard. Nick turned the cheery tone the blighter had used on him at the club back upon him with full force. 'Harry!'

'Nicholas.' Harry turned towards him with an even broader smile than usual, and a voice oozing suspicion. 'Did you sleep well?'

The bed had been narrow, hard where it needed to be soft, and soft where it ought to be firm. And no amount of wood in the fireplace had been able to take the chill from the room. But he'd be damned before he complained of it. 'It was nothing less than what I expected when I accepted your kind invitation.'

Harry's grin turned malicious. 'And you brought a surprise with you, I see?'

Nick responded with a similar smile, hoping that the last-minute addition to the guest list had got well up the nose of his conniving host. 'Well, you know Elise. There is no denying her when she gets an idea into her head.'

'Yes. I know Elise.'

Anneslea was still smiling, but his tone indicated that there would be hell to pay if Tremaine knew her too well. Just one more reason to bolt for London and leave the two lovebirds to work out their problems in private.

He gave Harry a sympathetic pat on the back. 'And, since you do, you will understand how displeased she shall be with me when she hears that I've had to return to London.'

'Return? But, my dear sir, you've only just arrived.' The other man laid a hand on his shoulder. 'I would not think of seeing you depart so soon.'

Nick tried to shake off his host's friendly gesture, which had attached to him like a barnacle. When it would not budge, he did his best to ignore it. 'All the same, I must away. I've just had word of an urgent matter that needs my attention. But before I go, I wanted to thank you and wish you a M—'

Anneslea cut him off in mid-word. 'Received word from London? I fail to see how. It is too early for the morning post, and, given the condition of the road, I doubt we will see it at all today.'

Damn the country and its lack of civilisation. 'Not received word, precisely. Remembered. I have remembered something I must attend to. Immediately. And so I will start for London and leave Elise in your capable hands. And I wish you both a Mer—'

'But surely there is nothing that cannot wait until

after the holiday? Even if you left today you would not arrive in London before Christmas Day. Although you might wish to be a miserable old sinner for this season, you should not make your servants work through Boxing Day to get you home.'

Nick sighed, trying to manage a show of regret. 'It cannot be helped. I have come to tell you I cannot stay. Pressing business calls me back to London. But although I must toil, there is no reason that you cannot have a Merr—'

Before he could complete the phrase sliding from his lips, Harry interrupted again. 'Ridiculous. I will not hear of it. In this weather it is not safe to travel.'

Damn the man. It was almost as if he did not want to win his bet. Which was obviously a lie, for he had seen the look on Anneslea's face at the sight of his wife. The man was as miserable without her as she was without him. Nick stared out of the nearest window at the snow lying thick upon the drive. 'It was safe enough for me to arrive here. And the weather is much improved over yesterday, I am certain. If I depart now I will have no problems. But not before wishing you a M—'

'Not possible.' Harry gestured at the sky. 'Look at the clouds, man. Slate-grey. There is more snow on the way, and God knows what else.' As if on cue a few hesitant flakes began falling, increasing in number as he watched. Anneslea nodded in satisfaction. 'The roads will be ice or mud all the way to London. Better to remain inside, with a cup of punch and good company.'

Nick looked at the mad glint in his host's eye and said, 'I am willing to take my chances with the weather.'

There was a polite clearing of the throat behind them as a footman tried to gain the attention of the Earl. 'My Lord?' The servant bowed, embarrassed at creating an interruption. 'There has been another problem. A wagon from the village has got stuck at the bend of the drive.'

Anneslea smiled at him in triumph. 'See? It is every bit as bad as I predicted. There is nothing to be done about it until the snow stops.' He turned back to the footman. 'Have servants unload the contents of the wagon and carry them to the house. Get the horses into our stable, and give the driver a warm drink.' He turned back to Nick. 'There is no chance of departure until we can clear the drive. And that could take days.'

'I could go around.'

'Trees block the way on both sides.' Harry was making no effort to hide his glee at Nick's predicament. 'You must face the fact, Tremaine. You are quite trapped here until such time as the weather lifts. You might as well relax and enjoy the festivities, just as I mean you to do.'

'Is that what you mean for me?'

'Of course, dear man. Why else would I bring you here?'

The man was all innocence again, damn him, smiling the smile of the concerned host.

'Now, was there anything else you wished to say to me?'

Just the two words that would free him of any further involvement in the lives of Lord and Lady Anneslea.

Nick thought of a week or more, trapped in the same house with Elise, trying to explain that he had thrown over the bet and her chance at divorce because he had her own best interests at heart. 'Anything to say to you? No. Definitely not.'

Rosalind stared at the bare pine in the drawing room, wondering just what she was expected to do with it. Harry had requested a tree, and here it was. But he had requested decorations as well, and then walked away as though she should know what he meant by so vague a statement. The servants had brought her a box of small candles and metal holders for the same, sheets of coloured paper, some ribbon, a handful of straw, and a large tray of gingerbread biscuits. When she had asked for further instruction, the footman had shrugged and said that it had always been left to the lady of the house. Then, he had given her the look that she had seen so often on the face of the servants. If she meant to replace their beloved Elise, then she should know how best to proceed—with no help from them.

Rosalind picked up a star-shaped biscuit and examined it. It was a bit early for sweets—hardly past breakfast. And they could have at least brought her a cup of tea. She bit off a point and chewed. Not the best gingerbread she had eaten, but certainly not the worst. This tasted strongly of honey.

She heard a melodious laugh from behind her, and turned to see her brother's wife standing in the doorway. 'Have you come to visit me in my misery, Elise?'

'Why would you be miserable, dear one?' Elise stepped into the room and took the biscuit from her hand. 'Christmas is no time to look so sad. But it will be considerably less merry for the others if you persist in eating the *lebkuchen*. They are ornaments for the tree. You may eat them on Twelfth Night, if you wish.'

Rosalind looked down at the lopsided star. 'So that is what I am to do with them. Everyone assumes that I must know.'

'Here. Let me show you.' Elise cut a length of ribbon from the spool in the basket, threaded it through a hole in the top of a heart-shaped biscuit, then tied it to a branch of the tree. She stood back to admire her work, and rearranged the bow in the ribbon until it was as pretty as the ornament. Then she smiled and reached for another biscuit, as though she was the hostess, demonstrating for a guest.

Rosalind turned upon her, hands on her hips. 'Elise, you have much to explain.'

'If it is about the logs for the fireplace, or the stuffing for the goose, I am sure that whatever you plan is satisfactory. The house is yours now.' She glanced around her old home, giving a critical eye to Rosalind's attempts to recreate the holiday. 'Not how I would have done things, perhaps. But you have done the best you can with little help from Harry.'

'You know that is not what I mean.' Rosalind frowned at her. 'Why are you here?'

She seemed to avoid the question, taking a sheet of coloured paper and shears. With a few folds and snips, and a final twist, she created a paper flower. 'The weather has changed and I was not prepared for it. There are some things left in my rooms that I have need of.'

'Then you could have sent for them and saved yourself the bother of a trip. Why are you really here, Elise? For if it was meant as a cruelty to Harry, you have succeeded.'

Guilt coloured Elise's face. 'If I had known there would be so many guests perhaps I would not have come. I thought the invitation was only to Nicholas and a few others. But I arrived to find the house full of people.' She stared down at the paper in her hands and placed the flower on the tree. 'The snow is still falling. By the time it stops it will be too late in the day to start for London. We will see tomorrow if there is a way to exit with grace.' She looked at Rosalind, and her guilty expression reformed into a mask of cold righteousness. 'And as for Harry feeling my cruelty to him? It must be a miracle of the season. I have lived with the man for years, and I have yet to find a thing I can do that will penetrate his defences.' The hole in the next ginger-bread heart had closed in baking, so she stabbed at the thing with the point of the scissors before reaching for the ribbon again.

Rosalind struggled to contain her anger. 'So it is just as I thought. You admit that you are attempting to hurt him, just to see if you can. You have struck him to the core with your frivolous behaviour, Elise. And if you cannot see it then you must not know the man at all.'

'Perhaps I do not.' Elise lost her composure again,

and her voice grew unsteady. 'It is my greatest fear, you see. After five years I do not understand him any better than the day we met. Do you think that it gives me no pain to say that? But it is—' she waved her hands, struggling for the words '—like being married to a Bluebeard. I feel I do not know the man at all.'

Rosalind laughed. 'Harry a Bluebeard? Do you think him guilty of some crime? Do you expect that he has evil designs against you in some way? Because I am sorry to say it, Elise, but that is the maddest idea, amongst all your other madness. My brother is utterly harmless.'

'That is not what I mean at all.' Elise sighed in apparent frustration at having to make herself understood in a language that was not her own. Then she calmed herself and began again. 'He means me no harm. But his heart…' Her face fell. 'It is shut tight against me. Are all Englishmen like this? Open to others, but reserved and distant with their wives? If I wished to know what is in his pocket or on his calendar he would show me these things freely. But I cannot tell what is on his mind. I do not know when he is sad or angry.'

Rosalind frowned in puzzlement. 'You cannot tell if your husband is angry?'

'He has not said a cross word to me—that I can remember. Not in the whole time we have been married. But no man can last for years with such an even temper. He must be hiding something. And if I cannot tell when he is angry, then how am I supposed to know that he is really happy? He is always smiling, Rosalind.' And now she sounded truly mad as she whispered, 'It is not natural.'

It was all becoming more confusing, not less. 'So you abandoned your husband because he was not angry with you?'

Elise picked up some bits of straw and began to work them together into a flat braid. 'You would think, would you not, that when a woman says to the man she has sworn herself to, that she would rather be with another, there would be a response?' She looked down at the thing in her hands, gave a quick twist to turn it into a heart, and placed it on the tree.

Rosalind winced. 'Oh, Elise, you did not. Say you did not tell him so.'

Elise blinked up at her in confusion. 'You did not think that I left him without warning?'

'I assumed,' said Rosalind through clenched teeth, 'that you left him in the heat of argument. And that by now you would have come to your senses and returned home.'

'That is the problem. The problem exactly.' Elise seemed to be searching for words again, and then she said, 'After all this time there is no heat.'

'No heat?' Rosalind knew very little about what went on between man and wife when they were alone, and had to admit some curiosity on the subject. But she certainly hoped she was not about to hear the intimate details of her brother's marriage, for she was quite sure she did not want to think of him in that way.

'Not in all ways, of course.' Elise blushed, and her hands busied themselves with another bunch of straws, working them into a star. 'There are some ways in which we are still very well suited. Physically, for example.'

She sighed, and gave a small smile. 'He is magnificent. He is everything I could wish for in a man.'

'Magnificent?' Rosalind echoed. Love must truly be blind. For although he was a most generous and amiable man, she would have thought 'ordinary' to be a better description of her brother.

When Elise saw her blank expression, she tried again. 'His charms might not be immediately obvious, but he is truly impressive. Unfortunately he is devoid of emotion. There can be no heat of any other kind if a person refuses to be angry. There is no real passion when one works so hard to avoid feeling.'

Rosalind shook her head. 'Harry is not without feelings, Elise. He is the most easily contented, happy individual I have had the pleasure to meet.'

Elise made a sound that was something between a growl and a moan. 'You have no idea, until you have tried it, how maddening it is to live with the most agreeable man in England. I tried, Rosalind, honestly I did. For years I resisted the temptation to goad him to anger, but I find I am no longer able to fight the urge. I want him to rail at me. To shout. To forbid me my wilfulness and demand his rights as my husband. I want to know when he is displeased with me. I would be only too happy for the chance to correct my behaviour to suit his needs.'

'You wish to be married to a tyrant?'

'Not a tyrant. Simply an honest man.' Elise stared at the straw in her hand. 'I know that I do not make him happy. I only wish him to admit it. If I can, I will improve my character to suit his wishes. And if I cannot?' Elise gave a deep sigh. 'Then at least I will have the truth. But if he will not tell me his true feelings it is impossible. If I ask him he will say that I am talking nonsense, and that there is nothing wrong. But it cannot be. No one is as agreeable as all that. So without even thinking, I took to doing things that I suspected would annoy him.' She looked at Rosalind and shrugged. 'He adjusted to each change in my behaviour without question. If I am cross with him? He buys me a gift.'

'He is most generous,' Rosalind agreed.

'But after years of receiving them I do not want any more presents. Since the day we married, whenever I have had a problem, he has smiled, agreed with me, and bought me a piece of jewellery to prevent an argument. When we were first married, and I missed London, it was emerald earbobs. When he would not go to visit my parents for our anniversary, there were matched pearls. I once scolded him for looking a moment too long at an opera dancer in Vauxhall. I got a complete set of sapphires, including clips for my shoes.' She shook her head in frustration. 'You can tell just by looking into my jewel box how angry I have been with him. It is full to overflowing.'

'Then tell him you do not wish more presents,' Rosalind suggested.

'I have tried, and he ignores me. Any attempt to express displeasure results in more jewellery, and I am sick to death of it.' She began to crush the ornament she had made, then thought better of it, placing it on the tree and starting another. 'Do you wish to know of the final argument that made our marriage unbearable?'

'Very much so. For I am still not sure that I understand what bothers you.' Rosalind glanced at the tree. Without thinking, Elise had decorated a good portion of the front, and was moving around to the back. Since the Christmas tree situation was well in hand, Rosalind sat down on the couch and took another bite from of the biscuit in her hand.

'Harry had been in London for several days on business, and I was reading the morning papers. And there, plain as day on the front page, was the news that the investments he had gone to look after were in a bad way. He stood to lose a large sum of money. Apparently the situation had been brewing for some time. But he had told me nothing of the problems, which were quite severe.'

'Perhaps you were mistaken, Elise. For if he did not speak of them, they could not have been too bad.'

The tall blonde became so agitated that she crumpled the straw in her hand and threw it to the floor. 'I was in no way confused about the facts of the matter. They referred to him by name, Rosalind, on the front page of *The Times*.'

That did look bad. 'Surely you do not hold Harry responsible for a bad decision?'

'I would never do such. I am his wife, or wish that I could be. Mine is the breast on which he should lay his head when in need of comfort. But when he returned home, do you know what he said to me when I asked him about his trip?'

'I have not a clue.'

'He said it was fine, Rosalind. *Fine!*' Elise repeated

the last word as though it were some unspeakable curse. 'And then he smiled at me as though nothing unusual had happened.'

She paced the room, as though reliving the moment.

'So I went to get the paper, and showed him his name. And he said, "Oh, that." He looked guilty, but still he said, "It is nothing that you need to worry about. It will not affect your comfort in any way." As if he thought that was the only thing I cared about. And then he patted me on the hand, as though I were a child, and said that to prove all was well he would buy me another necklace.'

She sagged onto the settee beside Rosalind and stared at the straws littering the floor. 'How difficult would it have been for him to at least admit that there was a problem in his life, so that I did not have to read of it in the papers?'

'He probably thought that you were not interested,' Rosalind offered reasonably. 'Or perhaps there was nothing you could do to help him.'

'If I thought it would help I would give him the contents of my jewel case. He could sell them to make back his investment. They mean nothing to me if all is not well. And if that did no good, then I would help him by providing my love and support,' Elise said sadly. 'But apparently he does not need it. And if he thinks to keep secret from me something so large that half of London knows it, then what else is he hiding from me?'

'It is quite possible that there is nothing at all,' Rosalind assured her, knowing that she might be wrong. For she had often found Harry closed-mouthed about things that pained him greatly. It was quite possible that Elise's suspicions were well grounded. She wished she could slap her foolish brother for causing his wife to worry, when he could have solved so many problems by telling her the whole truth.

'And when I told him, in pique, that I quite preferred Nicholas to him, for he at least had the sense to know that I was capable of reading a newspaper, Harry smiled and told me that I was probably right. For Nick had finally come into his inheritance. And at that moment, he had the deeper pockets. But Harry said he could still afford to buy me earrings to go with the new necklace if I wished them. So I left him and went to London. And he bought me a whole new wardrobe.' The last words came out in a sob, and she stared at Rosalind, her eyes red and watery. 'Is that the behaviour of a sane man?'

Rosalind had to admit it was not. It made no sense to open his purse when a few simple words of apology would have brought his wife running home. 'He was trying to get on your good side, Elise. He has always been slow to speak of his troubles, and even slower to admit fault. It is just his way.'

'Then *his way* has succeeded in driving me away from him. Perhaps that was what he was trying to do all along. He certainly made no effort to keep me. I said to him that perhaps I was more suited to Nicholas, and that our marriage had been a mistake from the start.'

'And what did he say to that?'

'That he had found our marriage most satisfactory,

but that there was little he could do to control how I felt in the matter.'

'There. See? He was happy enough,' said Rosalind. She picked up the ornament from the floor and offered it back to Elise, thinking that the metaphor of grasping straws was an apt one if this was all the ammunition she could find to defend her idiot brother.

Elise sniffed and tossed the straw into the fire, then took a sheet of paper and absently snipped and folded until it became a star. 'He said it was *satisfactory*. That is hardly praise, Rosalind. And the way he smiled as he said it. It was almost as if he was daring me to disagree.'

'Or he could have been smiling because he was happy.'

'Or not. He always smiles, Rosalind. It means nothing to me any more.'

'He does not smile nearly so much as he used to, Elise. Not when you are not here to see. Harry feels your absence, and he is putting on a brave front for you. I am sure of it.' There was truth in that, at least.

'Then he has but to ask me to return to him and I shall,' she said. 'Or I shall consider it,' she amended, trying to appear stubborn as she busied herself with the basket of ornaments, putting the little candles into their holders.

But it was obvious that, despite initial appearances, Elise would come running back to Harry in an instant, if given any hope at all. And Harry was longing for a way to get her back.

Rosalind considered. While neither wished to be the

first to make an overture, it might take only the slightest push from a third party to make the reconciliation happen.

And so she began to plan.

Chapter Seven

Harry watched Tremaine retreating to the library.
Merry Christmas, indeed. Apparently the miserable pest
had seen through the trap and was trying to wriggle out
of it, like the worm he was. But his hasty departure
would solve nothing, and his forestalling of the bet
would anger Elise to the point that there was no telling
what she might do. If she got it into her head that she
was being rejected by both the men in her life, she
might never recover from the hurt of it.

Thank the Lord for fortuitous weather and stuck
wagons. It would buy him enough time to sort things
again, before they got too far out of hand. And if it gave
him an opportunity to deal out some of the misery that
Tremaine deserved? All the better.

'Harry.' Rosalind came bustling out of the drawing
room and stopped her brother before he could escape.
'What is really going on here?'

'Going on?' He made sure his face showed nothing

but innocence, along with a sense of injury that she should accuse him of anything. 'Nothing at all, Rosalind. I only wished to entertain some members of my set for the holiday, and I thought…'

His little sister set her hands upon her hips and stared at him in disgust. 'Your wife is here with another man. And you do not seem the least bit surprised. As a matter of fact you welcomed her new lover as though he were an honoured guest.'

'In a sense he is. He is the object of a bet I have made with the other gentlemen. I guaranteed them that I could make Tremaine wish me a Merry Christmas.'

'Why on earth would you do that?'

He grinned. 'Perhaps my common sense was temporarily overcome with seasonal spirit.'

Rosalind frowned at him. 'Or perhaps not. Perhaps you have some plan afoot that involves ending the separation with your wife. Or did you bet on her as well? And what prevailed upon the odious Mr Tremaine to accept your challenge? I do not understand it at all.'

'Then let me explain it to you. I told Tremaine that I would facilitate the divorce Elise is so eager for, if he would come down to the country and play my little game. I knew he would take the information straight to Elise, and that she would insist they attend—if only for the opportunity to come back here and tell me to my face what she thought of the idea. I expect she is furious.'

'And you think by angering her that you will bring her closer to you? Harry, you do not understand women at all, if that is your grand plan.'

'But I know Elise.' He smiled. 'And so far it is going just as I expected it to.'

'If you know her so well, then you should have been able to prevent her from leaving in the first place. Do you understand what you have done to her to make her so angry with you?'

He was honestly puzzled as he answered, 'Absolutely nothing. As you can see from the house, her wardrobe, her jewels, she can live in luxury. And if this was not enough I would go to any lengths necessary to give her more. I treat her with the utmost respect. I do not strike her. I do not berate her in public or in private. I am faithful. Although I have never denied her her admirers, I have no mistress, nor have ever considered a lover. I want no one but her, and I am willing to give her her own way in all things.' He gestured in the direction of the library. 'I even tolerate Tremaine. What more can she ask of me? There is little more that I can think to give her.'

Rosalind paused in thought for a moment. 'You spoil her, then. But you must cut her off if she means to belittle you so. If she has a taste for luxury, deny her. Tell her that you are very angry with her over this foolishness and that there will be no more gifts. Tell her that you wish for her to come home immediately. That will bring her to heel.'

'Do not speak that way of her.' He said it simply for he did not mean to reprove his sister, since she got enough of that at home. 'Elise is not some animal that can be punished into obedience and will still lick the hand of its master. She is a proud woman. And she is my wife.'

'It seems she does not wish to be.'

'Perhaps not. But it is something that must be settled between the two of us, and not by others. And perhaps if you had lived her life…'

Rosalind laughed. 'I would gladly trade her life for mine. You will not convince me that it is such a tragedy to be married to an earl. Even in separation, she lives better than most ladies of the ton.'

He shook his head. 'You should understand well enough what her life was like before, Rosalind, and show some sympathy. For her parents were every bit as strict to her as your father has been to you. I met her father, of course, when I offered for her. Her mother as well. It would not have been easy for her if she had been forced to return home after the disaster with Tremaine. The man betrayed her, and so she broke it off with him. It was the only reason she was willing to consider my offer.'

Rosalind bit her lip, as though the situation was unusually distressing to her. 'A broken engagement is not the end of the world. And you saved her from any repercussions. It could not have been so horrible to have you instead of Mr Tremaine.'

He shrugged. 'Perhaps not. I have endeavoured to make her happy, of course. But in losing Tremaine she lost any dreams she might have harboured that her marriage would be based in true love. Her parents did not care what happened to her as long as her brother was provided for. It was for him that they came to England. They wished to see him properly outfitted and to give him a taste for travel. Her presence on the trip was little more than an afterthought.' He remembered her brother Carl, who was as sullen and disagreeable as Elise was charming, and gave a small shudder.

'Before I came into the room to speak to her father I heard him remonstrating with her before the whole family for her refusal of Tremaine. He called her all kinds of a fool for not wishing an unfaithful husband. Told her if her mother had seen fit to provide a second son, instead of a useless daughter, then the trip would not have been spoiled with tears and nonsense. Her father swore it mattered not to him who she might choose, and that if she wouldn't have me then he would drag her back home by her hair and give her to the first man willing to take her off his hands.

'When I entered, and she introduced me, I assumed he would show some restraint in his words. But he announced to me that if the silly girl did not take her first offer she must take mine, whether she wanted it or no. He complained that they had spent a small fortune in launching her at what parties were available to them in the winter. They had no wish to do it again in spring, when she might be shown to her best advantage and have a variety of suitors. She stood mutely at his side, accepting the abuse as though it were a normal part of her life.'

Harry clenched his fists at the memory, even after several years. 'If I was not convinced beforehand that she needed me I knew it then. How did they expect her to find a husband with the season still months away? My offer was most fortuitous.' He remembered the resignation with which she had accepted him, and the way she had struggled to look happy as he took her hand. 'And she has been most grateful.'

'Then why is she not living here with you, instead of at Tremaine's side in London?'

'While it was easy enough for her to break the engagement, it has been much harder to tell her heart that the decision was a wise one. And at such times as there is trouble between us, she cannot help but turn to him and wonder if she made a mistake.' He sighed. But he made sure that when he spoke again it was with optimism. 'But, since I can count on Tremaine to be Tremaine, if she thinks to stray, she always returns to me, sadder but wiser.'

'Is he really so bad, then?'

He made note of the curious look in Rosalind's eyes as she asked the question, as though she was both longing for the answer and dreading it.

'He is a man. No better or worse than any other. I imagine he is capable of love if the right woman demands it of him.'

A trick of the morning light seemed to change his sister's expression from despair to hope and back again. So he said, 'But Elise is not that woman and never has been. He was unfaithful to her, you know.'

'Perhaps the thing that parted them was an aberration. Things might be different should they try again.' Rosalind's voice was small, and the prospect seemed to give her no happiness.

He gave her a stern look. 'I'm sure they would be happy to know that their rekindled love has your support. But I find it less than encouraging.'

'Oh.' She seemed to remember that her behaviour was of no comfort to him, and said, 'But I am sure she could be equally happy with you, Harry.'

'Equally?' That was the assessment he had been afraid of.

Rosalind hurried to correct herself. 'I meant to say much happier.'

'I am sure you did. But I wonder what Elise would say, given the chance to compare? Until recently I could not enquire. For at the first sign of trouble, she rushed off to London to be with Nicholas Tremaine.'

Rosalind eyed him critically. 'And you sat at home, waiting for her to come to her senses?'

For a moment he felt older than his years. Then he pulled himself together and said, 'Yes. And it was foolish of me. For I knew how stubborn she could be. It is now far too late to say the things I should have said on that first day that might have brought her home. She has ceased arguing with me and begun to talk of a permanent legal parting. But despite what I should have done, or what she may think she wants, I cannot find it in my heart to let her go. There will be no offer of divorce from me, even if Tremaine can remain stalwart in his hatred of Christmas.' He frowned. 'Which he shows no sign of doing.'

He cast her a sidelong glance. 'This morning he seemed to think he could lose easily and escape back to London. But it does not suit my plans to let him go so soon. If there is any way that you can be of help in the matter…'

Rosalind straightened her back and looked for all

the word like a small bird ruffling its feathers in offended dignity. 'Is that why you invited him here while I am hostess? Because if you are implying that I should romance the man in some way, flirt, preen…'

He found it interesting that she should leap to that conclusion, and filed it away for further reference. 'On the contrary. I mean to make Christmas as miserable an experience for him as possible, and keep him in poor humour until Elise is quite out of patience with him. I was thinking something much more along the lines of an extra measure of brandy slipped into his glass of mulled wine. Enough so that by the end of the evening his mind is clouded. While good humour may come easy at first, foul temper will follow close on its heels in the morning. But the thought of you forced into the man's company as some sort of decoy?' He shook his head and smiled. 'No, that would never do. To see my only sister attached to such a wastrel would not do at all.' He watched for her reaction.

'Half-sister,' she answered absently.

He pretended to ignore her response. 'No, I think he should have more brandy than the average. I doubt laudanum would achieve the desired effect.'

'Laudanum?' She stared at him in surprise. 'Are you seriously suggesting that I drug one of your guests?'

'Only Tremaine, dear. It hardly counts. And it needn't be drugs. If you can think of a better way to keep him off balance…'

'But, Harry, that is—' she struggled for words '—surprisingly dishonourable of you.'

'Then, little one, you are easily surprised. You did not think I had invited the man down here to help him in stealing my wife? I am afraid you will find that I have very little honour on that particular subject. So I did not follow Elise to town to compete for her affections? What point would there have been? Look at the man. More town bronze than the statues at Westminster. He has so much polish I swear I could shave in the reflection. I did not wish to go to London and challenge the man, for I doubt I could compare with him there.'

Harry rubbed his hands together. 'But now we are on my home turf. He knows nothing about country living, or the true likes and dislikes of my wife. And he has no taste at all for the sort of simple Christmas diversions that bring her the most joy. It will take no time at all for him to wrongfoot himself in her eyes, and his disgrace will require very little help from me. When that happens I will be here to pick up the pieces and offer myself as an alternative, just as I did before. If you wish to help me in the matter of persuading Elise to return home, then I wish to hear no more talk of bringing her to heel. Help me by helping Tremaine to make an ass of himself. I will see to Elise, and things will be quite back to normal by Twelfth Night.'

Chapter Eight

Rosalind left her brother and his mad plans alone in the entry hall. If what he was saying was true, then their marriage must have been as frustrating as Elise had claimed. The man had no clue what was wrong or how to fix things. And, worse yet, he refused to stand up to his wife, no matter how much she might wish for it.

This would be more difficult than she'd thought.

As she walked past the door to the library she paused, noticing the mistletoe ball from the doorway had fallen to the floor. She stared down at it in dismay. That was the problem with bringing live things into the house in such cold weather. There was always something wilting, dying or shedding leaves. And even with the help of the servants, she was hard pressed to keep pace with the decay. She shook the tiny clump of leaves and berries, patting it back into shape and re-tying the ribbon that held it together. Then she looked up at the hook at the top of the doorframe. It was hardly worth calling a servant, for to fix the thing back in place would be the work of a moment.

She reached up, her fingers just brushing the lintel, and glanced across the room at a chair. She considered dragging it into place as a step, and then rejected the idea as too much work. The hook was nearly in reach, and if she held the thing by its bottom leaves and stretched a bit she could manage to get it back into place, where it belonged.

She extended her arm and gave a little hop. Almost. She jumped again. Closer still. She crouched low and leaped for the hook, arm extended—and heard the stitching in the sleeve of her dress give way.

The mistletoe hung in place for a moment, before dropping back on her upturned face.

'Do you require assistance?' She caught the falling decoration before it hit the floor and turned to see the head of Nicholas Tremaine peering over the back of the sofa. His hair was tousled, as though he'd just woken from a nap. And he was grinning at her, obviously amused. Even in disarray, he was as impossibly handsome as he had been the day she'd met him, and still smiling the smile that made her insides turn to jelly and her common sense evaporate.

She turned away from him and focused her attention on the offending plant, and the hook that should hold it. 'Have you been watching me the whole time?'

Tremaine's voice held no trace of apology. 'Once you had begun, I saw no reason to alert you to my presence. If you had succeeded, you need never have known I was here.'

'Or you could have offered your help and saved me some bother.'

He paused, and then said, 'If you wished assistance, you would have called for a servant. I thought perhaps you drew some pleasure from it.' He paused again. 'I certainly did.'

She reached experimentally for the hook again. 'You could at least have done me the courtesy to mention that you were in the room. Or in the house, for that matter. You said that you wished to be gone.'

He sighed. 'I assumed you had looked out of the window this morning and guessed the truth on your own. You were right and I was wrong. I am told by your brother that the roads are quite impossible, the drive is blocked, and I am trapped. So I have gone to ground here by the library fire, and I was doing my best to keep true to my word and stay out of your path.' She heard the rattle of china and glanced over her shoulder to see his breakfast things, sitting on the table beside the couch.

'When you realised that your plan was not working, you could have given me warning that I was being observed. It would have spared me some embarrassment.'

He gave a slight chuckle. 'It is not as if I am likely to tell the rest of the company how you behave when we are alone together.'

She cringed. 'I did not say that you would. I have reason to trust your discretion, after all.'

'Then are you implying that my presence here embarrasses you?' He let the words hang with significance.

It did. Not that it mattered. She turned back to look at him. 'Perhaps it is my own behaviour that embarrasses me. And the fact that you have been witness to more than one example of the worst of it.'

He laughed. 'If I have seen the worst of your behaviour, then you are not so very bad as you think.'

She gave him her most intimidating glare, which had absolutely no effect. 'Tell me, now: are you accustomed to finding Elise leaping at doorframes, like a cat chasing a moth?'

'No, I am not. But then, she would not have need to.' His eyes scanned over her in appraisal. 'She is much taller than you are.'

'She is tall, and poised as well, and very beautiful.' Rosalind recited the list by rote. 'She will never know how vexing it is to find everything you want just slightly out of reach. It all comes easily to her.' And Elise, who had two men fighting over her, would never have to cope with the knowledge that the most perfect man in London still thought of her as a silly girl. Rosalind glared at the hook above her. 'I must always try harder, and by doing so I overreach and end up looking foolish.'

'Perhaps you do.' His voice was soft, which surprised her. And then it returned to its normal tone. 'Still, it is not such a bad thing to appear thus. And I am sure most people would take a less harsh view of you than you do of yourself.'

She picked at the mistletoe in her hands, removing

another wilted leaf. Behind her, there was a sigh, and the creak of boot leather. And then he was standing beside her and plucking the thing from between her fingers.

She looked up to find Tremaine far too near, and grinning down at her. 'I understand your irritation with *me*, for we agreed to keep our distance,' he said. 'I have been unsuccessful. But what has that poor plant ever done to you, that you treat it so?'

She avoided his eyes, focusing on the leaves in his hand, and frowned. 'That "poor plant" will not stay where I put it.'

He reached up without effort and stuck it back in its place above their heads. Then he tipped her chin up, so she could see the mistletoe—and him as well—and said innocently, 'There appears to be no problem with it now.'

As a matter of fact it looked fine as it was, with him beneath it and standing so very close to her. For a moment she thought of how nice it might be to close her eyes and take advantage of the opportunity. And how disastrous. Some lessons should not have to be learned twice, and if he meant to see her succumb again he would be disappointed. 'Do not try to tempt me into repeating mistakes of the past. I am not so moved.'

He smiled, to tell her that it was exactly what he was doing. 'Are you sure? My response is likely to be most different from when last we kissed.'

Her pulse gave an unfortunate gallop, but she said, in a frigid tone, 'Whatever for? What has changed?'

'You are no longer an inexperienced girl.'

'Nor am I as foolish as I was, to jump into the arms of a rake.'

He smiled again. 'But I was not a rake when you assaulted me.'

'I assaulted you?' She feigned shock. 'That is doing it much too brown, sir.'

'No, really. I cannot claim that I was an innocent babe, but no one would have called me a rake.' He held a hand over his heart. 'Not until word got round that I had seduced some sweet young thing and then refused to do right by her, in any case.'

'Seduced?' The sinking feeling in her stomach that had begun as she talked to Harry was back in force.

'The rumours grew quite out of proportion to the truth when Elise cast me off. Everyone was convinced that something truly terrible must have happened for her to abandon me so quickly.'

Her stomach sank a little further.

He went on as though noticing nothing unusual. 'And it must have been my fault in some way, mustn't it? Although I was not exactly a pillar of moderation, I had no reputation for such actions before that time. But it is always the fault of the man, is it not? Especially one so crass and cruel as to refuse to offer for the poor, wounded girl because I was already promised to another. And then to deny her father satisfaction, for fear that I might do the man injury.' He leaned over her. 'For I am a crack shot, and a fair hand with a blade. And your father, God protect him, is long past the day when he could have hurt me.' He put on a face of mock horror.

'And when I refused to make a full explanation to my betrothed, or give any of the details of the incident? Well, it must have been because it was so very shameful, and not because it would have made the situation even more difficult for the young lady concerned.'

'You needn't have used my name. But I would not have blamed you for giving the truth to Elise. It was not your fault, after all.' She wished she could sink through the floor, along with the contents of her heart.

'When she came to me with the accusation, I told her that the majority of what she had heard was true. I *had* been caught in an intimate position with a young lady, by the girl's father. But I had not meant to be unfaithful to her, it would not happen again, and she must trust me for the rest.' He frowned. 'That was the sticking point, I am afraid. Her inability to trust. The woman has always been quick to temper. She broke the engagement and went to Harry. I happily gave myself over to sin. And thereby hangs a tale.'

'So you are telling me not only did I ruin your engagement, and spoil Christmas for ever, I negatively affected your character?'

'It is not so bad, having a ruined character. I have found much more pleasure in vice than I ever did in virtue.' He frowned. 'And after all this time the woman I once sought has come back to me.'

Her anger at him warred with guilt. Elise and Harry were in a terrible mess, and she might have been the cause of it all. But how could Tremaine stand there, flirting so casually, as though it did not matter? 'She might have come back, but she is foolish to trust you. What would she think of you, I wonder, if she found you and I here, alone together?'

'I think she would go running right back into Harry's arms, as she did once before.' He seemed to be considering something for a moment, before reaching out to brush his knuckles against her cheek. 'But enough of Elise. I know what she has done these past years, for we have been close, although not as close as I once wished. At no time did she ever mention that Harry had a sister.'

Rosalind cleared her throat, to clear her head, and stepped a little away from him, until he was no longer touching her. 'Half-sister.'

'Mmm.' His acknowledgement of her words was a low hum, and she thought she could feel it vibrating inside her, like the purr of a cat. 'If it was not a trick, as I first suspected, is there some reason that they kept you so well hidden?'

She swallowed hard, and when she answered her voice was clear of emotion. 'Harry and my father do not get on well. He was sent away to school when we were still young, and took the opportunity to spend all subsequent holidays with his own father's family, until he was of age. Then he came to London.' She hung her head. 'I remained at home, where I could not be an embarrassment to the family.'

He was still close enough that if she looked up she could admire his fine lips, see the cleft in his chin. And she remembered the feel of his cheek against hers, the taste of his tongue. She had lost her freedom over a few kisses from that perfect mouth. And somehow she did not mind.

She could feel him watching her so intently that she feared he could read her thoughts, and he said, 'What did you do in the country, my little black sheep? Did you continue in the way you set out with me? Were there other incidents of that kind, I wonder, or was I an aberration?'

Rosalind pulled herself together, pushed against his chest and stepped out of the doorway further into the room. 'How rude of you to assume that there were. And to think that I would tell you if I had transgressed is beyond familiar.'

He turned to follow her and closed the distance between them again. 'But that does not answer my question. Tell me, my dear Rosalind, have there been other men in your life?'

'You were hardly in my life. And I most certainly am not your dear…'

'Ah, ah, ah.' He laid a finger on her lips to stop her words. 'Whether I was willing or no, I was your first kiss. But who was the second?'

'There has not been a second,' she answered, trying to sound prim. But his finger did not move from her lips, and when she spoke it felt rather as though she were trying to nibble on his fingertip. His mouth curled, and she shook her head to escape from the contact. 'I learned my lesson, I swear to you. There is nothing about my conduct of the last years that is in any way objectionable.'

'What a pity.' He leaned away from her and blinked his eyes. 'For a moment I thought Christmas had arrived, in the form of a beautiful hostess every bit as wicked as I could have wished. But if you should have a change of heart and decide to throw yourself upon my person, as you did back then, I would make sure that you would have nothing to regret and much more pleasant memories.'

She turned away and looked out of the window, so that he could not see the indecision in her face. The offer had an obvious appeal. 'How dare you, sir? I have no intention of, as you so rudely put it, *throwing* myself upon your person.'

'Did you have that intention the last time, I wonder?'

'I have no idea what I thought to accomplish. It was the first time I had drunk anything stronger than watered wine, and I did not know my limitations. One cup of particularly strong Christmas punch and I lost all sense.'

He raised his eyebrows. 'And how is the punch at this house?'

'Nothing I cannot handle.'

'If you have returned to the straight and narrow, then you are no use to me at all.' He turned and walked away from her, throwing himself down on the couch as though he had forgotten her presence. 'Whatever shall I do now, to give Elise a distaste of me? For if that fool brother of yours does not come up to snuff soon and reclaim his wife, I am likely to end up married to her after all.'

She looked at him in surprise, and then she blurted, 'Do you not mean to marry Elise?' It was none of her business, but it turned the discussion to something other than herself, which suited her well.

'Elise is already married.' He said it flatly, as though stating the obvious, and stared up at the ceiling.

It was her turn to follow him. She stood before him, hands on hips, close enough so that he could not pretend to ignore her. 'Elise is separated from Harry. If she can persuade him, she will be divorced and free. What are your intentions then?'

'Divorce is by no means a sure thing,' he hedged. 'I would have to declare myself in court as her lover. And even then it might amount to nothing. But it would drag the whole affair into the public eye.'

'Do you have issues with the scandal of it?'

He shrugged. 'If I did, then I would be a fool to escort her now. It is no less scandalous to partner with her while she is still married.'

'Would you think less of her should she be free? Would she be beneath you? Because that would put things back to the way they were before I spoiled them.' She sighed, and dropped her hands to her sides, remembering the look in her brother's eyes when he had seen his wife in the doorway. 'Although it would hurt Harry most awfully.'

Nicholas gave her a tired look, and stretched out on the couch with his feet up and a hand over his eyes. 'There is nothing wrong with Elise, and no reason that I would find her unfit to marry if she were free. Save one.' He looked as though the words were being wrenched out of him. 'I do not love her.'

'You do not…' Rosalind looked confused. 'But she has come back to you again, after all these years. And when I spoke to her, she seemed to think…'

'What she understands to be true is in some ways different from what I have come to believe.' He turned his head to her, and there was a look of obvious puzzlement on his face. 'At one time I would have liked nothing better than to meet her in church and unite our futures. But in the years since she turned me down in favour of Harry?' He shrugged. 'Much time has passed. I still find her beautiful, and very desirable—for, while I am circumspect, I am not blind to her charms. I enjoy her company, and I value her friendship above all things. But I seriously doubt, should we marry, that I will be a more satisfactory husband than the one she already has. Once the novelty began to pale she would find many aspects of my character are wanting. And for my part? She broke my heart most thoroughly the first time she chose another. But I doubt when she leaves me this time that it will cause similar damage.'

'How utterly perfect!' Rosalind reached out and pulled his boots onto the floor, forcing him to sit up.

'Oh, really?' He was eyeing her suspiciously. 'And just why would you say that?'

She sat down on the couch beside him, in the space his legs had occupied, trying to disguise her obvious relief. 'I will explain shortly, if you can but answer a few more questions to my satisfaction. If you do not want her, then why did you take her back?'

He scratched his head. 'I am not sure. But I suspect that force of habit brought her to me, and force of habit keeps me at her side.'

'That does not sound very romantic.'

'I thought at first that it was lust. A desire to taste the pleasures that I was once denied.' He gave her a significant look. 'But our relationship has not yet progressed to such a stage, and I find myself most content with things as they are.'

'You two are not…? You do not…?' Rosalind took her most worldly tone with him, and hoped he could not tell that she lacked the understanding to ask the rest of the question. For she was unsure just what *should* be happening if the relationship had 'progressed'. But she had wondered, all the same.

'We are not, and we do not.' He was staring at her in surprise now. 'Are you seeking vicarious pleasure in the details of Elise's infidelity? For you are most curious on the subject.'

'Not really.' She gave him a critical appraisal in return. 'I think it is quite horrid that she left Harry, and even worse that you took her in. But if it was all for an ember of true love that smouldered for years, though untended, it would give me some measure of understanding. And I would find it in my heart to forgive her.'

'But not me?' he asked.

'I would suspect you of being an unrepentant rogue, Tremaine, as I do in any case. For you seem ready to ruin my brother's marriage not because you love deeply, but because you are too lazy to send Elise home.'

He flinched at her gibe. 'It will probably spoil your low opinion of me, but here is the real reason I encouraged her to remain in London. I recognise a friend in dire need, and I want to help her. She is lost, Miss

Morley. She will find her way right again, I am sure. But until that time better that she be lost with me than with some other man who does not understand the situation and chooses to take advantage of her weakness.'

'You are carrying on a public affair with my sister-in-law for her own good?'

Tremaine smiled. 'And now please explain it to your brother for me. I am sure he will be relieved to hear it.'

'I think Harry doubts your good intentions.'

His smile widened to a grin. 'I know he does. I think he invited me down here for the express purpose of keeping me away from Elise during the holiday. To the susceptible, Christmas can be a rather romantic season. I believe we both know what can happen in the proximity of wine and mistletoe.'

He looked at the ceiling and whistled, while she glared steadfastly towards the floor.

'Do you know how he attempted to trick me into this visit? By offering to divorce his wife if I won his silly bet. He probably thought I could not resist the challenge of besting him. Little did he suspect that I would tell Elise all, and she would insist on coming as well. It must gall him no end to see the two of us here.'

Rosalind cleared her throat. 'I think you would be surprised at how much he might know on that matter. But pray continue.'

Tremaine laughed. 'For my part, were I a jealous man, I would be enraged at the amount of energy my supposed intended spends in trying to attract her husband's attention by courting mine. She means to go back to him, and he is dying to have her back. There is nothing more to be said on the matter.'

'I will agree with that,' said Rosalind. 'For I have never met a couple better suited, no matter what they might think.'

He nodded. 'We agree that they belong together. And she does want to come home to him, since he did not come to London and get her. So be damned to Harry's machinations for the holidays. I have devised a plan of my own.'

'Really?' Someone else with a plan? She could not decide if she should meet the news with eagerness or dread.

'Harry's scheme, whatever it might be, requires my eagerness to win his wife away from him. In this he does not have my co-operation. I have kept her safe from interlopers for two months now, but it is time she returned home. I was hoping to find my host, lose the bet, and make a hasty escape before Elise realised what had happened. In no time, I would have been back in London. And she would have been back here with Harry, where she belongs.'

She shook her head. 'Until such time as Harry loaned her a coach so that she could leave him again. Which he will do, the moment she asks. It will do no good at all if you leave only to have Elise following in your wake.'

Tremaine grimaced in disgust. 'Why on earth would Harry lend her a coach? I have brought her as far as Lincolnshire. If he lacks the sense to hold on to her once he has her again then you can hardly expect me to do more.'

Rosalind replied, 'Elise's main argument with the

man seems to be that he is too agreeable. And he has admitted to me that he would deny her nothing. If she wished to leave, he would not stop her.'

'Damn Harry and his agreeable nature,' he said. 'In any case, the snow is keeping me from the execution of my plan, since it required a rapid getaway and that appears to be impossible.' He stared at her for a moment. 'But finding you here adds an interesting ripple to the proceedings. Considering our history together, and the results that came of it, I thought perhaps…'

'That I would allow you to dishonour me again to precipitate another falling-out with Elise?' She gave him a sceptical glare. 'While I cannot fault you for the deviousness of it, I do not see what good it would do. You might have escaped marriage to me once, but I expect Harry would call you out if you refused me now.'

He glared at her. 'Very well, Miss Morley. You have proved my plans to be non-starters. I shall fall back on my last resort, of taking all my meals in this room and avoiding both the lord and the lady of the house until I can leave. Unless you have a better idea?' The challenge hung in the air.

She smiled back. 'I was hoping you would ask. For I have a far superior plan.' Or rather Harry had, if she could get Tremaine to agree with it. It would be quite hopeless if he meant to hide in the library the whole visit.

He favoured her with a dry expression, and reached for his teacup to take a fortifying sip. 'Do you, now?'

'Of course. You admit you are concerned with Elise's welfare. And, while I wish her well, I am more worried about Harry. If we are in agreement that what they need for mutual happiness is each other, then it makes sense that we pool our resources and work together to solve their difficulties.'

'Because we have had such good luck together in the past?'

She sniffed in disapproval. 'I would not be expecting you to do anything more than you have done already. Pay courteous attention to Elise. Be her confidant, her escort, her friend. But to do that you must come out of this room, participate in the activities I have planned, and see that she does as well. Your mere presence may be enough to goad Harry to action on the matter, if he is the one who must apologise.'

'That is exactly what I fear.' Tremaine shuddered theatrically. 'Although Harry seems to be a mild-mannered chap, I've found in the past that this type of fellow can be the most dangerous, when finally "goaded to action". If your plan involves me meeting with violence at the hands of an irate husband…'

'I doubt it will come to that.'

'You doubt? Miss Morley, that is hardly encouraging.' He spread his hands in front of him, as though admiring a portrait. 'I can see it all now. You and the other guests look on in approval as Harry beats me to a bloody pulp. And then, Elise falls into his arms. While I wish them all the best, I fail to see the advantages to me in this scenario.'

'Do not be ridiculous, sir. I doubt Harry is capable of such a level of violence.' She considered. 'Although, if you could see your way clear to letting him plant you a facer…'

'No, I could not,' He stared at her in curiosity. 'Tell me, Miss Morley, are all your ideas this daft, or only those plans that concern me?'

'There is nothing the least bit daft about it. It is no more foolish than taking a lover in an effort to get her to return to her husband.' She stared back at him. 'You will pardon me for saying it, but if that is the projected result of an affair with you, it does not speak well of your romantic abilities.'

'I have the utmost confidence in my "romantic abilities". But if you doubt them, I would be only too happy to demonstrate.'

She cleared her throat. 'Not necessary, Tremaine. But, since you are concerned for your safety, we will find a way to make Harry jealous that involves no personal harm to you. Is that satisfactory?'

'Why must we make him jealous at all? If I stay clear of him, and we allow time to pass and nature to take its course…'

'Spoken as a true city-dweller, Tremaine. If you had ever taken the time to observe nature, you would have found that it moves with incredible slowness. The majestic glaciers are called to mind. So deliberate as to show no movement at all. And as cold as that idea.'

He shook his head. 'Spoken by someone who has never seen the ruins of Pompeii. They are a far better example of what happens when natural passions are allowed their sway. Death and destruction for all who stand in the way. Which is why I prefer to keep my distance.'

'You have seen them?' she asked eagerly.

'Harry and Elise? Of course. And I suspect that, although they do not show it outright—'

'No. The ruins of Pompeii.'

He stopped, confused by the sudden turn in the conversation. 'Of course. I took the Grand Tour. It is not so unusual.'

She leaned forward on the couch. 'Were they as amazing as some have said?'

'Well, yes. I suppose. I did not give it much thought at the time.'

She groaned in frustration. 'I have spent my whole life sequestered in the country, drawing the same watercolours of the same spring flowers, year after year. And you have seen the world. But you did not think on it.'

'You are sequestered in the country because you cannot be trusted out of sight of home,' he snapped.

'Because of one mistake. With you.' She pointed a finger. 'But I notice you are to be trusted to go wherever you like.'

'That is because I am a man. You are a girl. It is an entirely different thing.'

'Please cease referring to me as a girl. I am fully grown, and have been for some time.' She glared up at him. 'My diminutive stature has nothing to do with youth, and should not render me less than worthy— despite what Elise might have to say on the subject of what constitutes a good match.'

He was staring at her with a dazed expression. 'Indeed. You are quite tall enough, I am sure. And what does Elise have to do with it?'

'She was speaking on the subject of her marriage to Harry,' Rosalind admitted. 'I still find it very hard to understand, but she seemed to think it important that Harry was tall.'

Tremaine furrowed his brow, and took another sip from his cup. 'That makes no sense. He is no taller than I, certainly. Perhaps even a little shorter.'

'But just right in the eyes of Elise, I assure you. She made a point of assuring me that physically he is a magnificent specimen, and that they are very well suited.'

Tremaine choked on his tea.

'Is something the matter?'

'Not at all. It is just I think you have misunderstood her.'

'Whatever else could she mean?'

He was looking at her in a most unusual way. 'Perhaps at another time we can discuss that matter in more detail. But for now, do not concern yourself with it. I suspect it means that there are parts of married life that she is eager to resume. And that I have brought her home not a moment too soon. We need not concern ourselves with Harry's good qualities. If we wish success, we would be better served to improve on his deficiencies. And, much as I dislike the risks involved, we must do what is necessary to make him reclaim his wife's affection.'

Rosalind smiled at his use of the word 'we'. Perhaps they were working towards the same end, after all. 'My thoughts exactly.'

He returned her smile. 'Well, then. What does she want from him that we can help her achieve?'

'I know from experience that Harry can be the most

frustrating of men.' She frowned. 'If he does not wish you to know, it is very hard to divine what it is that he is thinking. Hence our current predicament. I have no doubt that he adores Elise. But she cannot see it, even after all these years.'

Tremaine frowned in return. 'Can she not see what is obvious to the rest of us?'

'I think she wishes him to be more demonstrative.'

'Which will be damned difficult, you will pardon the expression, with her hanging upon my arm. If he has never made any attempt to dislodge her from it, I fail to see what I could do to change things.'

She patted him on the arm in question. 'You have hit on the problem exactly. She wishes him to *do* something about you.'

Tremaine ran a hand over his brow. 'And I would rather he did not. Is there anything else?'

'She wishes he would talk to her so that she could better understand him.'

He furrowed his brow. 'They have passed the last five years in silence? That cannot be. I would swear that I have heard him utter words in her presence. Is it a difficulty of language? For I have found Elise's comprehension of English to be almost flawless.'

Rosalind closed her eyes for a moment, attempting to gather strength. 'She wishes him to speak about important matters.'

'Matters of state, perhaps? How odd. She has shown no interest in them when speaking to me.'

Rosalind burst forth in impatience. 'This has nothing

to do with English lessons or a sudden interest in politics, Tremaine. Elise wishes Harry to speak openly about matters that are important to *her*.'

'Oh.' He slumped in defeat. 'Then it is quite hopeless. For he would have no idea what that would be. The minds of women are a depth that we gentlemen have not been able to plumb, I'm afraid.'

'Don't be an idiot,' she snapped. 'There is nothing so terribly difficult to understand about women, if you make an effort. We two are conversing well enough, aren't we? You do not require the assistance of a guide to understand me?'

He paused for a moment and answered politely, 'Of course not. But you are more direct in your communication than Elise.'

She smiled graciously, preparing to blush and accept the compliment.

Then he said, 'Almost masculine.' He paused again. 'And why do you persist in calling me just Tremaine, and not Mister? If you prefer, you may call me Nicholas.'

'I do not.' She stood up and moved away from him. 'Nor do I think your behaviour proves you worthy of an honorific. Tremaine will do. And you may continue to call me Miss Morley. And now that we have got that out of the way, are we in agreement about the matter of Elise and Harry? Will you help me?'

'Since it is likely to be the only way you will allow me any peace? Yes, I will help you, Miss Morley. Now, go about your business and let me return to my nap.'

Chapter Nine

Harry sighed in satisfaction as he climbed the stairs towards his bed. The day had gone well enough, he supposed. The house had buzzed with activity. Wherever he went he had found people playing at cards or games, eating, drinking and merrymaking, with Rosalind presiding over all with an air of hospitable exasperation. The only faces that had seemed to be absent from the mix were those of Tremaine and his wife.

The thought troubled him, for he suspected that they might be together, wherever they were, enjoying each other's company. And it would be too obvious of him to pound upon his wife's door and admit that he wished to know if she was alone.

He almost sighed in relief as he saw her in the window seat at the top of the stairs. She was just where she might have been if there had been no trouble between them, sitting in her favourite place and looking out onto the snow falling into the moonlit park below.

He stepped up beside her, speaking quietly so as not to disturb her mood. 'Beautiful, is it not?'

'Yes.' She sighed. But it was a happy, contented sigh, and it made him smile.

'I expect it will make tomorrow's trip into the trees a difficult one.'

'You still mean to go?' She looked at him in obvious surprise.

'Of course. It will be the morning of Christmas Eve. We went out into the woods together often enough that I have come to think of it as a family tradition. Would you like to accompany me?'

She looked excited at the prospect, and then dropped her gaze and shook her head. 'I doubt that would be a good idea.'

He laughed. 'It is not as if we are planning an assignation. Only a sign of friendship. If we cannot be lovers we can at least be friends, can't we?'

'Friends?' The word sounded hollow and empty coming from her. She was making no attempt to show the world that she was happy with their situation.

It gave him hope, and he continued. 'Yes. We can have a truce. If you wish Tremaine to be your lover, then why can I not occupy the position he has vacated and be your trusted friend?'

'You wish to be my friend?' Now she looked truly puzzled.

'If I can be nothing else. Let us go out tomorrow, as we have done in the past. We will take Tremaine with us, so that he can share in the fun. If he is what you want, then I wish to see him well settled in my place before I let you go. Tomorrow I will pass the torch.'

'You will?' If she wanted her freedom, his offer should give her a sense of relief. But there was nothing in her tone to indicate it.

'Yes. I had not planned on your visit, but now that you are here it is a good thing. We cannot settle what is between us with you in London and me in the country. If you wish an end to things, then it is better if we deal with them face to face, without acrimony. Only then will you truly be free.' He let the words sink in. 'You do wish to be free of me, do you not?'

'Yes…'

There was definitely doubt in her voice. He clung to that split second of hesitation as the happiest sound he had heard in months.

'Very well, then. If there is nothing I can do that will make Tremaine lose the bet, on Twelfth Night I will honour my word and begin divorce proceedings. For above all I wish you to be happy. Merry Christmas, Elise.'

'Thank you.'

She whispered it, and sounded so very sad that it was all he could do to keep from putting his arms around her and drawing her close, whispering back that he would never let her go.

'Let us go to bed, then, for it will be an early morning.'

She stood and walked with him, towards their rooms.

Would it be so wrong to take her hand and pull her along after him to his door? Although her manner said that she might not be totally opposed to the idea, neither was there proof that she would be totally in favour of it. It would be best if he waited until he had a better idea of what she truly wanted.

He put his hands behind his back and cleared his throat. 'About our disagreement of yesterday, over the arrangement of the rooms. After we had gone to bed, I realised how it must look to you. And I apologise if you took it as an effort to control your behaviour. You have made it clear enough to me that it is no longer any business of mine what occurs in your bedroom. If there is a reason that you might wish to lock the connecting door, I will allow you your privacy.'

'For what reason would I wish privacy?' She sounded confused by the idea. Perhaps even after two months Tremaine was an idle threat to their marriage. She shrugged as though nothing could occur to her, and gave a tired laugh. 'In any case, what good would it do to lock the door against you? You have the key.'

He held his hands open in front of him. 'I have all the keys, Elise. I could open the door of any room in which you slept. You must have realised that when you came home. But do you really think me such a villain that I mean to storm into your room without your permission and force myself upon you?'

She caught her breath and her eyes darkened. For a moment his threat held definite appeal.

Then he cleared his throat and continued, 'Am I really the sort who would take you until you admitted that there was no place in the world that you belonged but in my arms and in my bed?'

She froze for a moment, and then glared at him. 'No, Harry, you are not. On more careful consideration, I think that I have nothing to worry about. Goodnight.'

And, perhaps it was his imagination, but the way she carried herself could best be described as stomping off to her room. When the door shut, he suspected that the slam could be heard all over the house.

The next morning Harry was up well before dawn, had taken breakfast and dressed in clothes suitable for the weather before going to roust Tremaine. He could not help but smile as he pounded smartly on the door to the poor man's bedroom. He could hear rustling, stumbling noises, and a low curse before the door in front of him creaked open.

Tremaine stood before him, bleary-eyed and still in his nightshirt. 'Eh?'

'Time to get up, old man.'

Tremaine squinted into the hall and croaked, 'Is there a problem?'

'No problem at all. Did I forget to tell you last night? So sorry. But you *must* be a part of today's proceedings. Elise is expecting you.'

'Then come for me in daylight.'

'No, no. What we are about must be done at dawn. And on the morn of Christmas Eve. There is no better time. Pull on some clothes, man. Warm ones. Your true love is awaiting you in the hall.'

At the mention of Elise Tremaine's eyes seemed to widen a bit. Then he stared back at Harry, as though

trying to gauge his intentions. At last he sighed with resignation, and muttered something that sounded rather
like, 'Damn Rosalind.' Then he said, 'A moment.' And
then he shut the door.

'A moment' proved to be the better part of a half an
hour. Tremaine appeared at the door again, no happier, but
reasonably well dressed for Harry's purposes, in a fine
coat of light wool and soft, low shoes. He stepped into the
hall and shut the door behind him. It was only then that
he noticed the axe in Harry's hands. 'What the devil—?'

Harry nudged him with the handle and gave him a
mad grin. 'You'll see. You'll see soon enough.'

Tremaine swallowed. 'That is what I fear.'

'Downstairs.' He gestured Tremaine ahead of him,
and watched the cautious way the man passed him.
There was a tenseness in his shoulders, as though his
back was attempting to climb out of his coat while his
head was crawling into it. His neck seemed to have disappeared entirely. He did not relax until he saw Elise,
pacing on the slate at the foot of the stairs, probably
assuming that Harry would not cut him down dead in
front of a lady.

'There you are.' Elise was trying to display a mixture
of irritation and trepidation at what was about to occur,
but she could not manage to disguise the same childlike
excitement that she had shown whenever they had done
this in the past. It made Harry happy to look at her. 'I
was not sure if you would still hold to the practice.'

Harry smiled. 'Perhaps if you had not come home I
might have forgone it. But if you are under this roof then

Christmas will be every bit as full as you would wish it to be. And if we are to do it at all, then we must bring Tremaine, so he will know what is to be expected of him next year.'

If she meant to rescue the poor man, she gave no indication of it. Instead, she nodded with approval. 'Let us go, then.'

'Go where?' Tremaine had found his voice at last.

'Outside, of course. To cut the Yule Log.'

'Oh, I say. You can't mean…'

'A massive oak. I have just the thing picked out.' He turned back to his wife, ignoring the stricken look on Tremaine's face. 'You will approve, I'm sure, Elise. The thing is huge. Sure to burn for days, and with enough wood for two fireplaces.'

'Really?' She was smiling at Harry as though he had offered to wrap her in diamonds. Any annoyance at the chill he would take tramping about the grounds in a foot of fresh snow was replaced by the warm glow of her presence.

But the Christmas spirit did not seem to be reaching Tremaine. He grumbled, 'Surely you have servants to do this?'

Harry shook his head. 'I could never expect them to do such. It is tradition that we choose one ourselves. Elise is very particular about the choice, and she enjoys the walk. I could not begrudge her the experience.'

Elise looked at Tremaine in disapproval. 'You are not dressed for the weather.'

'Here—we can fix that.' Harry removed his own

scarf and wrapped it twice around Tremaine's neck, pulling until it constricted. 'There. All better. Let us proceed.' He opened the front door wide and shepherded them through.

Elise took to it as he had known she would. Though she might claim to adore the city, she needed space and fresh air to keep her happy. She strode out into the morning, with the first glints of sunlight hitting the fresh snow, twirled and looked back at them, her face shining brighter than any star. 'Isn't it magnificent?'

Harry nodded in agreement. As he looked at her, he felt his own throat close in a way that had nothing to do with the tightness of a scarf. She was so beautiful standing there, with the dawn touching her blonde hair. And he thought, *You used to be mine.* He chased the thought away. He would make her come home again. For if he had lost her for ever he might just as well march out into the snow, lie down and wait for the end.

He looked around him—anywhere but at Elise. For until he had mastered his emotions he could not bear to look in her face. And he saw she was right: with a fresh coating of snow over everything, and frost and icicles clinging to the trees, it was a most beautiful morning indeed.

Tremaine merely grunted.

'This way.' Harry pointed to the left, up a low hill at the side of the house. 'In the copse of trees where we used to picnic.' He set off at a brisk pace.

Elise followed him easily in her stout boots and heavy wool skirt. 'You do not mean to take the tree where we…' She was remembering their last picnic in the oak grove, and her cheeks were going pink in a way that had nothing to do with the cold.

He cleared his throat. 'Not that one, precisely. But very nearby. This tree is dying, and we will have to take it soon in any case. Why should it not serve a noble purpose?'

Behind them he could hear Tremaine, stumbling and sliding and cursing his way up the hill. He was falling further behind as Elise drew abreast of Harry.

She said softly, 'I am still amazed that you are willing to do this after what has gone on between us. Although you always complied with my wishes, you complained about the bother of it in years past.'

He appeared pleased, and looked at the ground. 'Perhaps I did. But I found, though I meant to leave it off, that the habit was ingrained. Although I complained to you, perhaps I enjoyed it more than I knew.' He glanced back over his shoulder. 'In future you will have Tremaine to complain over it, when he takes my place. But for myself I mean to spend a quiet hour on a winter morning, watching the sun come up.'

She smiled at him in approval, and then blushed and looked away. He glanced back again, so that she could not see his answering smile, and called, 'Keep up, Tremaine, or you shall miss the best part.'

The tree he had chosen had been carefully notched by a servant, so that most of the work was done and it would fall correctly. In truth, there was so little left to do that it was fortunate the thing had not fallen on its own in the storm. A few blows of the axe would give the impression to his lady love of manly competence without undue exertion.

He stepped around to the far side and swung the axe into the wood. It struck with a satisfying clunk that made Tremaine flinch. 'See? We strike thusly.' Harry swung again, and felt the unaccustomed labour jar the bones of his arms. After several Christmases just like this, at least he was prepared for the shock. It was much better than it had been the first time his wife had suggested the activity. 'It takes only a few strokes to do the job.' He smiled at his adversary again. 'Step away from that side, sir. For the tree is likely to come down when I least expect it.' He took a short pause, turned so that Elise could not see the expression on his face, and stared at Tremaine, not bothering to smile. 'I would hate for an accident to befall you.'

Tremaine fairly leapt out of the way, standing safely behind him. The man was terrified of him.

Harry grinned to himself and swung again. 'It is a dangerous business, using an axe.' *Clunk*. 'No end of things can go wrong. Should the handle slip in my hands, for example.' *Clunk*.

He glanced up at his wife's friend, who had gone bone-white with cold and fear. Harry offered him the axe. 'Here. You must try. For I expect Elise will wish you to learn the ways of this.'

Tremaine muttered low, under his breath, 'If you think next year will find me chopping wood for the holiday, you are both quite mad. I have no property in the country, nor do I plan to acquire one. And I seriously doubt that I will be motivated to march through Hyde Park with a weapon in my hands, doing damage to the landscaping.'

'Oh, Nicholas,' Elise laughed. 'What a droll idea.'

But Tremaine took the axe from Harry's hands, and looked relieved to have disarmed him. Harry stepped back as the other man took a mighty swing at the oak, overbalanced, and fell on his seat in the snow.

'Hmm. It does not seem that you have the hang of it yet. Best let me finish it after all.' He retrieved the axe, and a few more chops and a stout push was all it took. There was a loud cracking noise, and he put out an arm to shield Elise. Tremaine scrambled to safety, away from the falling tree.

It crashed to the ground and they stared at the thing for a moment—Tremaine in disgust, and Elise with obvious satisfaction. Then Tremaine said, 'I suppose now you will tell me that we must drag it back to the house?'

Elise giggled, and Harry said, 'Oh, no. Of course not. This is still much too green to burn. This is the log for next year's festivity. Some people save the cutting for Candlemas, but we have always done it on Christmas Eve morn. And this year it is my gift to you, Tremaine. You will need it next year, when you celebrate Christmas with Elise.' He gestured to the enormous tree on the ground before them. 'You can take the whole thing back with you when you return to London. The servants will take care of it in good time. They are just now bringing in last year's log. We shall see it when we go back to the house.'

'Mad.' Tremaine stared at them in amazement. 'You are both quite mad.' Then he turned from them and stalked back to the house, sliding ahead of them on the downward slope.

Harry looked after him. 'I do not think Tremaine appreciates my gift.'

Elise looked after him as well, trying to look stern, although a smile was playing around her lips. 'That was horrible of you, you know. To drag the poor man out in weather like this. And so early in the morning. He abhors mornings.'

Harry tried to focus on the snow-covered back of the retreating man. Not on the beautiful woman at his side and what her smile might tell him about her intimate knowledge of Nicholas Tremaine's morning routine. 'A pity. For it is the most beautiful time of day. You still enjoy mornings, do you not? Or have your ways changed now that you are not with me?'

'I still enjoy them,' she admitted. 'Although they are not so nice in the city as they are here. It is the best time to ride, though. For many are still sleeping from the night's revelry, and the park is nearly empty.'

'Oh.' He tried not to imagine what a handsome couple his wife and Tremaine would make on horseback in Rotten Row.

'But the city is quite empty at Christmas. And I will admit it would have been lonely to remain there.' She hesitated. 'I must thank you for inviting…Tremaine.'

She had remembered, too late, that she had not been included in the invitation. There was an awkward pause.

'I am glad that you chose to accompany him,' Harry said firmly. 'For I would not wish you to be alone. And I hope Christmas will be very much as you remember it.' He glanced down the hill towards the house. 'You have brought many changes to Anneslea since we married.'

'Really?' She looked surprised, as though she did not realise the merriment she'd brought with her when she'd come into his life. 'Was not Christmas a joyous time when you were a boy?'

He shrugged. 'Much like any other day. When I was small my father was often ill, and there was little cause for celebration. My stepfather, Morley, did not hold with foolishness on a holy day. And once I came here, to stay with Grandfather?' He shrugged again. 'It was a very quiet festival. There was dinner, of course. And gifts.' They had arrived back at the house. A footman grinned as he opened the front door, and they entered the front hall to the smells of pine and spices and an air of suppressed excitement. He looked around him. 'But it was nothing like this. Thank you.' His voice very nearly cracked on the words.

'You're welcome, Harry.' Her eyes were very round, and misty blue in the morning light. Then she looked away from him quickly, letting a servant take her outer clothes and enquiring about tea, which was already poured in the library, just as it had been in years past. It was still early, but any guests who had risen would be in the dining room taking breakfast. For a time it would be just the two of them, alone together.

In the library, she glanced around the room with a

critical eye. And Harry noted with some satisfaction that she seemed unconcerned by the presence of only two cups on the tea tray. Apparently, after his disgrace in the woods, she did not care that Tremaine would be left to fend for himself.

'Do you mean to have Rosalind here for Christmas from now on?' she said softly.

'It depends, I suppose, on whether Morley allows it. But I do not know what I would have done without her help this year.'

Elise looked up from her cup, her eyes still wide with sympathy. 'Does she know that the family recipes as they are written are not accurate?'

'Eh?'

'Rosalind. There are changes in the Christmas recipes, and she should remember to remind Cook.'

Harry waved a dismissive hand. 'I expect she will manage as best she can. It will be all right.'

'Perhaps I should help her.'

'No,' Harry said, worried that her sudden interest in the menu was likely to take her away from him again. 'There is no need, I'm sure. No one will notice if things are not quite up to standard.'

She stared at him. 'Really, Harry. You have no idea how difficult a house party can be.'

He looked warmly at her. 'Only because you made it look so easy, my sweet. But you need not bother.' He gave a slight sigh. 'I will want you here tonight, of course. When it is time to light the Yule Log. For it is still very much a part of you, since you helped me to choose it. And I've still got a piece of last year's log, so that we may light the new one properly.'

Her agitation seemed to fade, and she smiled a little, remembering.

'If we have any regrets from the old year we can throw them on the fire,' he announced. 'Next year we shall start anew.'

She set her teacup down with a click. 'And behave as if none of this has happened?'

He sighed. 'Is it really necessary to retread the same ground? If you are ready to come home, then I see no reason to refer to any of this again.'

'If I am ready to come home?'

He had spoken too soon, and ruined all that had gone before. For the coldness had returned to her voice, and she was straightening up the tea things and preparing to leave him.

'Perhaps I should go to my room and dress for the day. If you will excuse me?'

He followed her to the door and in a last act of desperation held up a hand to stop her as she crossed the threshold, touching her arm and pointing above them. 'Mistletoe.'

She frowned. 'You can't be serious.'

'Not even for old times' sake?'

'Certainly not.' She reached up and caught the thing by a twig. She pulled it down, then threw it to the floor at his feet.

He stared at it, unsure whether to be angry or sad. 'Pity. I would have quite enjoyed it. I think it is your kiss

I miss the most. But there are so many things about you that I miss it is hard to tell.'

'Miss me?' She laughed. 'This is the first I have heard of it. It seems to me that you are managing quite well without me, Harry.'

'It bothers you, then, that I have put Rosalind in charge?'

'Not particularly.'

'But something has made you unhappy again. Are you ready to discuss why you are here?' he asked.

'Whatever do you mean?'

'You have come back to me, Elise, just as I knew you would. It was no real surprise, seeing you. I had a devil of a time persuading Tremaine to take the invitation, but I knew if he came you would not be able to stay away. And I was right.' He looked at her, searching her expression for some evidence that she was weakening again.

'It should not be so terribly strange that I would wish to return with him. I lived here for several years, and associate many happy memories with the place.'

Harry sighed. 'Do you really? When you left I thought you never wished to see the place again. Or was it just the owner you wished to avoid? Because you must have known I'd be here as well.'

'I hold you no ill will,' she insisted, staring at him through narrowed eyes and proving her words a lie. 'And, since you have not said otherwise, I assume you agree that our separation is for the best.'

'You wished to part, not I. Do not mistake my unwillingness to beg for you to return as agreement.' And then his desire to hold her got the better of him, and he stepped even closer. 'There is very little separation between us at this moment.' He grabbed her wrist and pulled her to him, so her body rested tight against him.

'That is none of my doing and all of yours.' But she did not push him away.

He calmed himself so as not to alarm her. Then he put his mouth to her ear and whispered, so softly that only she could hear, 'Kiss me, Elise. Just one more time. I will enjoy it, and you will as well. I would make sure of the fact.' He felt her tremble and knew that he was right. When his lips met hers he would make her forget all about her argument with him. She would think of nothing but how he made her feel, and that would be the end of their troubles.

'I did not come here because I missed your kisses.' She pulled away from him, and the small rejection stung worse than all the others combined.

'And yet you were the one to come home.'

'For a brief visit. There are things in my room…'

'Things?' He laughed, for he had been sure that she would come up with a better lie than that when they finally had a chance to speak. 'If that is all you wanted, then you could have saved me a small amount of personal pride had you come alone, in January, rather than trailing after Tremaine when the house is full of guests.'

'I am not trailing after him,' she snapped.

Harry took a deep breath, for it would not do to lose his temper with her. 'It is all right,' he responded. 'I've grown quite used to it, really.'

But clearly it was not all right to her. He had misspoken again, and she was working herself into a rage. 'You did not expect me to live for ever alone, once we parted?'

'That is not what I mean, and you know it. I knew when you finally left me that you would go straight to Tremaine for comfort. I have expected it for many years.'

Anger and indignation flashed hot in her eyes, as though she could pretend the truth was not an obvious thing and her leaving had been all *his* fault. 'When I *finally* left you? What cause did I ever give you to doubt me?'

'It was never a question of doubt, Elise.' He tried to keep his tone matter-of-fact, for there was no point in fuelling her anger with his. 'I have always known that I was your second choice.'

'How utterly ridiculous,' she snapped. 'I married you, didn't I? Are you saying you doubted my innocence?'

'I am saying nothing of the kind. I am saying that I was not your first choice when you wed. You might have accepted my offer, but Tremaine offered for you first. You might have chosen me, but you always regretted that it could not have been Nicholas. I have had to live with the fact for five years, Elise.' He struggled to hide the hurt in his tone, and instead his voice sounded bitter. 'I had hoped that you would put him behind you once you were married. I would not have offered for you otherwise. But I realised almost from the beginning that it was not to be the case.'

'You realised?'

There was something in the sound of her voice that was almost like an accusation, and he could feel his carefully managed control slipping away. 'It did not take you long to make up with the man. Less than a year. The quarrel that parted you would have mended easily had you been willing to wait. It was really most annoying to listen to you complain, at the end, about *my* lack of devotion. For you have been so clearly devoted to another. Did you expect me to remain for ever the be-nighted fool who had married you? In the face of your continued indifference? In time one learns to harden one's heart, Elise.'

He was almost shouting by the time he'd finished. And then he laughed again, at the shocked expression on her face. 'Although what you expect by accompanying your lover to our home for Christmas I cannot imagine. Did you hope to create a dramatic scene for the diversion of my guests? Is it not bad enough that you have finally worked up the courage to be unfaithful to me? Must you parade it in front of me as well?' He shook his head, and his voice returned to normal. 'I never in all these years felt you to be so cruel. Perhaps I did not know you as well as I thought.'

Which was foolish, for he had known all along that that was what she would do. He had wanted her to come with Tremaine, had planned for the eventuality. And now he was angry to the point of shouting because his plans had come to fruition. It made no sense at all.

But it was too late to call back the words, or to explain that he wished to discuss things with her in a rational manner. Elise's cheeks had grown hot with anger and shame, but no words were issuing from her lips, and she was staring at him as though she no longer knew him.

As he waited for her response, a part of him wanted to beg her forgiveness, forestall her reaction. But why should he take all the blame when she was the one who had left? It was long past time for her turn to be hurt and frustrated and embarrassed.

It did him no good to feel sure that he was in the right on this. Instead of vindication, he was suddenly sick with the taste of truth. He had spoken too much of it, all in one go, and it sat in his stomach like an excess of Christmas dinner.

Did she expect him to swallow his pride as well, before she was willing to come home? If the silence went on much longer she would see him on his knees, begging her to return.

Then she spoke, and her voice was cool and even. 'So I finally know, after all this time, what you really think of me. It is most gratifying that our separation has given you the ability to speak your mind. And I find I have nothing to add to it.'

Then she turned and walked from the room, leaving him all over again. He stared down at the mistletoe at his feet, and then kicked it savagely aside, before gathering enough composure to meet his guests for breakfast.

Elise walked back towards her room, numb with shock. She could hear Harry turn and walk in the opposite direction, towards the dining room. She was glad of it, for if he spoke one more word to her she would burst into tears and not care who saw her. After all her complaints over not knowing her husband's true feelings, he had finally given them to her. And she found that she liked him better as he had been.

What had happened to the man she'd married? The amiable fellow who had tolerated her behaviour without question? In two months he'd been replaced by an angry stranger who looked at her with hard eyes and a mouth set in bitter disapproval. It was as though he was meeting her for the first time, and was thoroughly disappointed with what he saw.

Why had she come here? It had seemed like a sensible decision at the time. Either she would prove to herself and everyone else that she had put her marriage behind her, or she would make it up with Harry and go back to her old life. She had hoped that she would come back to the house and understand why he had married her in the first place. He would prove that he needed her, even if there were no children, and she would see that her fears were foolishness, and learn to accept his natural reserve as an aspect of his character, not a reflection upon her person.

For a moment she had been sure it was true. He had spoken so fondly of the changes she'd made in his life. And then had proved that he did not need her to preserve them. The last thing she had expected was to find him getting on with things without her help.

And, even worse, that he would come out and admit that there had been a problem from the first, just as she had suspected. Worse yet, it did not sound as if she could easily gain his forgiveness, and the love she wanted. He had spoken as though he had no hope for a closer relationship with her. He had offered for her never expecting to receive her love, or to give his in return. But they could have drifted along in peace and pleasantry had she not chosen to rile him in an effort to fix things.

Rosalind was approaching from the other end of the hall, and Elise reached out to her in desperation. 'I need to talk to you. There is a problem.'

Rosalind replied, 'If it is about the eggs I must argue that they are not at all my fault. I hardly think if one makes a simple suggestion to Cook that a touch more seasoning would be appreciated, that it should result in so much pepper as to make the whole tray inedible. Lord Gilroy took a large portion and grew so red in the face that I feared apoplexy. I—'

Elise grabbed her sister-in-law by the wrist and pulled her into the drawing room. 'It is not about the eggs.'

'What else has gone wrong, then? It is so early in the day that there cannot be more.'

'It is your brother. He is angry with me.'

Rosalind smiled with satisfaction. 'And you have no trouble recognising the fact? That is wonderful news. For it means you are beginning to solve your difficulties.'

'It is not wonderful. It is really quite horrible. He thinks I am faithless.'

Rosalind stared at her and made a face. 'Did you think that taking a lover would assure him of your fidelity? I know things are different in Bavaria, Elise. But they can't be as different as all that.'

'Nicholas is only a friend, nothing more.' She squeezed Rosalind's arm. 'You must believe me. I would never be untrue to Harry.'

Rosalind disengaged her arm and said, 'While I have no trouble believing you, it is what Harry thinks that matters.'

'If Harry were really bothered he should have said something before now.' She realised too late how defensive she sounded—and how guilty.

Rosalind was looking at her in annoyance. 'You have said yourself that Harry does not speak about anything that bothers him. Did you think that this would be different?'

'Perhaps I was trying to make him jealous.' It was difficult to say the words, for they proved that she had known what she was doing was wrong.

Rosalind nodded. 'You were lonely. And by his silence Harry made it easy for you to stray. He is lucky the situation is not worse than it is.'

Elise let out a small sigh of relief. At least Rosalind did not hold her weakness too much against her. 'I wanted Harry to notice me. But now that he has, what am I to do? I would send Nicholas away, but with the weather he cannot get to the end of the drive, much less back to London.' And then she remembered the offer she had made to get him to bring her home. 'And I will have to apologise to Nicholas as well, for I fear I have given him the wrong idea of my feelings.'

Rosalind stared at her, offering no help.

Elise continued. 'We are all stuck here together, the

house is full of strangers, and if we argue everyone in London will hear of it. What am I to do?'

Rosalind replied with a helpless shrug. 'I assumed you would not have come here if you did not have some idea how to proceed once you had talked to Harry. Did you not have a plan? Everyone seems to be full of them nowadays. It is quite the thing.'

'I was so angry with him I did not think.'

'And he was not angry enough. And now you are less angry, and he is more so.' Rosalind nodded. 'In no time at all balance shall be achieved and you shall both be equally annoyed.' She said it as though this were supposed to be good news, and wiped her hands on her skirts.

Elise shook her head. 'But I do not wish to be annoyed with Harry. I wish us to be happy together. If I return to find that we are both still cross, leaving will have been an exercise in futility.'

Rosalind stepped past her towards the hall, gaining speed as she went. 'There is nothing more I can do for you at the moment. I must run to the entry hall and decorate the Yule Log, so that tonight we can throw the whole thing into the fire and burn those same decorations to ashes. I am sure I will be in a much better mood to discuss futile behaviour, after that is done.'

Chapter Ten

Rosalind hurried down the hallway, taking sips from the cup of tea in her hand. It was tepid. But since she had not managed lunch, it was all she was likely to have until supper, and it would have to do. Since the moment she had arisen there had been something that needed doing, or fixing, or seeing to. Harry's friends seemed to think that the food was either overcooked or raw, they found their rooms too hot or too cold, and the servants could not manage to please any of them without constant supervision.

After watching her decorate the Christmas tree, she had nurtured hopes that Elise would see the chaos, take control of the house, and set things to right again. But after one conversation with Harry the woman could not manage to do anything more useful than wring her hands.

It was most distressing.

As Rosalind passed the open door of the library she noticed that the mistletoe was no longer in its place. Was there something wrong with the thing that it could not seem to stay fixed to the door? Was the nail loose? Tremaine had placed it quite securely yesterday. What had happened now?

She searched the floor and found it had not fallen, as she'd expected, onto the doorstep, but had pitched up against the wall, several feet away. Someone must have kicked it by mistake, for it did appear somewhat the worse for wear. She glared at it, as though blaming it as a troublemaker, then shook it roughly and gave it a half-hearted toss in the direction of the hook above her.

It hung for a moment, and then dropped back into her teacup, splashing the contents onto her bodice. Unlike yesterday, there was no sound of muffled laughter. But she took a chance before acting further.

'Tremaine, I need you. Get up from that couch and be of use.'

There was a sigh from the other side of the room. 'How did you know I was here?'

'I have been everywhere else in the house, for one reason or another, and I have not seen you all day. So, by process of elimination, you must be hiding in the library—just as you promised you would *not*.'

'And what in God's name do you mean to involve me in now? I have had quite enough of the festivities, and the fun, as you call it, has barely begun. Do you know what your brother attempted this morning?'

'Whatever it was, he has managed to annoy Elise no end.'

'Annoy her?' Tremaine's angry face peered from

behind the couch. 'When I left them they were as happy as lovebirds. It seems she was not bothered by the sight of her husband threatening me with an axe, or attempting to freeze me to death. And I have ruined my best pair of shoes by walking through the snow. My valet is beyond consolation.'

'As I have told you before, Tremaine, Harry means you no real harm. He is only teasing you because seeing you in a foul temper amuses him. My brother thinks that you have a lack of Christmas spirit, and I'm afraid I must agree with him.'

Nicholas punched the couch cushions in disgust. 'I do not deny the fact. And, since Harry has sufficient spirit for two men, he pretends that he wishes to share it with me.'

She looked down at the dripping mistletoe in her hand, gave it another shake to remove the tea, and reached for the doorframe again. 'If you would be so kind as to take it, then you could save some of us a world of effort. I can be every bit as persistent as my brother, if you give me reason. And if you try to avoid my scheduled activities, I will find a way to force your participation in them. It would be easier for both of us if you could at least pretend to enjoy them.'

He stood and walked slowly towards her. 'I will participate, Miss Morley. But you far overstep the bounds of our limited acquaintance if you think you can make me enjoy the fact. I am a proper gentleman of the ton. And as such I live by certain rules. Conversation should flow freely, but truth should be kept to an absolute minimum. In the Christmas season truth runs as freely as wine.' He made a sour face. 'But the wine is endlessly seasoned with cloves. And therefore undrinkable.'

'So you have an aversion to truth? And cloves? I can do little about the cloves, for they are all-pervasive, but I suppose spontaneous honesty is reason enough to avoid the holiday. Harry and Elise are proving that even if the truth is spoken it is oft misinterpreted. And then there is the very devil to pay. He has finally admitted that he is angry with her.' Rosalind looked heavenward for understanding. 'And yet, she is surprised.'

Tremaine shook his head in pity. 'He'd have been better to hold his tongue. When it comes to women, if you admit to nothing you will have less to apologise for later.'

'I find the fault is with her. One should never ask a man to reveal the contents of his mind if one does not already know what they are.' Rosalind smiled. 'But until they have fought they cannot make up. Some progress has been made. And the game I have chosen for tonight will be perfect to rejoin the two of them. They will be back in each other's arms and laughing together in a matter of minutes. I suspect, once that has happened, the temptation will be great to stay where they are. But you must help fill out the room so that it doesn't look too suspicious.' She looked him up and down. 'You need do nothing more strenuous than take up space. In less than an hour you will be back on that couch, and none the worse for it.' She tapped the mistletoe against her teacup, awaiting his response.

He yawned, as though to prove that taking up space

was near the limit of his endurance. And then he said, 'How can I resist you when you put it so appealingly? Here, now. Will you stop fooling with that accursed thing.' Her tapping had turned into a nervous rattling of china, and with surprising alacrity he snatched the kissing ball out of her hand and put it in place on the hook, above her head. And then he stood perfectly still, totally alert, looking down at her. His mouth turned into a curious smile.

She felt the bump as her back met the doorframe, for she'd scrambled out of reach of his arm without even re-alising it.

And then he laughed. 'You are much more cautious than you once were.'

'And you are no less prone to flirt. But, since I know you wish to return to London alone, I see no point in in-dulging you.' She took another step, which brought her back into the hall and well out of harm's way. 'I will expect to see you in the drawing room this evening, Tremaine. And we will see if you are still so interested in fun and games when my brother is present to chaperone me.'

After a hearty Christmas Eve dinner, Harry gathered the guests in the drawing room for the lighting of the Yule Log. Elise was pleased to see that the trunk of the ash they had chosen the previous year was large enough to fill the fireplace from end to end.

Rosalind had spent a good portion of the afternoon draping it with garlands of holly and ivy, tied on with red bows, until it was almost too pretty to burn. And she had sighed dramatically as she directed the servants to put it on the grate.

Harry produced a charred piece of last year's log and doused it liberally with brandy before thrusting it into the embers and watching it flare to life.

The crowd gave an appreciative 'Ahh' and several people stepped closer to offer toasts.

When Harry felt ceremony had been properly served, he touched the old log to the new and held it until the decorations upon the new log caught. Then he threw his torch into the fireplace.

'There you are, my friends. The Yule Log. May it burn long and joyfully. If you have any regrets of the previous year, now is your chance to throw them upon the fire and start anew.' He looked significantly at Elise as he reached into a basket of kindling and tossed a handful of pine needles upon the fire, watching them flare.

Elise stared at the basket of needles, and at the crowd around them. Did he mean her to do penance, in front of all these people? But what good would it do to stand in front of the guests and wordlessly declare herself a failure as a wife? Even if she could prove herself sorry for her indiscretion with Nicholas, there was so much she could not change. Without a miracle, next year was likely to be as barren as this had been.

When she did nothing, he gave a moment's thought and added a second handful of needles to the fire. Then he smiled, changing easily back into the jovial host. 'Come, everybody—wassail and mince pies!' He made a few steps in the direction of the refreshment table, until he was sure that the guests were well on their way, then turned back to face Elise on the opposite side of the fire.

'Elise. A word, please, in the study.' Harry beckoned to her to follow him and left the drawing room, walking down the corridor and away from the crowd. His smile was as pleasant as it had always been, with none of the rancour it had held that morning. But his tone was that of a husband who took it for granted that a command would be obeyed.

It rankled her to see him falling right back into the pattern of the last five years. Even though she no longer lived with him, he was acting as though there was nothing strange between them, and ordering her from room to room while pretending that she was free as a bird and could do as she liked.

She hesitated. If she wished to come home, then she must learn not to fight him over little things. But if he did not want her back, then what was the point of obeying? At last she sighed, and nodded, and followed him to the study, letting him shut the door behind her.

He turned and faced her, and he must have seen the anger growing in her—and the shame. For a moment he seemed at a loss for words. He held his hands out in front of him and opened his mouth. Then closed it again, and put his hands behind his back, pensive. At last he said, 'I notice that you did not throw anything onto the fire tonight. Am I to take it that you have no regrets?'

'Of course I have regrets,' she said. 'But do you think a handful of burned pine needles and dead silence is a sufficient apology?'

He shrugged. 'Sometimes, when one does not know what to say, it is better to keep silent.'

'But not always.' She looked earnestly at him. 'It is possible, when one cares deeply about another person, to forgive harsh words said in the heat of the moment.'

He frowned and stared at the ground. 'But not always.' He dipped a hand in to his pocket, removing a jewellery box. 'I have your Christmas gift.' He offered it to her.

'Harry…' And now she was at a loss for words, but her mind was crying, *Tell me you didn't*. Their marriage was in a shambles, and he meant to gloss it all over with another necklace. At last she said, 'This is not necessary.'

He gave her another empty smile. 'Gifts rarely are. It defeats the point, when one has ample means but denies necessities to someone all year, to mete them out at Christmas, pretending that they are gifts. That is miserliness in the guise of generosity.'

She pushed the box back to him. 'I mean that it was not necessary for you to buy me a present. I do not wish it.'

'How do you know? You do not know what is inside.' He held it out to her again.

'It is not the contents of the box that concern me. I do not wish another gift from you, Harry.'

For a moment she thought she saw pain in his eyes, before he hid it in sarcasm. 'And yet you have no trouble with my paying for your apartment or settling your bills? You take things from me every day, Elise.'

He was deliberately misunderstanding her, so she struck back at him. 'If it bothers you so, then set me free. Then I would not take another thing from you, Harry.'

He nodded. 'Because you prefer Tremaine, now that he can afford to buy you the things you need?'

'His inheritance has nothing to do with my leaving you.'

'It was merely a fortunate coincidence that six months after his uncle died you went to London to be with him? You barely allowed him enough time to mourn before you returned to his side.'

She started in surprise. It had not occurred to her when she had left how that might look to the casual observer. Or, worse yet, to her husband. 'If you think I left you because of Tremaine, then you do not understand the problem at all.'

'I understand the problem well enough. I have a wife who prefers the company of another.'

'If you wish to see it that way then there is little I can do to change your mind,' she snapped. 'But in truth you have a wife who left because she was tired of being held at a distance. I can understand, Harry, if you are not happy with me. Or if you do not wish to take me into your confidence. But if you do not want me, must you blame me for seeking companionship elsewhere?'

'I do not want you?' He laughed. 'You do not want *me*, more like. Has Tremaine shown you the letter? I assume that is why you are both here? So that he can win his bet and you can gloat over it.'

'That letter was foolishness itself. Do you think our marriage is some kind of joke? And it was most cruel of you to make me a part of it. I did not think you capable of such base behaviour.'

His eyes held the hooded look they had sometimes, and he looked away from her briefly before saying, 'You would be surprised what I am capable of when it comes to you, Elise. But my cruel trick succeeded in making you angry enough to return home for Christmas.'

She moaned in exasperation. 'Really, Harry. If all you wanted was a visit at Christmas, then you had but to come to London and ask me.'

He thrust the jewel box back into his pocket and glared into the fire. 'And the answer would have been no. Or you would have insisted that we discuss a divorce.'

It surprised her to see him looking so sullen. And without intending it, her tone became softer. 'At least we would have been talking again, and the matter of our future could have been decided one way or another. But you felt the need to trick me into doing what you wished instead of asking me outright, and taking the risk that my answer might not be to your liking.' She stared at him, willing him to understand. 'If you do not see the wrong in that, then perhaps you will never understand why I am unhappy with you.'

He grabbed a poker and jabbed at the logs in the grate. 'I understand you well enough to know that you were eager to come back to me for an argument. But I do not think you returned home to climb the hill with me at dawn and watch the sun rise, as you did this morning.'

She swallowed for a moment as the memory of that simple pleasure returned to her. 'You are right. And thank you for that. There is much we need to talk about, Harry. But it has been a long time since we have done something just for pleasure's sake. It felt good to put our differences aside for a few moments.' She hesitated. 'I enjoyed it very much.'

He set the poker aside, wiped his hands on a handkerchief, and then patted the box in his pocket, smiling. 'Then you will enjoy this as well.'

A lump of bitterness formed in her throat at the thought of the jewel box again. 'I brought nothing for you in exchange, you know.'

His voice dropped low. 'There is only one thing I want from you.' He stepped towards her and reached out, taking her hand in his. 'That is for you to return home to me, and for things to go back to the way they were.'

'I would not want to return to what we had, Harry,' she said, surprised that he had not seemed to notice the emptiness they'd shared. 'You cannot continue to pretend that nothing was wrong any more than you can buy my co-operation with jewellery.'

He shook his head in amazement, as though he really did not see a problem. 'I am not attempting to buy you, Elise. I should not need to. We are married, after all. You have been mine for five years.'

His words shocked her back to anger. 'So I am already bought and paid for? Is that the way you see me?'

'What a daft idea. I never said so,' he answered.

'Perhaps because you speak so rarely.'

'Then I will speak now, if you are willing to listen,' he said, and smiled. But for a moment, before the affability returned to his face, she saw frustration underneath. 'I did not mean that I had bought you. I meant that I should not have to buy you now. Do you expect me to outdo Tremaine in some way, to win you back? I had hoped that when we married your choice was fixed. But now I am not so sure.'

She threw her hands into the air. 'I have been gone from your house for two months, Harry. And your best response, after all this time, is that you are "not so sure" I am gone.'

He scoffed. 'You did not expect me to take this division between us seriously, did you? It would serve you right if I went ahead with the divorce you seek and left you to marry Tremaine. But I have forgiven you for it. Now, let us put aside this silly quarrel. I will give you your Christmas present, and we can return to the main room and explain to Tremaine that his presence is no longer required.'

He offered the box to her again, and she knocked it from his hand onto the floor. 'It does not matter to me, Harry, if you have "forgiven" me for leaving. For if you think so little of me, and take our marriage for granted in such a way, how can I ever forgive you?' And with that she stormed from the room.

In the drawing room, Rosalind grabbed Nick by the arm, almost jostling the cup of wassail from his hand.

'Dear God, woman,' he drawled. 'Can I not enjoy a moment's peace?'

'The guests are getting restless. We must start the games soon. Harry has gone off somewhere.' Her eyes darted to the open doorway. 'And Elise appears to be in a state and is headed for her room. Stop her!' She gave him a shove towards the open door that spilled even more of his punch. 'I will find my brother.'

Nick stumbled out into the hall and hurried to catch up with Elise. 'Darling, where are you headed at such an alarming pace? The night is young, and I long for your company.'

She turned on him with a glare, and responded in a torrent of unintelligible German.

He grinned. 'I gather you have been talking to your husband?'

'That man. If I spend one more moment in his company I swear I shall go mad.'

He gestured to the drawing room. 'Then spend a moment with me. I have brought you a cup of wassail.' He held his cup out to her.

She took it, and stared down at it. 'This cup is empty, Nicholas.'

He slipped an arm around her waist, guiding her back to the party. 'Perhaps it is only waiting to be filled. Optimism, Elise. We need optimism at times like this. Twelfth Night will be here soon enough, and then we shall go back to London and I will help you to forget all about this.' He gave her waist a little squeeze.

She blinked, as though just remembering what she had promised him. 'That will be wonderful, Nicholas. I can hardly wait.' But she said it with a sickly smile that proved she had not been living for the moment they would become one. 'I believe I might need a cup of punch after all.'

'I thought you might.' He shepherded her to the refreshments and she downed a cup of wassail, hardly stopping for breath. It was not flattering to see that the thought of intimacy with him required so much fortification. Alcohol could not help but make Harry more appealing to her, so he reached for the ladle and helped her to a second cup.

'I have found another who is willing to play,' Rosalind announced from the doorway. She was ignoring Harry's lack of enthusiasm as she hauled him back into the room by his elbow. 'The more people we have, the more fun it shall be.'

As they passed, Harry stared at Nick's hand, which was still resting on his wife's waist while he plied her with liquor. Harry shot him a look of undisguised loathing before turning to his sister. 'Yes, Rosalind. I think we should all like a diversion.'

'And what exactly is this game we are all so eager to play?' Nick asked dryly.

'Blind Man's Bluff,' Rosalind said. 'And, Harry, as host you must go first.'

Nick thought to remind her that it was rarely polite to put guests last, but he could see the stubborn glint in Rosalind's eye and elected not to challenge her.

'I will blindfold you, and you must identify your guests.' She was tying a handkerchief around Harry's face, and spinning him so that he lost all direction.

Guests who were not interested in playing moved to the corners of the room. Elise looked to the exit with longing, and then to Harry, as though trying to decide between the two.

But Rosalind hurried to close the door, and put her back to it, making the decision for her. 'Quiet, everyone, let Harry try to find you.'

Nick swore silently, and nudged Elise towards the centre of the room and into the game. With Rosalind blocking the door, his escape was thwarted as well. If Harry's eyes were covered, there was little he could do to affect the man. It would have been an excellent opportunity to get away. He shot Rosalind a murderous look.

She shrugged and cocked her head towards the other players, as though telling him to pay attention to the game.

While Nick was distracted by her, Harry lumbered past him, on his blind side, and stamped mercilessly on his toe. 'Eh—what was that?' He stumbled, turned back as though to find Tremaine, and then veered left at the last minute, catching another guest by the shoulders. 'Let me see.' He patted at the man, placing his hands on an ample stomach. 'Cammerville. I do not need eyes to tell it is you.'

The gentleman laughed and sat down.

'That's one down.' Harry swung his arm out wide through the open air and laid hands on a young lady, reaching carefully to touch her hair. 'And the younger of the Misses Gilroy, I believe. For there are your pretty curls.' Then he marched purposefully towards Elise, who took a deep breath and froze like a rabbit, waiting to be caught.

Nick hoped that the game they were really playing would be over once Harry had caught his wife. Elise looked more resigned than happy to be playing, but at least she was no longer as angry as she had been in the hall. But Harry stopped at the last moment and turned, moving across the room again, away from his wife.

Elise put her hands on her hips and glared at his back in disgust.

On his way to wherever he thought he was going, Harry managed to catch himself on a small table and tip it, sending a carafe of wine cascading down the leg of Nick's best buff trousers.

He stifled an oath and mopped at the stain with his handkerchief.

Rosalind glared at him, making frantic gestures that he should hold his tongue and keep to the spirit of the game.

'I have upset something,' announced Harry, grinning without remorse.

Rosalind reached him from behind and spun him, giving him a forceful shove to send him back towards Elise.

Harry lurched again in the direction of his wife, only to catch another woman by the shoulders. 'And this is the elder Miss Gilroy. For I have danced with you before, and recall you as being most slim and just this tall.' The girl dissolved into a shower of giggles.

Elise's countenance darkened with the clouds of a returning storm. As Harry made another pass through the room, instead of avoiding him she stepped in front of him, so that he could not help but run into her.

He swung his arms wide again, turned suddenly, and reached high instead of low, catching Tremaine by the throat. 'What's this, then? Have I caught the turkey for tomorrow's dinner?'

He gave a warning squeeze, and Nick gagged slightly.

'Oh, no. Not a turkey at all. It is Tremaine. I recognise that artfully tied cravat. You're out of the running, old man. Sit down.' He released his throat, spun him around and gave a sharp push to his shoulders that sent him stumbling towards the sofa. 'And stay out of my way.'

The other people in the room laughed knowingly.

He turned again, 'How many is that, then? Almost everyone? But there must be someone left.' He walked deliberately past his own wife again.

Elise was getting angrier by the minute, and was now actively trying to be found—repeatedly stepping into his path, only to be avoided as he seized and identified someone else.

Nick was near enough to Rosalind to hear her fervent whispering. 'Don't toy with her, Harry. Do not toy with her. She does not appreciate it.'

But either Harry did not hear or did not care. He was still pretending that he did not know the location of his wife. He groped in the empty air to the right of her, and when she moved into his path he turned again. It was plain to all there that he was deliberately avoiding her.

'Where is she?'

Several guests laughed, and a young girl called out, 'Behind you. Look behind you.'

At last, Elise could control her temper no longer. 'If you seriously wish to find her, she will be in her bedroom. With the door locked.' Elise gave her husband an angry shove, then marched past him and through the drawing room door.

The room went silent, waiting to see what would happen next. When Harry yanked off the blindfold he looked, for a moment, as though he were torn between staying and following her. And then he smoothed his hair and let out a hearty laugh, to prove that there was nothing seriously wrong.

The guests relaxed and laughed with him.

Rosalind caught Nick before he could leave the room to find Elise. He frowned at her. 'You need some practice, I think, in your tying of the blindfold. Your brother could see us all, clear as day.'

She let out an exasperated puff of air. 'Of course he could. It would make little sense for him to have wandered around blind.'

'That is the point of the game, is it not?'

'When you are in a room with your wife and her lover it is never a good idea to be blind.'

'He has pretended blindness on the subject long enough,' said Nick, with a growing understanding of Harry's predicament.

'But now it is long past time for him to stop pretending.' She glared in the direction of her brother. 'I am so angry with Harry that I can hardly speak. He must have known what I was about by tying the handkerchief the way I did. I gave him an excellent opportunity and he wasted it. But if I question him on it, he will claim that he knows his wife better than I. And she will return to him in her own good time and there is little else to be done about it.'

'You gave him no choice but to act as he did, Rosalind. I had my doubts, when he welcomed me into his home, but the man does have his pride. He wants his wife back, but he does not want to be forced to admit the fact in front of an audience.'

'And why ever not? Admitting that you love your wife is nothing to be ashamed of.'

Nick shook his head. 'Perhaps not. But to solve this problem someone must be willing to sacrifice their pride. And each one is still hoping that it can be the other.'

'It might be easier for us to reconcile them were they not so perfectly suited in their bullheadedness.'

He glared at her. 'It might also be easier if you would include me in the plans that you are making. At least a small warning would have been welcome just now. The man positively mauled me, and I had to stand there and take it in good humour.'

'It serves you right,' she said with vehemence. 'You are quite horrible, you know.'

'I am no worse than I have ever been.'

'And no better than you should be. Harry is right in one thing, Tremaine. You need to change your ways. And, while it pains me to see Harry and Elise struggling with pride, I have no compunction in sacrificing yours. If this season gives you a chance to do penance, then so be it. You may start afresh in the New Year.'

'What if one suspects that no matter what one does the next year will be no different from the last?' He shook his head. 'I find it no cause for celebration.'

'Only if you are unhappy with your life,' she said. 'I

thought you claimed to be content. If so, another year of the same will not bother you.'

Damn her for making him think on it. For as he did he realised that he was far too bored to claim contentment. 'And you are so content in yours, then?' He gave her a sour smile.

She lifted her chin. 'My view of the future is somewhat more optimistic than yours. I do not worry myself over the things I cannot change, and apply myself diligently to those things that I can. I view the New Year as a promise that things do not always have to be the same.' She held out a hand. 'While the book is closing on 1813, there is no telling what 1814 will bring us. You might be a better man.'

Nick stood too close to her, and was satisfied to see the flash in her eyes that proved she was not so immune to his charms as she pretended. 'Are you still convinced there is something wrong with me as I am now?'

Instead of responding playfully to his comment, she looked at him in all seriousness and said, 'Yes, there is. You wonder how it is that you manage to be in such trouble with Harry, and why your life does not change from year to year. But you have only your own behaviour to blame for it.' She glanced towards the hall, in the direction of the absent Elise. 'I saw the two of you together when I brought Harry into the room. And I saw the look you gave her as she left. Do not tell me that you were not about to follow her. It is more than difficult, trying to get the two of them to co-operate and reconcile. If you can muster enough sense to set her free, then it will be much easier for all of us.'

Chapter Eleven

The next day, Nick was lying on his back on the library sofa, struggling to enjoy the peace and quiet of Christmas afternoon. The roads to the village were better, but still suspect. So the party had forgone church and let Harry lead them in morning prayer in the dining room. After luncheon, the servants had hitched up sleighs, and Harry had taken the majority of his guests to go ice skating on a nearby stream. Others had retired to their rooms. There had been no sign at all of Elise since she had taken to her room the previous evening.

He felt a touch of guilt over that point. But jollying her back into good spirits would mean he must forfeit the afternoon, which was going just as he preferred it: dozing with a full stomach, in air scented faintly with pine and punch, and none of the frenetic eagerness to make fun where none was needed. Nor did he wish to give Rosalind Morley fuel for her spurious argument that he did not know how to let well enough alone when it came to his ex-intended. If Elise needed cheering, then perhaps it was time for her husband to do the job.

It had occurred to him that if he wished any real peace, it would be a far better idea to stay in his own bedroom than to stretch out in a common area, where he was likely to be interrupted at any moment. But he had rejected the idea for the illogical reason that it would give him too *much* privacy. Rosalind would not think to look for him if he rested in his room. And he had to admit that he was growing to expect a disruptive visit from the sweet Miss Morley as part of his daily routine. He had promised to stay out of her way, and he had meant to be true to his word. It was no fault of his that she insisted upon searching him out.

His mind ran over and over their conversation of the previous evening. She seemed to think that he was still to blame for the troubles between Harry and Elise, even though he was doing everything in his power to rejoin them. Had he not brought her home? Was he not doing his best to stay clear of them while they sorted out their difficulties?

And had he not immediately fallen back into his role of devoted admirer the minute he'd seen Elise's unhappiness? Damn it all, he did not want to lie with her any more than she wanted his attentions. But the suggestion of it had been enough of a distraction to coax her back to the punch bowl.

Now, despite nagging doubts about the wisdom of it, he would leave Elise to have her sulk. He would be sure to point the fact out when Miss Morley put in an appearance with whatever scheme she was currently hatching. There was no telling what chaos she was likely to bring with her when she came today. He smiled. Although she was a most annoying young lady, at least she did not bore him.

Nick glanced at his watch, and was surprised to see it was almost three. Several hours had passed in relative silence, and he should have been able to settle his mind and get the sleep he'd been craving. Although the library sofa was much more comfortable than the miserable mattress his host had allotted him, he could not seem to find peace.

He looked over the back of the couch at the mistletoe, still hanging in its proper place above the door. On impulse he rose and removed it from the hook, dropping it on the floor under a table. Then he went back to his place by the fire and pretended to sleep.

Rosalind came into the room a short time later, but took no notice of the missing decoration. Instead, she strode directly to his hiding place, coming round to the front of the couch to slap at the sole of his boot. 'Wake up, Tremaine. I have plans for you.'

He pretended to splutter to consciousness, looked up at her, and hurriedly closed his eyes again. 'Then I am most assuredly still asleep. Please leave me in peace.'

'There is much work to be done if you wish to go home alone.'

'Far more than that, I wish to go home alive. And the best way to assure my safety is to stay right here, far away from Harry. The man laid hands on me yesterday. He cannot be trusted.'

'You are being silly again. It was an innocent game.'

When she scolded him, her curls bounced in a most amusing fashion, and he had to force himself not to smile at her. 'The game was innocent enough. But I do not trust some of the players any further than I can throw them.' No more than he trusted Rosalind. He suspected that she had other reasons for wishing him to play.

'You have nothing to fear from Harry. I have known the man almost a quarter of a century. Although he might threaten, he would never do you bodily harm.'

He laughed. 'When you reach that advanced age, little one, and make such claims, then I shall take your word.'

She glared down at him. 'Twenty-five is not an advanced age, and it is most unflattering of you to call it so. The fact that I am near to it does not put me so far beyond the pale.'

Four-and-twenty? But she could barely be eighteen now. He was convinced of it. He looked at her more closely. But hadn't he thought the same thing when he had met her the first time? And that had been years ago. If she was twenty-four, then… He counted upon his fingers.

His silence must have unnerved her, for she said, 'Do not fall asleep again, Tremaine. The festivities have not been so strenuous as to require rest in midday. And if you mean to imply that my conversation bores you to unconsciousness, I swear I shall box your ears.'

He gave a little cough. 'Twenty-four?'

'Twenty-five next month.'

'But you are…'

She gritted her teeth. 'Older than Elise. Just barely. And still single. But I look much younger and always have. Or were you about to say *tiny*? For if you mean to comment on my lack of height as well as my advanced age then you will have nothing more to fear from Harry. I will do more damage to you than he ever shall.'

For a moment, he could swear that he was looking at the same gamine he had found in the hallway at the Grenvilles' ball, five Christmases ago. The only change in her was the cynical glint in her eyes and the determined set to her mouth. 'You look no different than you did when I first met you.'

She put her hands on her hips. 'Considering how well our first meeting went, I hardly know what you mean by that. But I shall assume you mean to compliment me. I hope you are not so cruel as to torment me with my appearance? There is little I can do to change it.'

'I thought you much younger when we first met. You were standing in the doorway of the ballroom, behind a potted palm, watching everyone else dance.'

She smirked. 'You remember that now, do you?'

'I never forgot it.'

'But when my father caught us kissing you announced, "I have never seen this girl before in my life." I assumed that we were keeping to the established lie and pretending that our dance had never occurred.'

'It was only an hour before we kissed. So technically I had not met you before. Not before that night, at any rate.'

'Technically?' She nodded sceptically. 'My father

assumed that I had kissed a man without even taking the time to learn his name. It was very awkward for me.'

'But when we danced,' he said haltingly, 'you told me that you were not yet out.'

'I'd have made my come-out in spring, if Father had allowed me to remain in London. Twenty would have been a bit later than the other girls, of course. But not too late.' There was a wistful note in her voice, and she took a moment to crush it before continuing in a normal, businesslike tone, 'But a come-out is not necessary for a happy life. Only so much foolishness.'

'You were nineteen?'

'As were you, once.' There was another long pause as she came to understand him. 'You mean when we first met? Well, yes. Of course I was. You did not think I had escaped from the schoolroom to accost you? It was only my father's stubbornness, not my age that left me lurking outside the ballroom instead of dancing with the others.'

'But you were nineteen,' he repeated numbly.

'The night we met?' She shrugged. 'It did not matter. My father has very strict ideas on what is proper and improper for young ladies. Girls who are not out should not dance, no matter their age.'

As he remembered that night, he knew there had been girls much younger at the party, giggling in corners, begging for gentlemen to stand up with them and being no end of a nuisance—just as there were in the house today. He had assumed Rosalind to be one of them. But she had been of marriageable age, and yet still denied the pleasure of adult company. Her actions made more sense.

'That was rather strict of him.'

'Perhaps. But there was little to be done about it.'

'And you say you had not tasted wine unwatered?'

She stared at him, as if daring him to doubt her. 'I had not. If you were to speak to my father on the subject, I still have not.' She made a face. 'He does not approve of strong spirits. He drinks his wine with water as well, and forgoes brandy entirely. He says that consumption of alcohol by gentlewomen is most improper.' She smiled. 'It is fortunate for me that I am the one who does the pouring in our household. For, while he trusts me to follow his wishes, he really has no idea about the contents of my glass.'

He tried to imagine what it would be like to have to forgo wine with a meal and could not comprehend it. It was as if she had been trapped in childhood, with no escape on the horizon. 'And he still does not allow you to travel to the city, even after years of good behaviour?'

'I am not encouraged to leave the house at all. He sent me to Harry, of course, because my brother was in need. But I suspect that says more about his disapproval of Elise than anything else.' Rosalind made another stern face. 'He has much to say on the subject of foreigners and their strange ways, and he is none too secret about the satisfaction he feels at Harry's marital difficulties. He will expect a full report of them when I return home. Which will be very soon, should he get wind of the festivities I have organised. I do not care to hear what he will say when he finds out that I have been stringing holly on a Yule Log.'

'How utterly absurd,' Nick replied. 'It is an innocent enough diversion, and most enjoyable.' If one could manage to ignore the nuisance of going into the woods and focus on the blazing fire in the evening. He gave a nod to her. 'And I must say, the thing was most attractively decorated, before Harry set it to light.'

Rosalind looked amused. 'Are you a defender of Christmas now, Saint Nicholas?'

'I do not defend Christmas so much as believe that small pleasures are not a threat to character or a black mark upon the soul.'

'On that point you and Harry agree. It is one of the reasons I see so little of Harry, for he cannot abide my father's treatment of his mother, nor of me. And Father has very little good to say about him.' She sighed. 'But my father means well by it, although he may seem harsh to others. It has done me no real harm. And I must admit, I bring much of his censure on myself. For I have a tendency to small rebellions, and can be just as stubborn as Harry when I've a mind.'

It made Nick unaccountably angry to see her resigned to her future, caring for a man who was obviously impossible to please. And the idea that she had to moderate a temperament which he found quite refreshing, irritated him even more. He said, 'If a wild bird is caged long enough, even for its own protection, it will beat its wings against the bars. If it does itself an injury, whose fault is it? The bird's or the one who caged it?'

'If you are attempting to draw some parallel between me and the bird, then I wish you would refrain from it.

The fault would lie with the bird. For, while such creatures are lovely to look at, they are seldom held up as an example of wisdom and good sense.'

She was standing close enough to him that the smell of her perfume blended with the pine boughs on the mantel and the other inescapable smells of Christmas, turning the simple floral scent she wore into something much more complex and sensual. It was just as tempting as he remembered it, and just as hard to ignore. He wondered if it had been the same for her. For all along she had been old enough to understand temptation, but lacking the experience to avoid it. He smiled in sympathy. 'It seems I have done you an injustice, Miss Morley. For this explanation of your behaviour on the night we met puts the event in a whole new light.'

'I thought we had agreed not to speak of that again,' she muttered, and tried to turn away.

He put a finger under her chin and urged her to look up at his face. 'After you were forced to apologise repeatedly for something which was no real fault of yours? What you were doing was not so unusual, compared with other girls of your age. If you lacked seasoning or sense, it was because your family did not train you to know what was expected of you. They thought that they could confine you until the last possible moment and then thrust you into the light, where you would exhibit flawless behaviour with no practice. When you failed, it was more their fault than yours.' He hung his head. 'And mine as well. I might have behaved quite differently had I known the circumstances involved. And I do not remember at any time giving you the apology that you deserve in response.'

She swallowed. 'It is not necessary.'

'I beg to differ.' He moved so that he was standing before her, and said, 'Give me your hand.'

She was obviously trying to come up with a response that would make things easier between them, but none was forthcoming.

So he reached, and took her hand in both of his. 'I am sorry for what occurred that night,' he said. 'The fact that you were behaving without caution did not require me to respond in kind. If anything, I should have been more circumspect, not less. You have been punished inordinately for it, although I have always deserved the majority of the guilt. Please forgive me.'

He was staring into her eyes, and it made things difficult. For it reminded him of the way she'd looked at him that night, and how it had made him feel, and why it had been so easy to throw caution to the winds and kiss her when he had known he had no right to.

But this time she managed to look away from him, instead of drawing nearer. 'Of course,' she said, and then she closed her eyes and dropped her head, as though praying that humility would be sufficient to bring this awkward scene to a close.

He brought her hand to his lips and held it there. Her skin was soft against his, and he lingered over it for longer than a simple apology would warrant, imagining what it might be like to kiss her palm, her wrist, and all the rest of the white skin leading to her lips. And then he smiled, remembering that this was what had caused the problem five years ago. The suspicion that all parts of Rosalind Morley were eminently kissable, and his sudden, irresistible compulsion to test the theory.

And now she was looking up at him again, over her outstretched hand, as though the kiss were causing her pain when he suspected that it was an excess of pleasure that was the problem. Should he take another liberty with her, she would yield—just as she had the last time. And he would probably run away from her—just as he had been running his whole life, from any situation that smacked of responsibility.

And so he released her, smiling. 'There. I hope it is settled at last. There is nothing wrong with you, Rosalind Morley. Nothing at all. Never mind what your father says, or what others might think of you. You are perfect just as you are.'

It occurred to him, in an idle, confusing way, that it would take a lifetime to catalogue the things about her that were perfectly suited to his temperament.

'Thank you.' Her voice sounded hoarse, as though it were difficult for her to speak. He wished that she would call him Tremaine, and return some sharp rebuke that would put things back to normal between them. But instead she murmured, 'I must go. To see about…something. And you must come as well. I…' She touched her hand to her forehead, trying to remember, and then looked into his eyes again and went very still.

Her vision cleared and she muttered, 'Apples. That is it. We are bobbing for apples. Harry is there. I have managed to get Elise to come out of her room, but she is looking very cross with him, and threatening to go back to bed with a megrim.'

'So I must let your brother drown me to put her into good humour again?'

'If you would be so kind.'

She held out her hand to him, and he was more than ready to follow wherever she might lead. But when he smiled at her, she looked so worried that he put on his most perturbed expression and yawned. 'The least you could do is deny it, you know. If you wish me to behave, you will do much better with flattery than you do with the truth.'

'If I flatter you, it might cause your head to swell more than it already has.' She gave him her usually cynical smile. 'I dare not risk it, Tremaine. Come on, then. We can finish this business by New Year if we apply ourselves to it.'

Chapter Twelve

Rosalind pushed him into the hallway ahead of her, announcing, 'I have found him.'

Harry beamed in triumph. 'And about time. Do not think that you can avoid the party, Tremaine. It is hardly keeping in the spirit of the bet if you do not try.'

Nick sighed, and prepared for a dunking. 'Very well, then. What have I to do to get you to leave me alone?'

'Play our little game.' Harry led him into the hall and gestured expansively towards the centre of the room. 'We have all had a turn, and the other guests are eager to see how you fare.'

True to his word, there was a large crowd gathered around a basin of water, and the air smelled of apples. The daughter of a lord was holding a fruit in her hand and shaking the water from her pretty blonde locks, and everyone was laughing heartily and congratulating her on her success.

There were calls of encouragement from the crowd, accompanied by drunken laughter.

Tremaine approached the pan of water with caution, and looked down at the abused fruit floating there. He stalled. 'And I am to…?' He looked down into the water again.

'Put your face in, grab an apple and bite.' Harry was grinning.

He knew that Harry would never be so foolish as to kill him in front of witnesses. The worst that would happen would be a wet head. Embarrassing, of course. But not so terrible, really. It would be over in a minute. Nick stepped up to the basin, bent awkwardly at the waist, and placed his face near the water.

He dutifully chased one of the remaining apples around the edge of the pan, while Harry stood behind him, pretending to offer encouragement.

'You have nothing to be afraid of.'

Harry was laughing at him, the miserable bastard. But he could hear Elise laughing too, so he soldiered on.

'The water is not so very deep. You will not drown,' Harry said. And then he whispered, directly into Nick's ear, 'I'm right behind you.'

Nick leaned too close to the water, trying to escape him, and took a quantity of it up his nose. He gasped and shot upright again, coughing, to the laughter of the crowd around him.

Harry clapped him smartly on the back to clear his lungs. 'There, there. You have it all wrong. You are not to drink the water. You are to eat the apple. Try again.'

He glared at Harry and stared at Rosalind. 'This is part of your brilliant plan, is it?'

She gave him a frustrated smile, and said, 'Take your turn and let others have a chance.' She rolled her eyes and cast a significant glance at Elise.

'Very well. But if anything untoward occurs I will hold you responsible, even in the afterlife.'

'Tremaine, do not be an ass.' She pushed past her brother, took him by the back of the neck, and pushed his face down into the water.

This time he had the good sense to hold his breath, and came up dripping, with an apple in his mouth. To complete the humiliation of it, Elise was leading the crowd who laughed at his discomposure.

'That was not so bad, was it?' Rosalind grabbed him by the collar and pulled him out of the way of the next player. Then she took the apple from his mouth and offered him linen to dry his face.

'Did I perform to your satisfaction?' he asked, tipping his head to drain the water from his ear.

'You were most amusing. Elise is laughing again—at you, and in front of Harry. That cannot but help put him in a good mood.' She took a bite from the apple that he had caught.

He watched her slender fingers caressing the fruit, her red lips, so memorably kissable, touching the place where he had bitten, the delicate workings of her pale throat as she chewed and swallowed. And suddenly he knew how Adam must have felt when Eve came to him with a wild scheme that he knew would end in disaster.

He had agreed, because how could he have refused her, even if it meant the ruin of all?

'It will not be long, I think, before Harry decides his pride is not so very important.' She looked speculatively at Elise. 'Then perhaps I shall be able to turn the rest of the party over to his wife.'

'And when she is back as mistress of this house what shall you do?' he whispered. 'Do you mean to see Pompeii, then? Once you have your freedom?'

The apple froze, halfway to her mouth, and she gave him a blank stare. 'What do I mean to do? Harry is right, Tremaine. You are an idiot. Harry will send me home after the holidays. I will return to Shropshire and my needlework, my jelly-making and my good works.'

He snorted at the idea. 'Do you miss home so much?'

'I do not miss home in the slightest. But where else am I to go?' She took another bite of the apple.

He watched her lick a drop of apple juice from her lip, and fought down the desire to suggest some good works she might try that had nothing to do with making jelly. 'Now that you have left your father's house, you might enjoy travelling. For you seem to have a taste for adventure.'

She laughed. 'Tell me, sir, when you are in the city, what do you drive?'

He thought for a moment. 'At this time I have several carriages. A curricle, of course, and a high-perch phaeton as well. Pulled by the finest pair of matched blacks in London.'

She gave a little moan of pleasure, and then looked

him square in the eye. 'We have a pony cart, which Father allows me to drive to the market in Clun. But only when the weather is fine and no one else is free to take me. The rest of the time I must walk.' She pulled a stern face, probably mimicking her father. 'But never alone. My father warns against the dangers present for young ladies travelling alone. But what they are I have no idea.' She gave a dry sigh. 'A trip to Pompeii might have seemed a lark to you, but it would be no more likely for me than a trip to the moon.'

Rosalind was making her future sound quite grim, so he rushed to reassure her—and himself—that it needn't be so. 'Do not fear, little one. Some day you will find a man who will take you to Italy.' Although he found that thought to be strangely annoying.

She spun the apple core on its stem, looking for a place to set it. 'I do not understand why everyone is so convinced that I cannot find a husband. As it so happens, I find them frequently enough. And then I find them wanting. I have had three proposals, just this year. All fine, upstanding men, who were willing to offer me a life no different from the one I have: full of restrictions and cautions and common sense. It appears being a wife is little different from being a daughter, and so I will have none of it. In this, at least, I am in full agreement with Elise. If a husband does not offer the love and respect I truly desire, and means to treat me no better than an overgrown child or an inanimate object, then it is better to do without.'

This took him aback. 'You have refused suitors?'

'Yes, I have. The rest of the world does not find me so repellent as you must, Tremaine.'

Here he was supposed to offer a compliment. But his glib tongue failed him, and the best he could manage was, 'I would hardly say you were repellent.'

She gave him a tired look and batted her lashes. 'I shall cherish your sweet words on my journey back to Shropshire.'

'But there must be some other alternative. Another place you could go…' He racked his brain for a better answer.

She set the apple core on the tray of a passing servant, and took back the linen she had given him to wipe her hands on it. 'There is not. The fact of the matter is this: I have no other female relatives, and a father who wishes help with his parish. When I am finished here I will go where everyone expects me to go. Where I am needed.' She tipped her head to the side. 'Although I must say the parish would be better off if my father was encouraged to marry the widow who comes to see to the cleaning of the church. She is a very organised woman, and a skilled housekeeper. He is very fond of her. They would make an excellent match.'

'If this woman is so well suited to your father, then why does he not offer for her?'

'Because then what would become of me? While the widow is suited to my father, I do not like her at all. And two women under the same roof would be one too many, when those women are not in harmony. Any progress my father has made in finding a new wife will be thwarted by my return home.'

He could not be sure, but he thought for a moment she glanced at him in a most strange way, and the pause before her next words was a touch longer than normal.

'Unless there is any reason that I should not go back to Shropshire.'

'When your brother is finished with you he means to send you back to your father, with no care for your future?' The thought rankled, for it was most sweet to see this girl doing everything in her power to help the brother who cared so little for her.

'When he presented the idea of a house party, he offered me my pick of the bachelor guests to prevent my flight.' She glanced around the room and frowned. 'Of course since he neglected to invite any single gentlemen, it has done me no good to entertain them. I have never seen so many happily married men, so many wives and children.' She gave another sidelong glance at Tremaine. 'You are the only unattached man in the house.'

'That was most unfair of him,' Tremaine agreed. 'But do not worry. I am sure when you least expect it you will find someone to suit your tastes.'

'The men who seek me out are hoping for a moderation in my character.' She glanced in the direction of Elise. 'Someone more like my sister-in-law, who has grown in the last few years from a naïve and somewhat awkward girl into a polished lady. I, on the other hand, am very much as you found me when we first met:

wilful, short-tempered, and prone to acting in haste and following with regret.'

He suppressed a smile. 'I will admit your personality is more volatile than Elise's.'

She shrugged. 'When the men of England come to value volatility over grace and candour over artifice, then I shall have my pick of them. Now, if you will excuse me, I should see to the other guests.' She walked across the room to Elise, and said something that made the other woman laugh.

He took a moment to admire the two women together, and had to admit they had little in common. Elise's cool beauty was paired with an equally cool wit. The sort that made a man long to melt the icy exterior and find the warm heart beneath. And Rosalind? Her kisses were as tart as Elise's were sweet. And her skin and hair tasted of cinnamon and pepper.

He stopped and blinked. It had been years, and yet he could remember everything about that single kiss as though he had stolen it moments ago. With each new sight of her, the past had come flooding back, sharper than ever. She smelled the same, her skin was just as soft, and her face held the same mix of devilment and innocence.

He glanced across the room at Elise, and tried to remember the kisses that he had shared with her the year they'd met. There had been months of dancing, laughter, and a few passionate stolen moments alone. But it was all a vaguely pleasant blur, and not nearly so clear as their time spent in friendship since. Try as he might, he could not sort the incidents of his engagement, supposedly the happiest time of his life, from his time spent with the dozens of other pretty girls he had known before and since.

But he could still remember every moment of the hour he had spent with Rosalind Morley. The way he had felt when he'd looked at her. The way she'd felt in his arms. And how he had known it would be wrong to kiss her and done it anyway. She had positively glowed with an unsuppressed fire, and he had been helpless to resist.

A sensible man would have pulled her out from under the mistletoe that night and sent her home to her father before anything untoward happened. It would have been far better to douse the fiery spirit, even if it had turned her tart wits to bitterness. Only a fool would have leapt into the flames and laughed as he burned.

A fool, or a man in love.

He turned away quickly and took a sip of his drink, hoping for a soothing distraction. But the spices in the mulled wine heated his blood rather than cooled it. Love at first sight. What an utterly prosaic notion. It lacked the sophistication of lust or the banal thrill of debauchery. It was gauche. Naïve. A simplistic explanation for a natural physical response to finding a beautiful young girl alone and willing, and taking advantage of the opportunity to kiss her senseless.

And running away had been a natural response as well. He had given little thought to what the girl might have felt over it. She would have given the incident too much significance, since she had nothing to compare it with. He knew better. That brief intimacy, and his resulting obsession with it, was a result of too much whimsy in a season given over to such behaviour. To avoid such revelry in the future was the best way to keep one's head and prevent further mistakes.

He had ignored the vague feeling that his perfectly acceptable engagement to Elise was a misalliance of the worst sort. And the faint sense of relief he'd felt when Elise had rejected him. The feeling that he was very lucky to be free of it. His subsequent inability to find anyone to suit him better was merely selectiveness on his part. It did not mean that he'd given his heart away on a whim, several Christmases ago, and lacked the courage to find the girl and retrieve it.

He shook his head. This was not an epiphany. This was temporary insanity—brought on by too many parlour games, too much punch, and a severe lack of oxygen from too many nights packed in tight at the fireside next to people who were happier in their lives than he. One did not make life-altering decisions based on a brief acquaintance with a girl, no matter how delectable she might be. And, even worse, one should not make them in the presence of mistletoe.

Should he manage to get clear of his attachment to Elise, if he wished for the change to be permanent he should run and keep running. It would be even wiser to give a wide berth to Harry Pennyngton and all of his extended family.

He took another sip of wine.

But where would be the fun in that?

His sip became a gulp, and he choked and spluttered on it, gasping to catch his breath.

A hand hit him sharply between the shoulderblades, to help him clear his lungs. And then hit him again out of sheer spite.

'Anneslea,' he gasped.

'None other.' Harry was grinning at him again, revelling in Nick's distress. 'First I see you nearly drown in the apple bucket, and now in a single glass of wine? It is a good thing I am here to take care of you. Heaven knows what might happen if you were left on your own.'

There was probably a double meaning in his words, just as there always was. But suddenly Nick found it impossible to care. He took in a great gulp of air, reached out and took Harry by the shoulders to steady himself, and announced, 'I am a faithless cad.'

Harry clapped him on the back again. But this time it was in camaraderie. 'You have realised it at last, have you? Good for you, sir. And a Merry Christmas to you.' Then he disengaged himself and headed back to the apple barrel.

Nick stared after Harry, wondering if the man had interpreted that as an apology, or just a random statement of fact. Apparently, he had come to some level of self-awareness. But what was to be done about it? If he ran to Rosalind with the news, he was not positive that his discovery would be welcome. And even if it was, he did not dare risk breaking her heart again until he was sure how things would come out.

But if all went as planned, Elise would be home for

good in a few short days, and Rosalind would be faced with a return trip to Shropshire. If he could bide his time until then, Rosalind might be open to possibilities that might prevent her homecoming.

He grinned to himself. Even if she had doubts about a future with him, it would take only a closed door, some mistletoe, and a few moments' persuasion to convince her of the advantage in total surrender.

Elise stared down at the apples floating in the basin and forced a bright smile. Her head still ached, and her eyes felt swollen and sandy from crying. But she had promised herself there would be no more sulking in her room. After last night's outburst it would not do to let the guests see that she was upset.

Of course her husband's continual rejection of her during the game had hurt her. He had known all the girls in the room by touch, and had joked and laughed with them. In his study, he had claimed to want her back. But he had shown no sign of it a moment later. And now she must smile and chat with the women he had hugged as though nothing was wrong.

She focused her attention on the apples and dipped her face into the water, deep enough so that it lapped at her cheeks, cooling the fire in them. And if, while submerged, she imagined either of the Misses Gilroy, plunged headfirst into the same water until their hair dripped and their gowns were ruined? Then at least no one could see it in her face.

She caught an apple easily in her teeth, and rose to

laughter and applause. She set the fruit on the small table beside the basin, and turned to find Harry right behind her, holding out a towel.

He grinned at her. 'Very good, my dear. Very good indeed.' And she noticed his eyes shift away from her face, lower, to the neckline of her gown.

She could feel a drop of water sliding slowly down her skin, ready to disappear into the hollow between her breasts. Was it this that was drawing his attention? She took the towel from him. And then, as though she were flirting with a stranger, she offered him a languid hand. He took it, and led her away from the apples.

She dabbed carefully at her face with the towel, taking care to leave the single drop of water quavering on the swell of her breast. When they reached a quiet corner of the room she paused and looked up, to catch him staring again. For a moment, she expected him to give her a guilty smile to acknowledge that he was behaving improperly, and fix his gaze upon her face. For this was her husband, not Nicholas or some other gentleman of the ton.

But, although he must know that she had caught him, he continued to stare at her body as though the passage of the water were of the utmost importance to him. He wet his lips like a man parched from too long without a drink, and gave a small sigh of longing as it disappeared from sight. When he met her gaze again, his eyes were a dark, smoky green. And for a moment she was sure that honour, pride and propriety meant nothing to him. Even though they were in a crowded hall, if she gave the slightest of nods he would bury his face between her breasts, find that drop and kiss it away.

She felt a thrill of desire, just as she always did when Harry looked at her with that strange intensity. But this time it was heightened by abstinence, and the fact that he was admiring her so obviously, in so public a place. If he had been brazen before she'd left she would have scolded him. Told him to wait for evening, until they were upstairs. And he would have laughed and complied with her wishes, banking his desire until they were safely behind bedroom doors.

But he had been behaving quite unpredictably of late. It was possible she might never again see that look in his eyes. And suddenly dread mixed with desire, and she knew that it was of the utmost importance to hold his interest.

So she played the coquette, just as she would with a gentleman whose affections were not guaranteed. She touched the skin of her throat with one hand, spreading the fingers until they gave the briefest caress to the track the water had followed, and then traced the neckline of her gown. 'It is surprisingly warm in the house today, is it not?'

'Indeed.' His reply was innocent enough, but his eyes followed the progress of her hand.

'The water was most refreshing.' She smiled at him, gazing through her lashes. 'I am surprised that you have not taken a turn.'

'Alas, I have no skill in apple-bobbing. But there are other games I prefer.' His voice was a purr, and the invitation it held was clear.

Would it be success or failure to give in to desire, just for a night? It would not solve their problems, but at least she would be sure that he still wanted her. 'But so many games require a partner. It is most frustrating to find oneself unmatched when one wishes to play.'

'Very,' he agreed.

She bit her lip and pretended to hesitate. 'You seemed quite taken with the young ladies of the Gilroy family during yesterday's game. Perhaps either of them would suit?' She waited for the assurance that he would much prefer someone else.

Instead, he said, 'It is an interesting idea. They are both lovely girls—well-formed, fair of face. And on the whole I find them both to be good company. Too young, of course. Although their mother remarked, after you had left the room, that Lord Gilroy always retires early. I suspect she is also in search of a partner.' And he glanced away from her, to Lady Gilroy, who was wearing a dress cut far too low for daytime, and bending over the apple barrel to call attention to the fact.

He looked back to Elise, and she could feel the jealous colour rising in her face, spoiling her efforts to appear coy and detached. 'It is no business of mine,' she snapped. 'I am sure it does not matter who you choose to partner you.'

He sighed. 'You are wrong, of course. I'm sure it would hurt some people very much.'

Me. It would hurt me. Even the thought that Lady Gilroy was interested caused an ache in her heart. It was even worse than seeing Harry's innocent flirting with her daughters. But she must remember where she was, and the number of prying eyes around her. For she had a shameless urge to grab him by the arm and plead with him to assure her she had nothing to fear.

He continued. 'Think of Lord Gilroy, knowing that his wife is eager to give her attentions to another. It is most difficult to suffer in silence.'

Suffering. He was right to call it that. For now, with each minute they were apart, she would know that he was free, and she would worry that he might choose to exercise that freedom. It did not matter that he did not care for her, nor that there were other women who would be a better wife than she had been. She was overcome with a desperate, selfish desire to have her old life back.

Harry was staring across the room in the general direction of Lord Gilroy. 'I suppose it is easier to let people think he does not care than to appear a tired old fool who cannot keep his wife satisfied.'

Oh, God. Perhaps it meant nothing. Perhaps he was only speaking of Gilroy, and not of himself. If it mattered to him, why had he not spoken? If he truly cared for her, then every smile that she'd given to Nicholas, every dance, every shared laugh, would have been like a knife in her husband's heart.

'Harry?' Her voice was shaking, as were her knees. In fact it felt as if her whole body were trembling, afraid of the answers to the questions she must ask him.

'Darling?' He reached out and took her hand again, gave it a squeeze of encouragement.

'Anneslea!' Lord Cammerville was tottering over to

them, smiling broadly and gesturing with his glass. 'So good to see you with your lovely wife at your side again.'

Harry gave a slight bow of pride.

Elise smiled as well, letting the curses flow in her mind. Why had the fat old toad chosen *now* to interrupt them?

'And how have you managed to keep that delightful sister so well hidden from society? You are truly fortunate to be surrounded by such beauty.'

'Hardly surrounded, Cammerville. This is the first time I've been able to enjoy the company of both of them for an extended period. Rosalind's father, the Reverend Morley, has very little faith in my ability to watch out for the girl, even though it is long past time for him to let her fly the coop.'

Elise turned her wrath upon the absent Morley. 'He is very foolish. There can be no better place for her than with you if she wishes an introduction to polite society.'

Harry gave a surprised smile in response to her small compliment. 'If you asked her father's opinion, I doubt it would be the same. I was eight when he married my mother, and he still looks on me as a wilful schoolboy with a decadent upbringing that has permanently flawed my character. Didn't think much of my late father or his family, I'm afraid. Couldn't abide Grandfather, who was Anneslea before me.'

Cammerville laughed knowingly. 'Tried to cane the title out of you, did he?'

Harry winced, and laughed in response.

'He beat you?' Elise stared at him in surprise. For he had never mentioned any such thing.

'Spare the rod and spoil the child,' Cammerville answered.

Harry nodded. 'And Morley was a firm believer in biblical retribution—especially when it concerned the sin of pride.'

'Why did you not tell me?' It was the wrong time to ask him, in a room full of people. But suddenly it was urgent that she know.

He considered for a moment. 'Have I not? Hmm. I thought I had.' He shrugged in apology. 'I find I am happier if I do not think on him much. As I am sure he is content not to think of me.'

'Is that why you left home so early? Rosalind said that you found it easier to stay at Anneslea with the old Earl. And that she hardly saw you at all until after she was grown-up.' She reached out and touched his sleeve.

He smiled at her in reassurance. 'That is the way we like to remember the facts, yes. I came to live with my Grandfather Pennyngton because Lincolnshire was closer to my school than our home in Shropshire. It was much easier to come here for holidays.' He shrugged again. 'But I suspect that if we measured the distance it would have been a much shorter trip to the rectory, and on roads that were better and less affected by weather. The truth of the matter was Morley would not have me at home, and I had no desire to return. Nothing my mother could say would sway him.'

'That was most unfair of him.'

'I cannot say I blame him overly. By the time I was thirteen I was nearly as tall as he was.' He gave Cammerville a knowing wink. 'The day came when I disagreed with his parental advice. So I snatched the stick from his hand and broke it over his back.'

Cammerville laughed so hard that tears ran from his eyes, and Harry laughed as well.

'You struck him?' Elise looked at him in continued amazement.

He must fear that she was angry with him for keeping secrets, for he hurried to say, 'I doubt that Rosalind has heard that story either. It is one of the many things that we do not discuss in my family. Nor do we dwell on the fact that Morley threw me, bag and baggage, from his house. But that is the real reason I ended up with my father's family.'

'That is horrible.' She looked back and forth between his smile and Cammerville's obvious amusement, and her lip trembled in sympathy for the little boy he had been.

Harry reached out and laid a comforting hand on her shoulder, as though surprised by her strong reaction to something that had been over and done with for almost twenty years. 'It was not so terrible. It was quite possible that I earned the punishment he gave me. After Father died I was well on the way to having an uncontrollable temper. Grandfather took me in and put me right. He taught me that one does not need to rage to accomplish what one desires. One can do as much by patience as one ever can with temper.'

'Perhaps you learned too well,' she murmured. 'But it was better, if Morley beat you, that you remained away.'

'And in time I demonstrated my improved character

to him, and he allowed me home to visit Rosalind.' He frowned. 'Of course it was too late to heal some wounds. I only saw my mother once before she died.'

'He separated you from your mother?' Her voice was an anguished bleat, and Cammerville laughed at her tender heart.

Harry blinked, and absently brushed a lock of hair out of his eyes. 'It had to happen eventually, once I went away to school. The miserable old goat brought the whole family up here for Christmas, after I was of age. Of course, he turned around in only a day and rushed them all home again. But I had a very nice dinner with mother and Morley that evening.' He put his arm around her shoulders and gave her a cautious hug. 'It was fine, really. And over very long ago. Nothing to be so distressed about.'

'Oh, Harry.' Now she was both tearful and slightly disgusted with him. And he was giving her such a puzzled look, as though he knew he had done something wrong but had no idea what it might be. Like a lost little boy.

She stamped her foot, trying to drive the sob back down her throat, and whimpered, 'Excuse me, Lord Cammervile.' Then she seized the towel from Harry's hand and hurried towards the door.

Behind her, she could hear Cammerville's explosive, 'Women, eh? They are an eternal mystery. Is it too early for a brandy, do you think?'

And Harry's response. 'Let us find Rosalind and see where she is hiding it. I feel strangely in need of cheer.'

Elise hurried into the hall before the tears could overtake her. Of all the times for her husband to open up and reveal his soul it would have to be when they were chatting with one of his more ridiculous friends, in a room full of people. Lord Cammerville must have thought her quite foolish to be near to crying over a story that they thought was nothing more than a common fact of boyhood.

But not to her. Never had she seen her father raise a hand to Carl. Nor had her brother reason to respond in anger to punishment. And the sight of Harry running a hand through his hair like a lost child, telling her how one mistake had cost him his mother…

She gulped back another sob.

'Here, now, what is the matter?' Nicholas reached out and seized her by the arms, arresting her flight. 'Crying in a common hallway? What is the cause?' He looked happier than she had seen him in months, but his expression changed quickly to concern.

'I have done something terrible.'

He looked doubtful. 'Surely not?'

'I have left my husband.'

'Not again.' He drew away from her in alarm.

'No. Before. When I left him to come to you, Nicholas.' And she took him by the arms, trying to get him to listen. 'I teased him, and it hurt. And then I left him when he needed me.'

'And you have noticed this now?' Nicholas shook his head in amazement. 'Very well. And what do you mean to do about it?'

'I do not know. You are a man. Tell me. What can I say to him that will make it all better?'

'Say to him?' Nick responded with his most rakish smile. He put his hands on her shoulders and looked deep into her eyes. 'Oh, darling, I doubt you need say anything at all to have a man at your feet. You have but to wait until the guests are safely asleep, and open your bedroom door. You will not need words after that.'

There was the sound of masculine throat-clearing, and an inarticulate noise of female distress. And then her husband and his sister walked past them, down the hall.

Harry looked his usual calm, collected self. But Rosalind was nearly overcome with emotion, her eyes darting from Elise, to Nicholas and back, trying to choose whom she should scold first.

When she slowed, Harry took her by the arm and pulled her along, refusing to let her stop. But as they passed he gave Nicholas an arch look that made the man carefully release Elise's arms, as though he were taking his finger off the trigger of a primed pistol. Then Harry smiled to his sister, and said, 'The brandy, Rosalind. Remember the brandy. We shall find a glass for you as well. Your father will not approve, but so be it.'

Chapter Thirteen

Rosalind's foul mood continued unabated through dinner, despite the small glass of brandy Harry had given her to calm her nerves. While he'd said it was flattering to have a sister so devoted to one's happiness as to be reduced to spluttering rage by the scene of one's wife and her lover in a position that could be considered by some as compromising, he'd assured her it was hardly a reason to ruin Christmas dinner.

His assurances that it did not require action had been met with frustrated cries of, 'Oh, Harry,' and elaborate threats on her part to chase down Tremaine and make him pay bitterly for his lack of manners.

A rumour from the cook that the evening's goose was past its prime and too tough to eat had driven the scene temporarily from her mind, and Harry had made a mental note to reward the kitchen staff generously on Boxing Day for the timely distraction. He had smiled to himself in satisfaction and poured another brandy. For, after seeing the tears in his wife's eyes over his tragic child-hood, he doubted that Tremaine, annoying though he might be, was making as much progress as it appeared.

After a dinner of goose that had been more than tender enough for his taste, Rosalind stood and an-nounced, 'Tonight, for those who are interested, we shall have dancing in the ballroom. Come and join us once you have finished your port.'

Harry followed her out of the dining room and down the hall to the ballroom. 'If you can still manage a ball, darling, you are a magician.'

'And how so?' Her gaze was defiant, her smile frozen and resolute.

'There are no musicians,' he said reasonably. 'They did not arrive today—probably because of the bad weather. I am certain we can forgo the dancing and no one will mind.'

'It is not the first problem I have had with this party of yours,' she said through gritted teeth. 'And I doubt it will be the last. But if we cancel the dancing then I will have to find a better activity to pass the evening, and I can think of none. Besides, the room has already been decorated and the refreshments prepared. The servants have moved the pianoforte to the ballroom, and I am more than capable of playing something that the guests can dance to.'

'But if you are playing then you cannot dance yourself,' he pointed out.

'It is only polite that I sit out in any case.' Her voice was cold reason. 'It is slightly different than I feared, but I was marginally correct. Your numbers are unbalanced, and in favour of the women. Several families have brought daughters, and there are no partners for them. Better that I allow the others to dance in my place.'

'But no one expects you to forgo the pleasure all evening,' he said. 'You do not have to play for the whole time.'

'Really it is no problem. I enjoy playing. And I will have the opportunity to sit down while doing it.' The look in her eye said if the party knew what was good for it, they would dance and be glad of it, because she did not wish to be crossed.

Harry put on his most fraternal smile. 'But you also enjoy dancing, do you not? I can remember the way you stood on my boots and let me waltz you around the drawing room.'

She gave him a pained look. 'Twenty years ago, perhaps. Then, it was not so important to have a partner.'

He clutched at his heart. 'I am no partner? You wound me, Rosalind.'

'You are my brother,' she said firmly. 'And if you are the only unpartnered man in the room I suppose it is not improper that we dance. But it would be far more pleasant for me if you stand up as a courtesy to the daughters of your guests than with me out of pity.' For a moment she did sound a bit pitiable. But then she snapped, 'If you cannot manage that, then perhaps you should dance with your wife. It is what you want to do, after all. It does no good to pretend otherwise. But for myself? I prefer to remain at the keyboard. Thank you very much.'

Guests had begun to filter into the room behind them, and she sat down and began to play a tune so brisk that they could not resist standing up to dance.

Harry did as she'd bade him and offered his hand to a blushing girl of sixteen. He was gratified to see the look on her face, as though the room could hardly contain her joy at being asked. When they stood out, he had an opportunity to view the others in the room.

His wife was standing up with Tremaine, of course. They made a most handsome couple, as they always had. Their steps were flawless, their smiles knowing. It was painful to see them together, so he smiled even wider and raised a glass of champagne in toast to them.

Rosalind sat at the piano, playing a seemingly endless progression of happy melodies. To look at her was to suspect that the instrument in front of her had done her an injury, and that she wished to punish it with enthusiastic play. Her eyes never wavered from the empty music stand in front of her, even though she was playing it all from memory, and her hands hammered away at the keys with an almost mechanical perfection. She seemed to focus inward, and there was no sign that the sights she saw were happy ones.

And suddenly Harry felt the fear that if something was not done he would see her in the same place next year, and the year after, ageing at the piano stool, the lines in her face growing deeper and her expression more distant as the world laughed and went on without her.

So he smiled his best host's smile, remarked to all within earshot that it was a capital entertainment, and encouraged them to help themselves to refreshment when the music paused. If they thought him a naïve cuckold, so be it. Perhaps after this holiday they would have no reason to. But, no matter what became of him, he would not allow Rosalind to become the sad old maid who kept his house.

He turned to the girl beside him, pointed to Rosalind, and enquired if she played as well.

'Not so well, sir. But I have lessons. And my piano master says I am his most proficient pupil.'

'I would see my sister stand up for a set. But first I must find someone to replace her at the instrument. Can you help me?'

The girl was radiant at the thought.

Very good, then. He was only being a good host by making the offer.

He went to Rosalind. 'Dear sister, I have a favour to ask of you.'

She sighed, but did not pause in her playing. 'Another favour? Am I not busy enough for you, Harry?'

He laughed. 'Too busy, I think. Templeton's daughter was remarking at what a fine instrument this appears to be, and it seems she is a musician. But obviously not much of a dancer, for she trod upon my toes on several occasions. If she is thus with the other guests it might benefit all to have her play for a time and rest from dancing. If you could give up your seat to her, I would be most grateful.'

Rosalind considered for but a moment. 'It would be for the best—if she does not seem to mind.'

'Very good. Have a glass of champagne, and I will see her settled here.

He installed the Templeton girl at the piano, then watched as his sister visited the refreshment table and became occupied with haranguing the servants about the dwindling supply of wine. When he was sure she would take no notice of him, he swallowed his distaste, refreshed his smile with another sip of wine, and strode into the room to find a partner for Rosalind.

'Tremaine—a word, if you please?'

It was always a pleasure to see the way the man cringed when Harry addressed him directly, as though snivelling and subservience were sufficient apology for all he had done.

'Harry?' He took a deep sip from his glass.

'I need a favour from you.'

'From me?' Now the man was totally flummoxed. And then suspicious. His eyes narrowed. 'What can I do for you?'

Jump off the nearest cliff. Harry pushed the idea to the back of his mind, readjusted his smile, and said, 'I need a dancing partner. Not for me, of course.' He gave a self-deprecating laugh. 'For m' sister. She will not stand up from the damn piano if she must stand with me. And you are the only man in the room who could pass, in dim light, for eligible.'

Tremaine looked past his usual partner towards Rosalind, who had seated herself next to a potted palm, almost out of sight of the crowd. His face took on a curious cast in the flickering light of the candles. 'And she does love dancing,' he said. His voice was distant, as though lost in memory.

Harry wondered if he needed to repeat his request, and then the man next to him seemed to regain focus.

'Of course,' he said. 'You are right. She should not be forced to sit out the whole evening because of some misplaced sense of duty to her guests.'

'Make her think it is your idea, for I doubt she will do it for me. She was most cross that I even suggested she dance before.'

'Yes. Yes, of course.' And Tremaine strode across the room and passed by Elise as though she did not even exist.

Elise raised her eyes to follow him, and nodded with approval when she saw him go to Rosalind.

Tremaine smiled his cynical London smile and bowed to Rosalind, offering his hand.

Rosalind shook her head, gave him an outraged glare, and replied with something tart and equally cynical, which must have amused him. He laughed, and then repeated his offer, with a deeper bow and hands held open in front of him.

She tossed her head, and made a great show of getting up, against her better judgement, to take his hand and let him lead her into the room. But Harry could see the faint flush of guilty pleasure on her face, and the exasperated curve to the lips that had replaced her stoic lack of expression.

Harry went to stand next to the girl at the piano, who was looking nervous now that the attention was to be on her. 'Something simple to start, I think. You can manage a waltz, can you not? They are slow, and the beat is steady.'

The girl nodded and began.

When Rosalind realised what was about to occur, alarm flashed across her face, and the pink in her cheeks was replaced by white. She hissed something to her partner, stepped away from him, and made to sit down.

But Harry watched as Tremaine caught her hand easily in his and pulled her back into the dance, giving another slight bow before putting his arms about her.

She still hesitated for a moment, and then looked down at the floor and coloured again, as though she would be anywhere in the world but where she was. But as the dancing began she relaxed. Her small body settled into the circle of his arms like a sparrow seeking warmth in the winter.

For his part, Tremaine stood close enough to her that she could not see his face. He gazed over her head and past her, into the room. And wherever he was it was not in the present. His eyes were looking some-where very far away, some place that gave him both great happiness and great pain, for there was more sincere emotion in his eyes than Harry had ever seen. The man was in torment, and yet there was a faint smile on his lips.

For a moment Harry sympathised.

As the couple danced it was not with the easy, per-fectly matched grace of Tremaine and Elise, but as one person. Their steps were not flawless, but their mistakes matched their successes, and the false notes in the music did nothing to hinder them.

And then the dancing was over, and Rosalind pulled away from him and rushed from the room.

After a moment's hesitation Tremaine went after her, his urbane lope failing to disguise the speed of his response.

Harry sighed. That answered that. It would be even more complicated than he had hoped. But it was just as he had always feared, and he could not pretend surprise.

Chapter Fourteen

Elise watched the couple on the dance floor too, trying to disguise her ill ease. They were an unusual pair, for Nicholas was a head too tall to dance easily with Rosalind. But they were attractively matched in colouring. And of a similar temperament. If circumstance had been different, and Elise had been hostess at Harry's side, she would have seated the two together at meals just to see what became of it. It was disturbing that the idea held such appeal. For it showed her how easy it would be to forget the man who had stood by her side for so long, and had so graciously escorted her back to this house, although he must have known what it might mean.

She watched the dancers take another turn, and saw the expression upon Nick's face. The most incorrigible rogue in London looked the picture of restraint—and none too happy about it. For a moment Elise flattered herself that it was for her benefit, to show his loyalty. But only for a moment. She knew the man too well for that. He must want the girl in his arms most desperately to make such a great effort not to want her.

And as he turned again she could see Rosalind. It was as though the girl were dancing to her favourite tune on the edge of a cliff—for she was clearly struggling not to enjoy the waltz, nor her contact with the man who danced with her.

So that was the way it was to be. It pained Elise to think that she had not matched the two long ago, for Rosalind needed a way to escape from her father, and Nick needed a steady hand to hold his. She shook her head at her own folly. Rather than help him she had stood in his way, making it more difficult for him to leave her. How great a fool she was, to realise it now that things had grown so complicated.

But perhaps it would be easier if Tremaine wished a parting as much as she did. At least she would not be obliged to break his heart before returning to Harry. For, after their conversation of the afternoon, she was sure she meant to return—if he would still have her.

She frowned. Had she gained anything by her two months away? She suspected that once she was back in his house, Harry would cease his complaints about her loyalty and drop easily back into the role of affectionate but distant husband. She must learn to tolerate his silences without complaint now he had shown her the reason for them. And she would not trouble him any more with Nicholas, or any other foolish flirtations.

Although Harry had not run to fetch her from London, he had at least admitted, aloud, that he wanted her back. And she knew she wanted to be with him, perhaps even more than she had before. If he was willing to overlook their barren union, then she should count her blessings. Most men would not have bothered to disguise their dissatisfaction with her, or to mask their disappointment in false smiles and silence. Perhaps she should learn to view Harry's self-restraint as a gift.

She saw Nicholas whisper something to his partner, and the girl started like a frightened fawn. Then she broke from him and left the room.

For a moment Elise thought to go after her, but she saw Nick glance once around the room to see if the other guests had noticed. Then he followed in the girl's wake.

'I wonder what has got into Rosalind?' Harry had come to stand by her side.

'She is probably overcome with the burden you have forced on her with this party. It was most unfair of you to saddle her with it at so little notice.' Elise gave him a mildly disapproving look, and then smiled to prove it a joke.

He smiled and answered back, 'Perhaps it is unfair to my sister to say so, but you would not have had the trouble she has. I have seen you rise to greater challenges than this without faltering. Should we go and see to her, do you think?' He paused dramatically. 'But wait. I saw Tremaine go after her. So I needn't worry. He is very good at taking care of women in distress, is he not?' His expression was supremely innocent, but he was obviously trying to make her jealous.

'I have always found him so,' she answered with an equally blasé look, ignoring the bait. If he did not wish to question her directly about what he had witnessed in the hall, then did she really need to explain it? And then she remembered how he had been in the afternoon. And she responded in kind, 'Sometimes things are not as they appear.'

He glanced at her, as though surprised at her acknowledgement. And then he gave a small sigh, of fatigue or relief, and said, 'So I assumed.'

The girl at the piano began another waltz, and he bowed to her, holding out a hand. 'Will you favour me with a dance?'

When she hesitated, he added, 'You need not read too much into it. It is only a waltz. I trust Tremaine will not mind if I borrow you for a few moments?'

He was working very hard to appear neutral, but she could see the challenge in his eyes.

So she answered it. 'It does not matter to me what Nicholas thinks.' And she took his hand and let him lead her onto the floor.

It felt so good to be back in his arms again that she had to struggle for a moment to keep herself from saying it aloud. Would it be too much, too soon, to admit tonight that she wished to come home? Though a truce had been declared for Christmas Day, she was not sure it would last. And it would serve her right if he wished to toy with her a bit, as punishment for leaving, before accepting her apology.

Her hopes rose when he said, in a carefully polite

tone, 'It is good to dance with you again. Yet another of the many things I've missed since you have gone.'

He was willing to make the first move, to make things easier for her. She leaned back to get a better look into his face, surprised at his choice of words. 'Oh, Harry. You loathed dancing.'

He laughed and shook his head. 'Not true. I made a great show of loathing it. Because I so liked the things you were willing to do to coax me into it.'

She blushed at the memory of long nights spent in his arms after various balls, and he laughed again.

'But now I must take what pleasures you will allow, with no more foolish dissembling to gain ground.' He squeezed her hand, and tightened his fingers on her waist as he spun her around the floor.

She relaxed and let him lead her, enjoying the feel of his strength. Tonight she would do as Nicholas had suggested and open the connecting door between their rooms. And everything would return to the way it was.

'I shall know better,' he said, 'when next I seek a wife.'

She stumbled against him. He was teasing her again. Or did he mean it? She tried to match his tone as she responded, 'Do you have plans of that nature?'

'It all depends on what the future holds for us. I shall know if Tremaine is serious about keeping you by his actions this holiday. If he is true to his word, then we shall see about the divorce.' He paused for a moment. 'If you still wish for it, that is.'

Here was her chance to admit that her feelings on the subject had changed. She approached the subject elliptically, as he had. 'I understand,' she said, 'that the courts of England are not likely to be co-operative in the matter of a divorce. Once the bonds between two people are set they are not to be easily broken.'

'That is probably for the best,' he answered. 'But there should be some regard to the happiness of the individuals involved. It would not be good to force someone to remain if they were truly unhappy.'

And she had been miserable.

That was why she had left. She had loved him dearly, and still did, but it had not been enough to make a happy marriage. If she came back to him, perhaps for a while she could pretend that his silence didn't matter to her. She would forgo the companionship of other men so as not to arouse his jealousy, and she would learn to speak around the things that were most important to her, so as not to upset the delicate balance between them. But if it was to be just the two of them, alone until death?

'We are not likely to have any children,' she blurted, unable to avoid the truth a moment longer.

He tensed. 'Are they necessary for a happy union?'

'I assumed, when you offered for me, that they must be a primary concern to you. There is the title to consider, after all.'

'Well, yes, of course.' He glanced around them. 'I just choose not to discuss it in the middle of a crowded ballroom.'

She all but forgot the promise she had made to herself to be patient with his reticence. Once she came home she might never get a second chance to say what she needed to. 'No, Harry. You choose not to speak of it at all. You have left me to guess your opinions on the matter.'

'We are speaking of it now, aren't we?' He lowered his voice, hoping that she would follow suit.

She looked from her husband to the people around them. 'I know. It is the wrong venue, if we do not want our problems known to all of London. But at least I know that you cannot walk away in the middle, before you have heard what I mean to say.' She took a deep breath. 'In daylight, you treat me like a child if I wish to discuss matters of importance. But at night it is clear that you know I'm a grown woman, for you do not wish to talk at all. You visit me regularly enough. But I assume that you are hoping for a result from those visits. It must be gravely disappointing to you.'

She felt his spine stiffen. And suddenly it was as though she were dancing with a block of wood. 'I was under the impression that you enjoyed sharing a bed with me.'

'I never said I did not.'

He began to relax again, and his fingers tightened on her waist in a way that offered a return to intimacy should she be inclined.

She continued. 'But, pleasurable or not, I am beginning to think that nothing will come of it.'

'Nothing?' He grew stiff and cold again. 'And I suppose you think you will do better with someone else? Is this one more way that you believe Tremaine to be my superior?'

'I did not say that.' For she was not the one that needed an heir.

'But neither are you denying it.' He stopped dancing

and released her. 'Go to him, then, and see if it is better. It is obvious that I have nothing that you want. And I certainly cannot buy you children.' Then he turned and left her alone on the floor.

Rosalind leaned against the closed door of the library and felt the breath come out of her in a great, choking sob. She had done an excellent job controlling her emotions, in regard to Tremaine. And now it was all collapsing. It had taken years to convince herself that her first response to him had been the result of alcohol and inexperience. She had been sure that if she met him again she would find him no different from a hundred other town bucks. He would be no more handsome, no quicker to take advantage of a foolish girl, than if he were a man of better character.

But in comparison to the other men of her experience he was still perfection: sharp-witted, urbane and funny. And at such moments as he chose to turn his attention upon her he was no easier to resist than he had been that first day. And when they danced…

It was not fair. It simply was not. To be in the arms of a man one barely knew and feel convinced that one was home at last, finally in the place where one belonged. To feel all the wrongness and confusion of the rest of her life vanish like a bad dream. And to know that when the music ended she would find that she had confused dreams and reality again. Nicholas Tremaine was the fantasy. Not all the rest.

If she could have a moment alone to gather her wits

she would return to the ballroom as though nothing strange had happened. She would claim any redness of the eyes as brought about by cinders from the Yule Log.

'Rosalind? Open the door, please. We need to talk.'

She glared at the wood, as though she could see through it to the man on the other side. 'I think we have talked more than enough, Tremaine. I have nothing to say to you at the moment.'

'I need to know that you are all right before I return to the dancing.'

'I am fine. Thank you. You may go.'

'Rosalind! Open this door.' He was speaking more loudly than necessary, perhaps so that he could be heard clearly through the oak.

She rubbed at the tears on her cheeks. 'Don't be an ass. I am perfectly all right. Go back to the dancing, and to your…your…usual partner.' The words came in little gasps. Even without opening the door it would be obvious to him that she was crying. She winced at having revealed herself so clearly.

'Now, Rosalind.' His tone had changed to coaxing. 'What you think you saw in the hall today—it was nothing.'

'Nothing?' she parroted back. 'Tell that to Harry, for he says much the same thing. But I am not blind, nor foolish, nor too young to know better. I can recognise "nothing" when I see it. "Nothing" is what we share. But you and Elise have "something".'

'Barely anything, really. We are old friends, just as I have told you. Exceptionally close, of course.'

'Everyone knows about your "close" friendship, Tremaine. As apparently they always have. Nothing has changed in all these years. Everyone here can talk of nothing else.' She tried not to think of that first foolish Christmas, when she had had no idea of the truth. And how much easier it had been to know only half the facts.

He cleared his throat. 'It is not quite as it once was. When I first met you, Elise and I had an understanding, and I was not free. Now? Now we have a different sort of understanding. And until I can sort it out I cannot call my future my own.'

'Your future is no concern of mine, Tremaine. Nor do I wish to speak of how it once was. Frankly, I would rather forget the whole thing. I wish it had never happened.'

There was a long pause. 'And is that why you ran from the room after we danced? Because it reminded you of the first time we waltzed? I remember it well.' His voice had gone soft again, quiet and full of seduction. 'You were spying on the other dancers. I put a finger to your lips, to let you know that what we were doing was to be secret, and I pulled you out of the doorway and waltzed you around the corridor.'

She remembered the finger on her lips, and the feel of his arms. And how, when she had been confused by the steps, he had held her so close that he could lift her feet from the ground and do the dancing for both of them, until she had dissolved into giggles. And then the giggles had changed to something much warmer, almost frightening. He had set her back down on her feet rather suddenly, and put a safe space between them to continue the dance. She wrapped her arms tightly around her own shoulders, trying to focus on the disaster that had ended the evening and not on how wonderful the dancing had been. But she would always remember her first waltz as a special thing, no matter what had come later.

His voice was quieter, more urgent. 'And I distinctly remember thinking, Ah, my dear, if only you were older…'

She dropped her arms to her sides. 'Really? Well, I am quite old enough now. And it makes no difference. Elise still leads you about like a puppy, and you still dawdle behind, sniffing after any available female. And if any of them get too close, you have Elise and your poor broken heart as an excuse to remain unmarried. Do not think you can play that game with me, Tremaine, for I know how badly it will end.'

'Rosalind.' He said it softly, and she waited for what might come next.

When nothing did, she said, 'Go back to the ballroom, Tremaine. And leave me in peace. Just as I wish you had done five years ago.'

There was another pause, before she heard the sound of his footsteps retreating down the corridor to the ballroom. She crept further into the room and went to sit on the sofa, where she had so often found Tremaine. She laid her hand upon the cushion, imagining that there was still some warmth there. Why did everything have to be so complicated, so unfair? She was quite sure that of the four of them she was the least to blame for the mess they were in. Why was *she* the one who was being punished? For she suspected that, despite what he might feel for her, in the end she would be no closer to Nicholas Tremaine than she had ever been. He was everything that she longed for and always had been. But for the fact that he did not want her, he would be perfect.

The door of the library opened and Elise stalked into the room, showing no respect for her privacy. She dropped down on the couch beside Rosalind and stared into the fire. 'I do not understand your brother in the slightest.'

Rosalind glared at her, wishing with all her heart that she would go away and take her close friend with her. 'Then you are truly suited. For neither does he understand you.'

'Harry claims to want me back. But now that I am here we do nothing but argue.'

'You were doing that before, were you not?'

'I was arguing. But he did not respond. And now?' She shrugged. 'It seems I can do nothing to please him. He misunderstands me at every turn, and I cannot convince him that I do not prefer the company of Nicholas.'

'Perhaps because he finds you in Tremaine's arms in a public hallway begging you to give in to his desires?'

Elise stared at her in confusion, and then said, 'Today? That is not at all what was going on.'

Rosalind cast a jaundiced eye upon her. 'And did you tell Harry that?'

'I told him that things were not as they appeared.'

'Small comfort. You will not unbend sufficiently to put his mind at rest, but you still think all your problems are caused by what he does or does not say?'

'You do not understand,' Elise argued. 'He becomes even angrier when I speak the truth.'

'Well, let me be forthcoming, since you set such a high price on honesty,' Rosalind snapped. 'You were unhappy before you left because you did not know his mind, but now that you know it you are still not satisfied. Perhaps you are the one who cannot be pleased, Elise.'

Elise shook her head. 'That is because he is not being logical. One moment he wants me, the next he tells me he would marry again. He tortures Nicholas, but tells me to go back to him. He wants our life to be just the way it was before I left. But if I must lie to him, and tell him all is well, then what good will it be to either of us?'

'Before he was trying to hide the truth, to keep the peace. But now that he must face facts, he is as angry and stubborn as you are.'

'Me?'

'Yes. You. You refuse to admit that you were happy, just as much as he refuses to admit his unhappiness. And if neither of you can manage a happy medium?' Rosalind sighed. 'Then I expect you will continue to make those around you even more miserable than you make yourselves.'

'We are making other people miserable?' Elise gave her a blank look. 'I fail to see how. Everyone here seems to be having a delightful time.'

Rosalind stood up and threw her hands in the air. 'I stand corrected. All is well, and everyone who matters is perfectly happy. And, since that is the case, I need not concern myself with the situation. I am going to my room.' She stalked to the door of the library. 'And it will serve you all right if I do not come out until Easter.' With that she stamped out of the room, allowing herself the luxury of both a muttered curse and a slam of the door.

Elise waited until she was sure that her sister-in-law had gone well away, and then followed slowly up the stairs to her own room. Was it only a few hours ago that she had been convinced her problems were almost over? And now Harry was angry with her and Rosalind even angrier. Only Nicholas was still her friend. But it was most unwise to rely on him any longer if he wished to be free. Rosalind was right: she was making everyone around her miserable.

Elise sighed in defeat. The sooner she learned to hold her temper and her tongue, the better it would be for all concerned. She would go to her husband, take all the blame onto herself, and beg him to take her back. Perhaps she would never have the sort of marriage she wanted, but anything would be better than the chaos around her now, and the aching loneliness she had felt when Harry had left her on the dance floor.

She sent her maid away and undressed hurriedly, leaving the clothes in a pile on the floor. She rummaged in the wardrobe for the dressing gown she had worn on her first night with Harry. Would he remember it after all this time? Perhaps not. But if Nicholas was right it would not matter overmuch. Once she had come back to his bed Harry would cease to be angry with her. And if she could lie in his arms each night, the days would not be so bad.

She wrapped her bare body in the silk and went to the connecting door. For a moment she was afraid to touch the knob. What would she do if he had locked it against her? But it turned as easily as it always had, and she opened the door and entered her husband's room.

To find it dark and empty. The candles had not been lit. The fire was banked low in the grate. And the bed was cold and still neatly made.

She hesitated again, and then went to it, climbing in and crawling beneath the covers to wait for Harry. The night wore on, and the linen was cold against her skin. So she pulled her wrapper tight around her, curled into a ball and slept, shivering through fitful dreams.

She awoke at dawn, still alone.

Chapter Fifteen

The next day, Rosalind felt even worse than she had after storming off to her room. She'd spent the night staring up at the ceiling, thinking of all the things that had gone wrong and all the ways the people in her life had failed her. And after a few fitful hours of sleep she had woken to find that her problems were not just a bad dream. The house was just as she'd remembered it: full of people she did not want to see ever again, and manned by servants who were just as slow and disobedient as ever. But, since it was Boxing Day, she was obliged to thank them for the fact, and respond to the lack of service with light duties and generosity.

After a cold breakfast she went down to the library, to take it all out on Tremaine. He was lounging in his usual place by the fire, eyes closed and feet up, as though the struggle of tying his own cravat had caused him to collapse in exhaustion.

She pushed his boots from their place of elevated

comfort. When they hit the carpet she glared down and kicked them for good measure. 'Get up this instant. You are required in the drawing room.'

He sighed. 'For what possible reason could you need me? Are there not enough drunken fools available to bend to your will? I swear, I still have the blue devils from last night.'

So the tenderness while they had danced was to be explained by an excess of champagne? She said, in a voice that she hoped was painfully loud, 'Then it is about time you learned moderation. A headache is no more than you deserve. Now, get up.'

He draped an elegant hand over his brow. 'Do you show such cruelty to all your guests, Miss Morley? Or do you reserve it especially for me? If I were in my right mind I'd return to London immediately.'

'Do not think you can fool me with idle threats. The roads have been clear for several days, but you are still lying about on this couch, insisting that you will leave at any moment. If you mean to go, then stand up and do it.'

'Very well, then. I admit it. I intend to stay for the duration of this farce, until I can see Elise safely back into the arms of her loving husband.'

She glared down at him. 'As always, I cannot fault you for your devotion to Elise. Let us hope, once she is settled and you are long gone from this place, that you can find some other woman who is worthy of such un-wavering affection. But for now you will have to content yourself with my company, and I need your help.'

He gave an elaborate sigh, to prove that her words

had little effect upon him. 'Very well. I am your humble servant, Miss Morley. What do you require of me now?'

'Elise is out of temper with Harry again. She looks as if she has not slept a wink. Harry is little better. He appeared at breakfast still in his evening clothes, smelling of brandy.'

'And what am I to do with that? Make possets and sing lullabies?'

Rosalind smothered the desire to kick him again, and to keep kicking him until she had made her feelings known. She took a deep breath and said, 'We are having charades. Elise adores the game, and I'm sure she will play to show the world that nothing is wrong. Harry means to remain in whatever room has the punch bowl, so he is easily controlled. I have prepared clues to remind them of the happiness that is married bliss. The game will either leave them in the mood for reconciliation or murder. At this point I do not really care which. Either would solve my problem.'

'And what do *I* have to do with all of this?'

She narrowed her eyes. 'You need merely be as you are—incorrigible, irritable and unbearable. Harry cannot help but shine by comparison.'

He sat up and glared back at her. 'You have no idea what it means to know of your confidence in me. You have decided I'm unbearable, have you?'

She lifted her chin and said, with all honesty, 'Yes. I have.'

'I was dragged here against my better judgement. For reasons that have nothing to do with the sincere celebration of the holiday and everything to do with schemes concocted by you and your brother. I am forced to be the bad example so that everyone else may shine. And yet you find fault with my behaviour?' He had gone white around the lips, and was looking at her with a curious, hard expression, almost as though she had hurt his non-existent feelings.

She shifted uncomfortably from foot to foot, and for a moment she was tempted to retreat. But then her anger at him got the better of her, and she retorted, 'You talk as though you are the injured party in all this. I am sorry, Nicholas, but you are not. In my experience, you are just as I have described you. You are wilful, self-serving, and have no thought to the comfort of anyone but yourself. Because of this, you are finally getting what you deserve.'

He stood up and came near to her. When he spoke, his voice was so soft that only she could hear it. 'You have a very limited experience where it concerns me.'

She shook her head. 'I have more than enough.'

He stared at her for a long moment, as though there was something he wished to say. Or perhaps he was awaiting a sign from her.

She glared all the harder, and deepened her frown.

At last, he said, 'In your eyes I will always be a monster who ruined you and then abandoned you. Very well, then. Let us play-act. And I shall be the villain, since you have cast the parts.'

He stepped past her and stalked to the door. On his way he stopped, looked down at the floor, and scooped up the tattered ball of mistletoe, which was out of place again. Then he turned back, glared at her, and threw the thing into the library fire.

Nick preceded Rosalind into the drawing room and took a place at the back of the room, arms folded. The little chit had all but told him that he was repellent to her, and now expected him to do her bidding like a common lackey. Rosalind Morley had never been anything but trouble to him from the first moment he had laid eyes on her—cutting up his peace, altering his plans, and disappearing in body but remaining stuck in his mind like a burr, a constant irritant to his comfort. He had wondered on occasion what had become of her after they had first parted. In moments of weakness he had even thought about enquiring after her, before common sense had regained the upper hand. If a single dance with her had turned into his life's most fateful kiss, there was no telling what a casual meeting or a friendly letter might become.

And his fears had proved true. For after only a few days in her company his life had been turned upside down. There she stood at the front of the room, with a false smile on her face, acting for all the world as if she did not even notice him. Which was a total falsehood. He could feel when they were together that she was attracted to him, and he had a good mind to go up there and drag her back to the library, to give her a demonstration of the flaws in his character. No matter what she might claim, once the door was closed it would take only a few moments to prove that her character was no better than his. And afterwards he would have her out of his system and could go back to London in peace.

At the front of the room, Rosalind continued to explain the rules in an excessively cheerful voice that gave the lie to everything he had just seen. 'First we must choose who is to guess and who is to help with the clues.' She scanned the crowd. 'I must stay here, since I already know the answer, but I will need two helpers.'

Elise came to her side immediately, and looked hopefully across the room to Harry.

Harry began to rise unsteadily from his chair. Very well, the two would play nicely together, just as Rosalind wished. But that did not mean that Nick had to waste his time watching over them. He began a subtle retreat towards the door, hoping that Rosalind had forgotten her original plan after his outburst in the library.

But she was ignoring Harry, and had turned her attention to the doorway. 'Mr Tremaine. You as well, I think.'

So she still meant to involve him in this? He turned back into the room and saw the dark look on Harry's face before the man collapsed back into his seat with an easy and devious smile. Whatever Rosalind had planned, the results were not likely to be as she expected. Nick strode to the front of the room, conscious of all eyes upon him.

'The rules are simple,' Rosalind announced to the group gathered before her. 'I have a riddle, and the answer is a three-syllable word. If you cannot guess the word from the riddle, we will act out the parts to help you. Here is the riddle:

Vows are spoken, True love's token, Can't be broken.'

She passed a folded piece of paper to Elise, and then to Tremaine.

Elise frowned.

Nick read it, then stared at Rosalind. 'This is a four-syllable word. Not three.'

She gritted her teeth. 'It does not matter.'

'I think it does if you mean people to guess the answer.'

She glared at him. 'And if I do not care for them to guess too quickly,' she whispered, so that Elise could not hear, 'it does not matter at all.'

She had that wild look in her eye again, that she normally used on mistletoe. And she was turning it on him. He glared back at her. 'You are right, it does not matter.'

'Here, Elise,' Rosalind said, smiling too brightly. 'You must take the first clue.'

Elise read the clue again and stepped forward. She stooped to lift an imaginary object and then remove from the ground another, which appeared to be a key. She made a great show of placing it in a non-existent lock and opening an invisible door to step through. There were the expected calls of, 'Doorknob,' 'Enter,' and Harry's muttered, 'Leave.'

'Don't be an idiot, Harry,' Rosalind whispered, loud enough so that everyone could hear. 'It is clear that she is coming back.'

'Clear to you, perhaps,' he responded, looking more sullen than Nick had seen him all week.

Elise frowned in his general direction, and then went back to her play-acting. She pretended to look back over the threshold and notice something on the ground, to go back to it and stare down and carefully wipe her shoes.

Whereupon Harry announced, in a clear voice, 'Husband.'

Elise's glare was incandescent, and to stop the outburst that she knew was coming Rosalind announced, 'I should think it is obvious. The answer is—'

Nick put his hand over her mouth, stopping the word. 'You cannot make the riddle and give us the answer,' he announced, giving everyone a false grin. 'Where would be the fun in that?'

'Door,' announced someone in the crowd.

Elise pointed to her feet.

'Feet.'

'Shoes.'

'Dirt.'

'Mmmmmmm,' said Rosalind, around the edges of his fingers.

At last someone shouted, 'Mat.' And he could feel Rosalind, sagging in relief against his hand. He released her.

She looked out at the other guests and announced, 'And now the next word. Tremaine, you must do this one.'

He gave a deep sigh and turned to face the crowd, making a great dumb show of pouring wine from a bottle into a glass. He drank from his imaginary glass, then held it up to the light to admire it, held it out to the crowd and deliberately ran his finger along the rim.

'Wine.'

'Drink.'

'Drunkard,' shouted Harry. 'Inebriate. Wastrel.'

Rosalind put her hands on her hips. 'It is not the person you are supposed to look at, Harry. It is the thing in his hand.'

'Philanderer,' Harry supplied, ignoring her guidance.

Nick took an involuntary step towards him, before regaining his temper and pointing to the imaginary glass in his hand.

'It starts with an R,' Rosalind supplied, and gave an encouraging look to the audience.

'Rascal. Reprobate,' Harry answered. 'Rake.'

'Now, see here…' Nick threw down his imaginary glass and balled his fists.

Rosalind muttered, 'Rim,' under her hand, until a member of the audience took the hint and shouted it.

Nick stalked back to where she was sitting. 'I have had quite enough of this. I wish a resolution to these issues as much as you do. But if it means that I must stand before the entire room while your brother attacks my character for the amusement of the other guests—'

She answered, making no attempt to whisper, 'Oh, really, Tremaine. Stop protesting and play the game. After all, you did steal the man's wife.'

'He did not steal me,' Elise announced. 'I went willingly.'

Tremaine and Rosalind turned to her and whispered in unison, 'This is none of your affair.'

She held up her hands and said, 'Very well, then.' And took a step back.

'Elise is right,' Tremaine muttered back. 'The current

problems are none of my doing and all of theirs. I am an innocent bystander.'

'Innocent? Oh, that is rich, sir. The picture of you as an innocent!'

'And now I suppose we are talking of what occurred the night we met? As I remember there were two involved, and not just one. And if that event had not transpired, then today it would be Harry attempting to steal Elise away from *me*.' He stopped. Perhaps that was exactly what would have occurred. For he could much more easily imagine Harry stealing Elise than he could imagine himself exerting the effort to take her away.

'As if Harry would ever do such a thing. Look at him.' Rosalind held out a hand. 'He is the picture of innocence.'

They paused in their whispered argument to look out at Harry, who smiled and offered a wave.

'And there you go again with your twisted notions of guilt and innocence.' Nick looked at Harry again. The man appeared to be harmless, just as he always had. But, from the first, there had been a resolute glint in his eye that did not match the mild exterior.

'He is wondering what we are arguing about.' Rosalind flashed a bright, false smile in the direction of Harry, and nudged Nick until he did the same. 'So, let us go back to the game for now. We will continue this discussion when there are not so many people present.' There was something in her tone that said they would be doing just that, as soon as the guests were out of earshot.

He nodded in agreement and thrust the last clue to Elise. 'Here, take this.'

'I think it is Rosalind's turn,' Elise responded meekly.

'Take it,' Rosalind said with finality, transferring her anger to Elise. 'The last clue.' Rosalind gestured to Elise as she walked to the front of the room.

'I certainly hope so,' Nick replied, then looked at the other guests. 'But it is a two-syllable word.'

Rosalind slapped his arm. 'I said it does not matter.'

'And I beg to differ.'

'Shh.' Elise stared at them, hands on hips, as though she were viewing a pair of unruly children, and they fell to silence.

Elise mimed reaching into her pocket and removing something.

'Handkerchief?' someone supplied.

Tremaine glared into the crowd. 'And how many syllables might that be?'

Elise held the object up between her fingers, then made a great show of opening it and reaching inside.

'Bag?'

'Reticule?'

'Purse.'

She gave an approving nod, and then removed something from it and counted objects out into her hand.

'Coins.'

'Pounds.'

'Notes.'

'Money!' shouted Harry, rising from his chair. 'No surprise that this clue should come from you, Elise. For it is the only thing you care about, is it not?'

Elise's hands dropped to her sides and her eyes narrowed. 'Harry, you know that is not true.'

His chin lifted. 'And I say it is. When I offered for you, your eyes fairly lit as I told you my income. And what were we arguing about the day you left? Now that Tremaine has come into his inheritance you are no longer at my side but at his.'

There was a fascinated murmur from the crowd around them, as though they were finally getting the Christmas entertainment they had hoped for when accepting the invitation.

'You still think this is all about money, then?' Elise laughed. 'And so you *would* like to think. For it removes any blame in this from you, Harry. You, who spent all these years trying to buy my affection. If you had been less quick to give of your pocket and more willing to share of yourself, then we would not be having this argument.'

He stood up. 'I have given you everything I can, Elise.'

'And I say you have not. For Nicholas is the one who has given me love.'

'Because it cost him nothing.'

Nick took another step towards Harry. 'First I was a drunkard, then a rake. And now I'm cheap, am I?'

Rosalind pulled on his arm to draw him out of the line of fire.

Elise stepped towards her husband. 'Even though I chose another, he has given me love and faithfulness and honesty.'

'Ha!' cried Rosalind, unable to contain herself. 'If you knew—'

'Not now.' Nick pulled her back. 'It will not help, Rosalind, I swear to you.'

Elise ignored the interruption. 'But for one misstep. And that was years ago.' She turned back to him and said, as an afterthought, 'It was a mistake ever doubting you, Nicholas.'

'No, it wasn't,' whispered Rosalind.

But Elise had returned her attention to Harry. 'And an even bigger mistake to marry *you*.' She swept from the room.

Harry dropped back into his seat, shocked into silence.

Nick turned to Rosalind, gesturing wide to encompass the mess she had made of things. 'There. See what you have done with your little game? She wants nothing to do with him now he has insulted her. I must go and see if I can mend the damage you have caused.'

She reached for his arm. 'That is the last thing you should do, Tremaine. Let them work this out for themselves. For it is your meddling that is the cause of half their problems.'

He laughed and pulled away from her. 'You dare to accuse me of meddling in the affairs of others, after the games you have had us playing? You have done more than I to tinker with something you do not understand. And a fine pass it has brought us all to.'

He was following Elise out through the door, even if his mind was telling him Rosalind was right. He would be better off to wash his hands of the whole affair.

'Go, then,' Rosalind shouted. 'Follow her, if her happiness means so much. Follow her, just as you always do. I hope it brings you what you deserve.'

The words struck him in the back like blows, but his feet did not slow their pace. She was right. The last thing he should be doing was following another man's wife down the hall to offer her comfort. If she was so in need of it then it was her husband who should provide it, not some other man.

And it was not as if Harry would deny her. He had been quick enough to sense her distress when he offered for her, and it had been plain to see from the man's enraptured expression after the wedding that his offer had had nothing to do with seizing an advantageous opportunity, and everything to do with his hopeless love for Elise.

If Nick had had the sense to keep himself out of their way the couple would have been able to solve their problem on their own. But here he was, still insinuating himself into a situation he had no real desire to join.

He stopped at the open door to the library and turned to make his retreat. But it was too late. Elise had caught sight of him. She gave a watery moan of, 'Nicholas,' and held a limp hand out to him.

And, as he had always done, he sighed and went to her.

'I swear what he said is not true,' she sobbed. 'It was never about your money. Or even about his. Perhaps at first it made a difference. It was nice that an earl had offered for me. And I thought, Oh, Nicholas shall be so jealous, when I accepted. For he could give me much more than you could back then. But mostly I was afraid that no one would want me at all.'

Nick nodded and sat beside her, putting an arm around her shaking shoulders.

'But once we were married it changed. He was so good to me, and so kind. I could not help having tender feelings for him. I felt very guilty about it at first. For it seemed like a final betrayal of what we had together. And that is why I have worked so hard to see that we remained friends.'

'And I have always been your friend in return.' He gave her a small hug. 'For I did not wish you to think you had been abandoned, just because your future did not lie with me.'

'But now?' She shook her head. 'I wonder if it has all been a mistake. Does he really care about me at all?'

'I am sure he does.' But why was the ninny tarrying? If he wished to keep his wife he must come and tell her so. 'Perhaps he is not good with words.'

'He was good enough with them back in the drawing room.' He could feel her tense. 'I think he has finally given me the truth of it, just as I wanted him to. But why did it have to happen in front of all those people? He thought me a fortune-hunter, and in secret he regrets marrying me. He is wrong. But I love him enough to want him to be happy, and to have a wife he respects. And a family. And that is why I cannot go back.'

Nick held her as she composed herself, and silently damned her husband to seven types of hell. If he could not come and force some sense into his wife, then at least he might have given Nick more powerful ammunition to defend him. For after the debacle in the drawing room, her assessment of her marriage appeared to be accurate.

'He cannot mind your spending too much. Even while you are away he supports you, does he not?'

'He is obligated. And I have accepted it because I could not think of another way. But I certainly cannot take his money after what he has said.' She paused, and then drew closer. 'Whatever might happen in the future, I cannot live as a burden on Harry any longer.' She paused again. 'Nicholas, do you remember our discussion before we came to this house, and my promise to you?'

'Vaguely.' He felt a wave of disquiet.

'When I said that if you did this for me there would be no more barriers between us?'

'Yes.' *No*. At least he did not wish to remember what he was sure she must be talking about.

'I may never be free by the laws of the land, but my heart has no home.' She paused again. 'It is yours if you still want it.'

After all these years, how could he tell her that he did not? She had expectations of him, just as surely as if he had offered for her. If her husband would not have her, then it was his responsibility to take on her care. Even if they did not marry, he could offer some sort of formal arrangement that would give her security. It would make her little better than a mistress in the eyes of society, but that could not be helped. Perhaps if they left London they could leave the scandal behind as well. But wherever he lived, it would mean that he could have nothing to do with Harry Pennyngton's sister, for the sake of all concerned.

'Of course, darling,' he said, closing his eyes and accepting the inevitable.

And he felt the relief in her, for she must have suspected by now that he did not want her either. He did not have the heart to tell her she was right.

She looked up at him, obviously expecting something. 'Is this not worthy of a kiss?'

'Of course,' he said absently, and kissed her.

She was still looking at him in the same strange way. 'A real kiss, Nicholas.'

'That was not?' He tried to remember what he had done.

She was smiling sadly. 'It appeared to be. But it was an attempt to save my feelings wrapped up in a pretty package. Can you not kiss me as though you mean it?'

'Now?' There was an embarrassing squeak in his voice that undid all his efforts at urbane sophistication. Kiss her as if he meant it? Now was as good a time as any. It was long past time. For how could one tell the person that the world had decided was one's own true love that one longed for freedom to marry another?

'Yes, Nicholas.' Her lashes were trembling, and there was a hitch in her voice. 'I can never go back to Harry. It is quite impossible. But that does not mean that I must be alone for the rest of my life. On my darkest days, I feared that there was some deficiency in me that rendered me unworthy of true love. Perhaps there was some flaw in my character that had left me without heart. At such times it has been a great comfort knowing that your love remained true after all these years. I would tell myself, If my husband does not want me, then at least there will always be Nicholas.'

He closed his eyes, trying to look as if he was gratefully accepting the compliment that all but sealed his doom. Did she not recognise the difference between love and flattery when it was right before her? It was not possible that Harry was devoid of the emotion that she was so convinced *he* held for her in abundance.

She held out her arms to him and closed her eyes, looking no happier than he felt.

What had that imbecile Harry hoped to prove by behaving as he had in the drawing room just now? And why would he not swallow his pride and come and get his wife this instant? Tremaine had a good mind to find the fellow and punch him in the nose.

He stared at the woman in front of him, stalling for time. 'Perhaps it would be better to wait until we are back in London.'

She searched his expression, trying to read the meaning in it. Then she leaned forward and touched the lapel of his coat, and dropped her gaze so that he could not see her expression. 'If we are to do it at all, there is no reason to delay. I cannot wait for ever in expectation that things will change between my husband and myself. It will soon be a new year, Nicholas, time to put the past behind me. And I think things will be easier between us once we have jumped this particular hurdle.'

'Oh.' His hand shifted on her shoulder, and he could not help giving it a brotherly pat. It wasn't terribly flattering to have the act of physical love viewed as a hurdle. If she would admit the truth to herself, she would see that she wanted this even less than he did.

'Yes. I am certain of it.' But her voice didn't sound the least bit certain, and he feared there were tears at the edge of it.

'If you are sure, then,' he said, and waited for her to come to her senses.

And then she stopped talking and came into his arms, all trembling beauty. That was the way it had always been with Elise. Almost too beautiful to resist, even though she had never been right for him. Her body pressed tight to his, soft and yielding, and her face tipped up to give him easy access for his kiss. Perhaps she was correct, and giving in to lust was all it would take to clear his head of romantic nonsense. So he tried to kiss her in the way she wished to be kissed, as though it mattered, and made every effort to drum up the old passion he had felt for her so long ago.

Her response to him was just as devoid of true desire as his was to her. After a time she pulled away from him and looked up, disappointment and awareness written plainly on her face. When she spoke, her voice was annoyingly clear of emotion. 'This is not working at all as I expected.'

'No,' he answered in relief. 'It is not.'

'I suppose it is too much to hope that you are feeling more than I am on this matter?'

'I am sorry, but I am not. If there were anything, Elise, I would tell you. But do not think that I am disguising my true feelings for you to save your marriage.

I will be your friend for ever, but I do not love you in the way you desire.'

She pulled away from him, stood up. And as she walked towards the door she looked sad, but strangely relieved. 'All this time I have been so afraid that I was supposed to be with you. And now? Things are not as I expected at all.'

He nodded, following her. 'I will admit to being somewhat surprised on that point as well. When you came back, I thought perhaps… But, no. I have suspected for some time now that it was not meant to be.'

She sighed in annoyance. 'And when did you mean to share this knowledge with me? For if you meant to take advantage of the situation, Nicholas Tremaine, I swear…'

He held up his hands in surrender. 'I do not know why everyone expects the worst from me, for I am utterly blameless in this. It is not as if I sought you out.'

'You have flirted with me all these years, Nicholas.'

'You and everyone else, darling. I am incorrigible. You have told me so on many occasions. And you never for a moment took me seriously. It is only since the trouble between you and Harry that you have given me real consideration. Frankly, I found it to be rather alarming, and most out of character for you. But I thought, as your oldest and dearest friend, that if you meant to do something foolish you might as well do it with me.'

'You thought you would spare me pain by entering into a dalliance with me?'

He smiled. 'Better me than another. I never claimed to be a noble man, Elise. I am a rake, pure and simple.

But I sought to be the lesser of two evils, and I think, after a fashion, that I have succeeded. Never mind what the world thinks has occurred. We have done nothing that your husband will not forgive.'

Her face darkened. 'And what makes you think that my husband cares to forgive me?'

Damn his tongue for speaking of Harry too soon. He did not wish, at this delicate juncture, to spoil progress towards reconciliation. 'I am merely saying that should you ever wish to return to him, my conscience is still clear. I have not broken your heart. I have not even truly engaged your affections.'

'Neither has he.'

Tremaine resisted the urge to inform her that a woman whose affections were not fully engaged would not be going to such trouble to exact revenge. 'Even so, if you do not wish to settle for less than a full commitment from your husband, you need hardly settle for less than you deserve from me.'

She considered the situation. 'You think that I should choose another lover, then?'

Once again he felt himself losing control of the situation. 'That is not what I said at a—'

'Tremaine!' Harry's hand fell on his shoulder, heavy as death, and yanked him away from Elise. Then Harry pushed him back to the wall, and stared into his eyes, too close. 'I have had quite enough of your interference in the matter of our marriage. It has been difficult enough to have you sniffing about the edges, waiting for my wife to stray. I have tolerated it for Elise's sake. But if you mean to cast her off and pass her on to some other man? You are a heartless cad, sir. You are filling my wife's head with nonsense, and you are to stop it this instant.' His face had the same amiable smile it always had, but this time the tone of his voice was menacing. 'Or I will be forced to take action.'

'Ha!' Elise's response was a shrill laugh. 'You will take action, now, will you? After all this time?'

Nick could feel the fists of the man holding him begin to tense on the lapels of his jacket. 'Elise,' he said in warning. 'Do not goad the man.'

Elise ignored him, as it had always been her nature to do. 'I have been gone for months, Harry. And I have been with Nicholas all that time.'

'But not any more,' Nick announced, hoping that it would end the matter.

She smiled with pure malice at her husband. 'I suppose you can imagine what has occurred?'

Judging by the look on Harry's face as he stared at Nick, he was doing just that.

Nick gave him an ineffectual pat on the arm. 'It does no good to let one's imagination run free and create scenarios where none has existed. She's all yours, old man, and always has been.'

'I am not,' Elise insisted. 'I am not some possession of yours, Harry. And if I wish to take one lover, or a dozen, there is no way you can stop me.'

'Oh, really?' Harry was angry enough to strike someone, and since he would never raise his hand to a lady, no matter how vexing she might be, Nick closed his eyes and waited for the punch. Then, just as suddenly as Harry had grabbed him, he pulled him off balance and pushed him out into the hall, slamming the door after him.

Nick hit the wall opposite the door and bounced off it, landing on the floor with a thump. He leaned his back against the wall in relief, and waited for his head to clear. The situation was solved at last. Judging by the look on Harry's face as the door had closed, Elise would be given no more opportunities to roam. And even if she did, Nick would be risking life and limb should *he* involve himself in the situation. In any case, she had admitted that he was not the true object of her affections. If she could not manage to solve the problems in her marriage she would not come back to him again, hoping to regain the past.

Which meant he was free.

What a strange thought. For he had been free all these years, hadn't he? There was no wife to tie him down. Since his break from Elise he had sampled all the pleasures available to an unattached man in the city. He had indulged whims to the point of boredom, and was more than ready to give them up and settle down. But there had been something holding him back from seeking an end to his solitude.

In the background there had always been Elise—unattainable and yet his constant companion. For even when she had married he had grown used to the idea that he was in some way still responsible for her happiness. He had feared that while she might tolerate his mistresses and small infatuations, and laugh at his penchant for opera dancers and actresses, any serious attachment of his to another would break her heart.

But if she was returning to her husband, this time it would be in soul as well as body. He stared at the closed door in front of him, then rose to his feet, surprised at the lightness of his heart. He would always be her friend. But it was as if some bond had snapped, a tie that had held him so long it had felt more like security than restriction. As though he had been staring at a brick wall so intently he no longer knew if he was outside or inside of it.

And now there was nothing to prevent him from doing what he suspected he had wished to do from the very first.

Chapter Sixteeen

Rosalind stopped to retie a bow on the Christmas tree, only to be rewarded by a shower of needles on the rug beneath. After Harry's embarrassing outburst, and the disappearance, one by one, of the key players in the domestic drama, the audience had escaped to the dining room for luncheon and gossip.

She was in no mood to hear the scene reworked by curious strangers, so had remained behind with the pretence of refreshing the decorations. She kicked the needles into a small pile at the base of the tree, only to see more fall onto the cleared spot of carpeting. The silly pine had no right to die on her so quickly. How was she to keep the candles lit even for one more night with the tree in this condition? Well, they could carve 'Happy New Year' on her tombstone if they were burned in their beds because of the decorations.

Not that she was likely to remain here much longer. If things had progressed as she thought, Harry had finally come to his senses and she would be back in her own bed in Shropshire long before Candlemas. And Tremaine was still full of excuses, and no closer to offering for her than he had been all those long years ago.

She walked to the drawing room door and stretched and strained until she had pulled down the mistletoe ball. Without thinking, she began to shred the leaves in her hands. What had possessed her to hang the things all through the house, so she could not get a moment's reprieve from them? Damn all mistletoe, anyway. She was likely to see everyone else in the house put it to good use, but gain nothing by it herself.

She could hear steps in the hall, clicking on the marble at the far end. Tremaine, she thought, for there was the distinctive tap of his fine leather boots. But he was coming indecorously fast. What had started out at a measured pace on the marble was growing faster with each step. She ducked her head out into the hallway to see if she had guessed correctly.

At the sight of her, he sped up. And when he reached the rug that began at the entry hall, it was at a dead run.

She looked both ways, searching for the cause of the disturbance. 'What is it? Is something amiss? Do I need—?'

In a moment he was upon her, pushing her back into the room, closing the door and yanking the destroyed plant from her hand. Then he pinned her against the doorframe, his hand twisted in her hair, the mistletoe crushing beneath it, and his lips came down to hers with surprising force.

It was just as wonderful as she remembered it from the first time they'd kissed: the smell of him, the feel of his hands, the warmth of his body near to hers. She opened her mouth, as he had taught her then, to find the taste of his tongue against hers was deliciously the same.

If she was not careful, the end result would be the same as well. He would kiss her, and then he would leave. So, no matter how much she was enjoying it, she gathered her will and pulled away from him, trying to appear shocked. 'Tremaine, what the devil are you doing?' she managed, before he overpowered her weak resistance and stopped her speech with another kiss.

Actually, there was no question of what he was doing. He was driving her mad, just as he had when she was young and foolish. She could feel her pulse racing to keep up with her heart, and felt the kiss from her mouth to the tips of her toes, and every place in between. It did not matter any more than it had the first time that this was wrong. She wanted it anyway.

He pulled away far enough to speak. 'What I am doing, darling, is settling once and for all the location of the mistletoe. You have been standing under it for days, a continual source of temptation. I feel I have done an admirable job of ignoring the fact. But no longer.'

She struggled in his grasp, shocked to find that his other hand had settled tight around her waist, holding her to him in a way that was much more intimate than the brief meeting in their past. The situation was getting quickly out of hand. 'I did not think it mattered to you.'

'And I find I can think of nothing else.' When he

realised that he was frightening her, he relaxed for a moment, smoothed her hair with his hand and looked into her eyes. There was a softness in his expression, a tenderness that she had not seen since the day they had first met. Then he smiled, and was just as wicked as he ever was. He kissed her again, into her open mouth, before she could remember to stop him, thrusting with his tongue, harder and harder, until she gave up all pretence of resistance and ran her hands through his hair and over his body, shocking herself with the need to touch and be touched.

'I suppose,' she said breathlessly when he paused again, 'that when someone catches us here you will insist that this is all my doing, just as you did before.' She regained some small measure of composure and pushed at his hands, trying to free herself from his grip. But as she struggled against him she suspected that, despite the trouble it would cause, total surrender was utterly superior to freedom.

'On the contrary. This time, if you wish, you may claim yourself the innocent victim of my animal lust.' And he kissed her again, dominating her easily, to prove that any attempt to escape him was quite futile.

'Really?' She smiled, delighted, and stopped fighting. His head dipped to nuzzle her neck. 'I have never been an innocent victim of anything before.'

He laughed against her skin. 'I thought not. I expect once we are married you shall prove even more difficult to handle than Elise would have been.'

Married? She did her best to frown at him, for it

would not do to appear too eager after all the time she had waited for this. 'I expect you are right. If, that is, I decide to marry you. You have not offered as yet, nor have I accepted.'

'I have owed you a proposal for over five years. I assumed your answer would be yes.'

'Never assume,' she said, a little breathlessly. 'I would rather die an old maid than spend another Christmas as I've spent this one—as someone's dutiful wife, cooking geese and tending to the ivy.'

He reached out and took her fingers, bringing them to his lips, drawing them into his mouth to suck upon the tips until she gasped. 'If you marry me, your hands will never touch another Yule Log.' He held them out, admiring the fingers and kissing each one in turn. 'But they would look very attractive wrapped around the reins of a curricle in Hyde Park.'

Her eyes sparkled. 'You would let me drive?'

He smiled back. 'We must see if you have the nerve for it. And you would have to be very good to me, of course. But if you indulge my every whim, how can I deny you yours? We will discuss that later.' He tucked a sprig of mistletoe into his pocket and kissed her again, until she was quite breathless.

'Later?' She caught at his hand as it reached to touch her breast. 'You are being quite wicked enough now, Tremaine.'

'Not hardly,' he answered back, then kissed her once more until she let him caress her. 'You have led a most sheltered life, Miss Morley. And you are utterly unprepared to deal with a reprobate such as myself. But I will be only too happy to educate you in the ways of the world. For instance, I'm sure you will agree that this is much more shocking than a few kisses under the mistletoe.' And his hand slipped beneath the neckline of her gown.

His fingers found her nipple and began to draw slow circles about it. He was right. Judging by the way it was making her feel, it was much worse than kissing. 'You mustn't,' she whispered, and then arched her back to give him better access. 'If someone finds us…'

He pinched her. 'Then I shall be forced to marry you immediately.' He sighed. 'Which is just what I mean to do in any case. I cannot wait another moment. I must have you, darling. And I cannot very well remain under this roof and do what I wish to do with you. I have just left off trying to seduce Harry's wife, and now I mean to ruin his sister? I must show some respect for the poor man. It is Christmas, after all. He deserves to be rid of me. And absconding with his hostess in the middle of a house party is a fitting gift, considering what kind of host he has been to me.' Then he smiled. 'But I have not given you a gift either, have I?' And his other hand slipped beneath her skirts.

'Tremaine, whatever are you doing?'

'You will know soon enough, love.' And she felt his hand caress the bare skin of her leg above her stocking. 'Now, speak. Will you have me?'

She had wanted nothing more for as long as she could remember. But she was afraid he would stop trying to persuade her if she gave in too easily. Was it the knowledge that he was touching her so intimately, or the touch itself that was so compelling? She smoothed down her skirt, to hide what his hand was doing, and tried to appear uninterested. 'I doubt my father will approve of you.'

'Then we shall not tell him until it is too late to matter.'

His fingers travelled up, until they could go no further, and then gave a gentle caress that caused her to gasp in shock. She decided it was definitely the touch that was affecting her, for he had increased the speed of his stroking and was driving her mad with it. His fingers played in a gentle rhythm against her body, reaching places that she had never thought to touch, and creating a jumble of new sensations that made it much easier to feel than to think.

She could barely hear him as he said, 'Now that the roads are clear, it's Gretna for us, my love. And then to bed.'

'I have never…never…never been to Scotland,' she gasped, and grabbed his shoulders for support, trying and failing to hold on to common sense as the feelings built in her.

'Then it will be a day of firsts for you.'

He held her in place against the wall, one hand tightening upon her breast and the other teasing between her legs. She was not sure what was happening, but she knew at any moment that she would have no choice but to say yes, most emphatically, to anything he might ask.

So she closed her eyes and leaned her head back against the wall. With her last strength she whispered,

'Show me Pompeii, Tremaine, and I am yours for ever.'
And then she gave herself over to him, and dissolved in
pleasure at his touch, accepting his proposal repeatedly
and with surprising enthusiasm.

He laughed and kissed her throat. 'Tomorrow, if you
ask for it, I will give you the world. But tonight,
Vesuvius is nothing compared to what you shall have.'

Chapter Seventeen

Elise had heard Nicholas's body strike the wall with some considerable force. It had surprised her, for although she knew Harry was strong enough, he was not usually given to displays of brute strength. But now, as he turned back to face her, she began to wonder if she had ever known him at all.

It was not yet noon, his clothing was a mess, and he smelled of brandy. His face had not seen a razor that morning, and a slight stubble emphasised the squared set of his jaw. Everything about him seemed larger, more intimidating than she remembered, and he was advancing on her in a way that might have seemed threatening if she hadn't known that it was only Harry Pennyngton. But then he reached her, and before she quite knew what was happening he had taken her in his arms and crushed her body to his in a kiss she could almost describe as ruthless.

'Harry, whatever are you doing?'

'What I should have done months ago,' he said through gritted teeth. 'We are going to settle what is between us once and for all.'

'I thought it was settled,' she said.

'For you, perhaps. Since dear old Harry has allowed you to do whatever you want, in the vain hope that you will grow tired of wandering and come home. But I am done with patience.'

'If you think that I am so easy to control as all that, you had best think again, Harry.' She squirmed in his arms, expecting him to release her, but instead he held her tighter, until she gasped with pleasure.

'Easy to control?' He released her then, and she swayed against him. 'You are more trouble than any two wives. I am sure that the sultans of Arabia do not have the challenges in dealing with an entire harem that I have with you.'

'If I am so much trouble, you had best divorce me and save yourself the bother.' She started towards the door.

But he was past her in a flash, and pushed her back into the library ahead of him. Then he stepped in after her and slammed the door. 'On the contrary, my dear. I have no intention of letting you go. Especially if you mean to throw Tremaine aside and take another lover.'

She stopped and stared at him. 'Whatever difference should it make to you, who I choose to be unfaithful with?'

'I have always known, should you choose to leave me, that it would be for Tremaine. For you have wondered from the first if your decision in marrying me was a wise one. But now that you have had a chance to compare us, I hope that I appear more favourably in your mind.'

'Harry,' she groaned, 'that is the most cold-blooded thing I have ever heard. If you are willing to stand aside and allow me a lover for purposes of comparison, then it proves you don't love me in the slightest.'

'Not a lover, Elise. Only Tremaine. He has been as regular a feature in our marriage as a dog, lying beside the fireplace. Lord knows, I have often had to kick the blighter out of the way to regain your attentions. But it is my good fortune that he has as much initiative as an old dog as well.'

'I beg your pardon?' she said indignantly. 'Nicholas Tremaine is a notorious rake, with a very passionate nature.'

Harry scoffed. 'And no threat at all to our marriage. If he were half the man you claimed he'd never have let me take you away. Failing that, he'd have hounded you day and night, until you could no longer resist the temptation and allowed him into your bed. Instead, I have borne his half-hearted flirtation with you in good humour, knowing that it would lead to nothing. That in the end you went to him, and not the other way round, should tell you everything you need to know about his grand passion for you.'

The words hit close to home, and she felt like a fool for not noticing earlier. But at least Harry did not seem jealous any more. And then, as though unable to resist, she taunted him again. 'If what you say is true, and he does not have a burning desire for me, then I am sure there is someone who does.'

Harry's eyes narrowed. 'Oh, Elise, I have no doubt of it. But if you think you will be allowed to seek any further than this room for such a man you are sorely mistaken.'

He was finally angry enough to show her the truth that she wanted to see, and his words sent desire pulsing to the centre of her being. She pushed him again. 'Seek in this room a man with sufficient passion to hold my attention? If you had sufficient passion, Harry, I would not be looking elsewhere.'

If she had hoped for a reaction there was none apparent. His smile was the same vaguely placid one that he often wore. But there was a strange light in his eyes that had not been there when last she'd looked.

'Very well, then. If you wish a demonstration of the depth of my feelings…'

Before she realised what he had done, he'd locked the door behind her, torn the key from the hole and pitched it into the fireplace.

She stared into the embers, and she thought she could see the metal as it heated to glowing. 'Harry, what the devil are you doing?'

'Making it impossible for you to leave the room before we have finished our discussion. I imagine the fire shall be almost out by the time I am finished with you, and then you will be able to retrieve the key and open the door.' He said it in a way that made her think discussion was the last thing on his mind, and she felt another thrill go through her—one that she had been missing for over two months.

'Now, let me describe to you how I am feeling.'

And then she felt the desire start to fade, for it seemed they were only going to have another silly argument. 'You are going to tell me *now* how you feel? After five years of nothing, you have told me more than enough of your feelings in the last few days. Must I hear more of them? For I have had quite enough.' But when she looked at him, staring into his eyes, she wondered if that was true.

'Really?'

'You have made it quite clear that I have lost your trust. And I am sorry, Harry. I know I've given you cause to doubt me. But until recently I did not think it mattered to you how I behaved. I am sorry. There—I have said it. Though we did comfortably well together, proximity has not made us into lovers. You deserve more. As do I.'

'More comfort than I have given you?' he sneered. 'My pockets are deep, Elise, but they are not bottomless.'

She slapped at his shoulder. 'I cannot make you understand, and I am tired of trying. I do not wish you to buy me a new dress, or a diamond, or even a larger residence, so that I can live in luxury without you. If you want, you can take it all back. Sell every last jewel and turn me out on the streets in my shift. I do not care a jot for any of it if I cannot have a marriage that is more than remuneration for services rendered.'

'Am I to understand that you wish a meeting of hearts, and not just an equitable living arrangement?' He smiled.

'Exactly.' She was relieved that at last he understood her. But she found it strangely disappointing that it might mean he'd let her go.

'What utter nonsense.'

'Harry, it is not nonsense at all. It is what I have longed for all my life.' She reached out a hand to push his shoulder, to move him out of her way. But he caught it easily, sliding his palm over hers, wrapping his fingers around it and squeezing tightly, rubbing the ball of his thumb slowly over the pulse-point beating on her wrist.

'But, Elise, what kind of a fool would I be to give my heart to you now, knowing that you have ignored it for so many years?'

'Me?'

'When I sought to court you, as smitten as any young buck in London, you all but ignored me. You struggled to hide your disappointment when you married me. Since that time, you have been everything a man could desire in a wife. I have had all I could want save one thing.'

She thought of the children that should be gracing their home, and felt a moment's pain.

'You have not loved me.'

She started.

'And so I have kept my distance as well. For there is nothing more pathetic than a man so lost in love that his wife leads him like an ape on a string for the amusement of the ton. But now, after you have left me, you expect me to show you the depths of my feelings and risk ridicule or indifference?'

It was as if he was throwing her own thoughts back at her, and she found she had no way to answer for them. There must be something she could say that would make it all right between them, but for the life of her she could not think of the words.

When he realised that a response would not be forthcoming, he sighed. 'Very well, then.'

She feared that she had lost him with her hesitation. And then he kissed her.

The strength of her reaction came as a shock, and she wondered how she had ever become convinced that he was taking her for granted with the casual affection he displayed. He seemed to put no effort into arousing her. But he had managed it all the same. Where Nicholas Tremaine's kisses had been skilled enough, but not particularly passionate, Harry's lacked grace in their eagerness to bring her pleasure. In the months they had spent apart he had forgotten none of what she enjoyed, and now he was using all of his accumulated knowledge against her, until she caught fire in his arms.

He was kissing her with every last ounce of desire, his tongue sliding past her teeth and his lips devouring hers. And it no longer mattered what he had said, or not said, whether he loved her, hated her, or cared neither way. She could not help it that a small moan of pleasure escaped her lips, and then a somewhat louder moan of disappointment when he pulled away from her.

His voice was low and husky when he spoke. 'Do you still doubt the state of my heart after all we have been to each other?'

He had brought her close to climax with the force of his kiss. So she gathered her breath and whispered, 'The fact that you are a skilled lover does little to tell me your true feelings.'

He allowed himself a satisfied grin. 'So I am a skilled lover, am I?'

She was near to panting with eagerness as she said, 'I am sure there are many as talented as you, who care only for the pleasure to be gained from the act of love and not the woman they share it with.'

'Really?'

'Nicholas, for instance—'

And his lips came down upon hers again, stopping her in mid-sentence. This kiss was rougher, and more demanding, and his hands held her tight to his body as he rubbed his hips against hers. He was hard and ready for her. When he felt her growing soft and weak in response, near ready to give in, he pulled away from her again.

'There will be no more talk of Tremaine, Elise. For I do not care what he thinks when alone with a woman. I can speak only for myself when I say that it is much more pleasurable when one has the love of one's partner. And if, after tonight, I have not gained yours, then there will be no point in our continuing. If you do not love me with your whole heart, then I do not want you back.'

He would not take her back? She was struck by the shock of the idea. For she had believed for so long that he did not love her, it was a surprise to think he had feared the same.

'You want my love?' she asked softly.

He buried his face in her neck, inhaling the scent of her. 'As I have wanted it from the first day we met. I still remember the first time I saw you, standing in a doorway at some party or other. I cannot remember anything else about that night but you. You wore blue satin, and it matched the colour of your eyes. I had to force my way through a crowd of suitors to gain your hand for a dance.'

'That was a long time ago,' she murmured, trying to ignore the feeling of his lips on her throat so that she could hear his words over the singing in her blood.

'Barely an instant. You are no less beautiful. You were so bright—glowing like a diamond.'

She tried to remember the last time he had spoken to her thus, with anything more than polite approval. 'I did not know you had noticed my appearance.'

He raised his head to look into her eyes. 'Every hour of every day. Just to look at you was a pleasure, and still is. But you belonged to someone else, and I thought there was no hope. Can you blame me, then, for using Tremaine's downfall to my advantage?'

She pulled away and looked at him in surprise. 'And how did you do so? For we were parted before you offered.'

For a moment the old Harry was back, hesitant, guarded, evasive. 'The anonymous note you received? Telling of his perfidy? It was from me.'

The shock of it shook her to her very core. 'You lied to me?'

'It was the truth. The girl involved was Rosalind. As much her fault as his. But he was not blameless, for it was his flirting that led her to disaster.'

'Rosalind?' And suddenly the pieces of Elise's life began to fall together. The strange behaviour of her sister-in-law, and the even stranger behaviour of Tremaine.

'I should have called the bastard out instead of keeping what he did a secret. But Morley wished the thing covered up, and rushed her back out of town. And then I saw my opportunity to hurt him, and to have you as well. I sent the note, and I would do it again in a heartbeat.' He squared his jaw in defiance. 'If you believe I won you through unfair means, then so be it. I would have done anything to part the two of you. That the man was too decent to dishonour my sister further and tell you the truth came as a great relief to me. For I realised too late that I had jeopardised her reputation further by hinting at the facts. But he was not honourable enough to marry her, and he deserved some punishment for it—not the reward of your love as well.'

'You deliberately ruined my engagement?' He had changed her life to suit his own desires, tricked her into his bed and pleasured her until she was helpless to resist. The thought should have enraged her. But the rush of emotion she felt was closer to lust than anger.

'I was mad with wanting you.' And then he added, as if it should mitigate what he had done, 'You would not have suited. Tremaine is too shallow, and would not give you the safety and security of home that you desire. You would have discovered it yourself eventually, to your own regret, if I had not intervened.' He frowned. 'But if I had known that I would never be free of the man, and that you would still be pining for him five years later, perhaps I would not have bothered.'

'I have not been pining for him,' she snapped. 'I have made every effort to be a good wife to you, just as you deserved.'

He snorted. 'I got what I deserved, all right. A woman beautiful, passionate, and in mourning for the man she had given up. But willing to do her duty to the husband she never wanted. I am not sorry for what I did to get you. I would do it again to have even a day with you in my arms, though your heart was divided. But, believe me, I paid the price.' He looked at her again, his eyes strange and sad. 'For I will always wonder what it would have been like had you loved me first.'

As he spoke, it sounded as though something was over. Which was strange, because perhaps nothing had ended at all.

'I cannot tell you what might have been,' she said. 'I only know that my future does not lie with Tremaine, no matter the past.'

Harry looked at her with a slow, hot smile that made her insides melt.

'And what do you mean to do tomorrow?' He pulled her a little closer, and her body shocked her with remembrance.

'Tomorrow?'

'Yes, tomorrow. If you mean to leave both me and Tremaine, and find another lover, it will have to wait for morning. I have plans for you tonight.'

'Harry, it is barely noon.' Her breath came out in a

little squeak. It surprised her, for it sounded almost as if she was frightened by her mild milquetoast of a husband.

'I am well aware of the fact. For now, it is you and me and the library fire, my love. And, by God, if you go out through that door tomorrow morning, I will see to it that you remember what you have left.' Then he pushed her back to the door and kissed her so hard that she thought her lips must bruise.

'Harry,' she gasped, when he allowed her a moment to breathe.

'Indeed.' He was after the hooks on her gown, pulling until she felt them give.

'Stop it this instant. This is my best dress.'

'I will buy you another.' She heard the faint pop of seams and the rip of lace and silk as he pushed the dress down to her waist and ran his tongue along the tops of her breasts, where they peeked over her stays, before setting to work on the laces at her back.

She slapped at his hands, trying to slow his progress, for desire was rising in her again. 'At least let us go upstairs to my room.'

His hands froze, and he looked up from his work. 'If you like your bedroom so well, then I will allow you to return to it. Tomorrow. But today I mean to have you, here and now, in whatever way I care to.'

She swallowed, and felt her knees go weak as another wave hit her. She let out a shaky sigh before saying, 'Suppose someone discovers us?'

'The door is locked.' He plunged a hand beneath her skirts and stroked between her legs, and then laughed in triumph because there was no way for her to hide the evidence of her desire.

'But they might hear.'

He stroked again, and slipped a finger into her, making her moan. 'I expect they will.' And he settled his mouth over a nipple and thrust again with his hand, harder and faster, until she shuddered and groaned his name.

He raised his head to look at her, critically, but with a small smile playing about his lips. 'There. That is how I prefer you. Unable to argue with me.'

It was difficult to argue when her body was crying for more. But, since he was growing more passionate with each objection she raised, she found the strength to disagree. 'Do not think you can persuade me so easily, Harry Pennyngton. I have no intention of giving you your way in this. Unlock the door and let me go.'

'She has found her tongue again,' he murmured. 'A sharp tongue, but a pretty mouth.' And he kissed her again, biting at her lips and taking what little sense she had left. Then he scooped her legs out from under her and carried her into the room.

She kicked. 'Put me down this instant.'

He dropped her onto the chaise longue and stood over her, undoing his cravat. 'You are down. Stay where you are while I get out of these blasted clothes. And know this: if you run, I will catch you.'

As she watched him undress, her heart was pounding so that she feared she would dissolve into ecstasy before he had even touched her. 'If you do not stop this instant I shall scream.'

He was grinning now. 'I certainly hope so—eventually.' He threw his jacket down beside her and pulled his shirt over his head. 'Our guests will find it the most diverting entertainment of the year, but it will not dissuade me from what I mean to do.'

She propped herself up on her elbows and made to swing her legs onto the floor. But he blocked her, and she kicked at his knee with her slipper. 'Harry, be reasonable.'

He glanced down at her as he stripped off the last of his clothing. 'I have tried for five long years to be reasonable, Elise. And today reason fails me.' Then he knelt on the chair, with his legs straddling her, caught her hands in his and pinned them to the cushion beside her head.

She had to admit that it was difficult, under the circumstances, to maintain a level head. He was poised at the entrance of her body, and she lifted her hips to greet him as he plunged into her.

He gave a long, slow stroke that was so good it made her gasp, then leaned away to look at her, trapped beneath him. 'There—that is more like it.'

'This changes nothing,' she said, but the words came out in short pants as he thrust again.

'You are the one who wishes change, not I.' His breathing was barely laboured, but she could see a sheen of sweat glowing on his body. 'For my part, you are perfect just as you are.'

She groaned. 'You say that now. But when we are clothed you will say nothing at all.'

'How would you know what I say, since you show no desire to be at my side?' His thrusts increased their tempo, bordering on violence, and she could feel the pressure building inside her, ready to break. 'At least when I bed you I know that you are not thinking of another.'

And in truth she could think of nothing at all but him, and what he could do to her. Her body was liquid, hot and wet. Release was moments away. A few more thrusts would send her spinning over the edge. And he knew what he was doing to her, for he had five years' practice in making her respond. He slowed again and began to withdraw. She bucked her hips under him, trying to deepen the penetration.

And then he gritted his teeth in a pained smile, and said, 'Speak my name. Tell me that you want me.'

'Harry,' she whispered.

He gave a single thrust. 'Louder.'

'Harry, please.' She pushed against him, wriggling her hips.

'That's better. Now, tell me there will be no other but me. Tell me, or I swear I will withdraw and leave you unfinished.'

'You can't,' she gasped.

'I can.' And he thrust gently, just enough to keep her on edge.

It was so good that she didn't care what came tomorrow if she could have this moment. 'Not fair,' she panted.

'All's fair in love and war,' he muttered against her throat, and thrust into her again.

'Love?' He was filling her senses, and she struggled to remember if he had ever used the word to her, even in jest.

He paused again, and then rocked gently against her until she was trembling under him, dying for release. 'You are the one that wants war, not I. Now, tell me you love me. That you will be mine for always.'

He was moving slowly inside her, awaking every nerve. She struggled to reach for him, but he held her fast. She whipped her head from side to side, until she found his wrist and rubbed her cheek against it, groaning. 'I am yours, heart and mind and body. Always. Please…' And she felt her body clench at the words, and then go to pieces in spasms of rapture.

He felt it too, and laughed, then fixed his mouth on hers and smothered her screams of pleasure as he pounded into her body. He fell shaking against her, helpless with the strength of his own release.

When she could catch her breath, she whispered, 'I do love you, Harry. Truly.'

In response, he released a surprisingly shaky sigh and whispered back, 'At last. I despaired of ever hearing you admit it. I have loved you to distraction since the first moment I saw you.'

'You have?' She could not keep the wonder from her voice.

'Indeed.'

'You never said so.'

He laughed. 'I thought I had made it abundantly clear when we came together.'

'I knew you were happy with me in that way,' she whispered.

He groaned. 'Delighted. Ecstatic. Delirious.'

'But I thought perhaps a good marriage should be more.'

'A good marriage is whatever we choose it to be, my darling,' he whispered back, and kissed her again. 'And while ours happens to be a very satisfying physical relationship, I feel it *is* more than that. Do you know how I have missed you since you have been in London? The sound of your voice, the sight of you each morning at breakfast, the little things you did to bring joy to my life every single day. My only regret has been that I gained you through trickery. I was afraid that some day you might discover the truth and I would lose you. It seemed as though I was for ever on guard, lest in some impulsive moment I revealed too much. But you left me anyway. The secrecy was for naught.'

He looked worried now that he had told her. Could that have been the great mystery all along? That he had loved her past all honour, since the very first? She felt the thrill of it go through her. And then she relaxed against him for what seemed like the first time. For why did she need to be wary of losing a man who wanted her with such uncontrollable passion? She noticed the way his arm drew her tight, as it always did after they made love, as though he would never let her go. Perhaps it had always been thus and she had never noticed.

She turned her face to him and kissed his chest. 'It was very wicked of you,' she said. 'But I think I can forgive it after all this time.'

He broke into a grin, then, and hugged her again.

She blinked. 'If you can forgive me for Tremaine. I did not understand how you felt.'

He stroked her hair. 'If you have come back to me, then what does the past matter?' He looked away from her then, and said, as though it did not matter, 'Of course it made me very jealous.'

She poked him in the ribs. 'You worked very hard at hiding it until just recently. I did not think you cared a jot for how I behaved.'

'I told myself that he would take no greater liberties than he had already, even when you were free. But if I was wrong…' He paused again, and said with difficulty, 'I understand how much you long for children. But I have not been able to give them to you.' He paused and touched her belly. 'If there is any reason why you might need to return to him, or any likelihood of an occurrence that we might need to explain, then it would be best if you told me sooner and not later.'

She could feel the tenseness between his shoulder-blades as he waited for her answer. But his grip on her did not loosen. It stayed as protective and gentle as ever, even as he discussed the possibility of raising another man's bastard. She looked up at him, and for the first time she was sure, beyond a doubt, that he loved her.

'Harry,' she whispered, and hugged him back. 'You have nothing to fear. There has never been anyone but you. Nor will there be.' She frowned, and then pushed forward with her own greatest fear. 'There will be no surprises of that kind because of my time away. But what if there are to be no surprises at all? Even after I come home? We have been together for years, Harry, and nothing has happened. It has been so long.' And she waited, afraid that he would turn from her again.

He smiled, and it was sad, and then he gathered her close to him again. 'It has. But we are not too old yet, I think. And if we are not blessed then we will have to content ourselves with the future God has sent us. In any case, there is not another woman in the world I would wish at my side.'

He reached for his jacket and pulled it over them, to try to keep back the chill. It was hopeless, for the narrow tails did little to cover their bare legs, and they struggled with it, tangling together until she was laughing again. Then he reached into a pocket and withdrew the box he had offered her before.

'Look what I still have for you. Will you accept your gift from me now? You have given me what I want.' He kissed down the side of her neck. 'Let me give this to you.'

Her laughter disappeared at the sight of the box. He had made her laugh. Made her believe in him again. But here he was with another jewellery box, likely to stop talking and spoil it all. 'Must you?'

He shook his head and smiled softly. 'You do not want more jewels? I fear I do not understand women at all. I certainly do not understand you, darling, although if you open this box you will see that I am trying to do better.' He hesitated. 'But, before you do, let me assure you that the thing you read in the paper was nothing. I swear. There is no problem with money that will not fix itself, given time. Do not think that the value of this gift implies a lack of funds.'

She leaned back to examine his face, and was surprised to see the trepidation there. It did seem that he was unusually worried about her response.

'Do not be silly, Harry. It is not the value of the gift that matters to me. It never has been. As I have told you, time and time again, I do not wish any more jewellery from you. But if you mean to give me the thing, and I can no longer avoid it, then let us get it over with.' She steeled herself and reached for the box.

He was obviously rethinking the wisdom of his gift, for he pulled it away from her at the last minute. 'We will see how serious you are when you say that. For the contents of this box are really nothing at all. Nothing more than foolishness. But when I made it for you I did not think how it might appear…'

'You *made* it for me?' Surely she had not heard him correctly.

But he nodded, and coloured like an embarrassed schoolboy. 'We will go to London and get you a real gift once the guests have gone…'

'We most certainly will not,' she said, and snatched the box from his hands, popping open the lid.

Inside, lying on a bed of velvet, as though it came from the finest jeweller in London, was a tiny straw heart, threaded through with the same ribbon she had used for the Christmas ornaments.

He poked it with a finger. 'I fear I am not much good at braiding, although I have seen you do it often enough.

I worked for the better part of an afternoon, and the results are still quite sad. But I wanted to give you my heart on a string for Christmas. You have always had it, you know. But I did not truly miss it until you were gone. I am empty without you.'

She kissed him then, with an enthusiasm that took him quite by surprise. She was crushing the box between them, and further mangling his gift, not caring in the least whether it was crooked, or crude, as long as it came from her darling Harry.

He pulled away, catching his breath. 'It is all right, then?'

'It is the most perfect thing I have ever seen.' She picked up the ribbon and held it out to him. 'Put it on me—for I mean to wear it until Twelfth Night.'

He was embarrassed again. 'Not in front of the guests, surely?'

'Until you wish to take it off me again.' She gave him an inviting smile and rubbed her bare leg against his. He sighed happily in response, and took the necklace from her.

There was a knock at the door.

Which they ignored.

His hands were at the back of her neck, fumbling with the ribbon, but his lips were on her throat, warming the place where the straw was lying. She snuggled back into the wool of his jacket, squirming against him to distract him, until he had to start all over again and give her even more kisses while he re-tied the bow.

The knock came again—this time more insistent. And a polite clearing of the throat which, if it was to be heard through the heavy oak door, must have been as loud as a normal man's shout. It was followed by the butler's soft, 'Your lordship? I would not normally trouble you, sir. Under the circumstances… But this is urgent.'

Elise wondered what it could possibly be that should be deemed that important, and hoped it was nothing Rosalind had done. For one more evening the house must run itself, without her help.

Harry rolled his eyes and gave an exasperated groan. He answered, 'A moment, please.' Then he slipped out from under the jacket and covered her up again, struggling into trousers and shirt, going barefoot to the door. He tried the knob, and then remembered the key, still hot in the coals. 'Do you have your keys, Benton?' he muttered. 'You must open the door from your side. I will explain later. Or perhaps not.'

A moment later, there was a rattling of the lock, and the door opened far enough for the butler to proffer a piece of paper.

Harry took it, unfolded the thing, and read in silence for a moment before exploding with an oath. 'Damn the man. Damn him to hell. For that is where I will send him once I catch him. I cannot believe the audacity.'

'What is it, dear? Who do you mean to send to hell?' She could not help but smile when she looked at him.

'Your lover.' He glared down at her. 'I dare say you will be none too happy with him either. Tremaine has run off to Scotland. And he has taken my sister. I swear, Elise, this is outside of enough.' He slapped the note in his hand. '"Dear Harry—" And whenever have I been the least bit *dear* to the blighter? "—I wish you well in this happiest of seasons." Ha! "May it bring you a happy reunion with our beloved Elise." Our beloved? The nerve of the man… "Since my services are no longer needed, I must away. And since you no longer need Rosalind as hostess she means to join me. We travel north to Gretna Green, and then to warmer climes. Do not expect to hear from us until spring, for Rosalind craves more adventure than Shropshire can offer, and I do not wish to deny her. Merry Christmas. Your new brother, Tremaine."'

Harry shook the paper again, and then crumpled it in his fist. 'The bastard has stolen my sister.'

'Your half-sister,' Elise reminded him. 'Who, lest you have forgotten, is well of age, and should have married long before now.'

'But to Tremaine?' Harry made a face as though he was tasting something foul. 'Tremaine.' He shook his head and mouthed the name to himself again. 'Why must it be him?'

'I think that should be plain enough. They love each other.'

'Well, of course,' he spluttered. 'I have known that for years. But I thought he would at least have the decency to court her as he should, make an offer and wait for the banns to be read. Instead he has rushed my little sister over the border like some lust-crazed animal. And he has done it while she was in my care. What am I going to tell Morley? I suspect when he hears of this he will burst from apoplexy.' Harry considered for a moment. 'Which means that some good has come of it, I suppose.' He stared down at Elise. 'You are taking this surprisingly well.' And he smiled at her, in joy and relief, and forgot all about Rosalind.

Elise supposed she was. After all they had been through perhaps she *should* feel something other than joy at the prospect of Tremaine happily married to someone else. But she could not.

'It was time for Nicholas to marry as well. He is a dear man, but he can be a bit of a nuisance. Now that there is someone to watch out for him, his character will be much improved.' She leaned on her elbow and stared at her husband, the love of her life, and fingered the heart at her throat. She gave a theatrical sigh. 'While I cannot begrudge your sister her happiness, I confess that it makes me feel somewhat undesirable.'

'Never,' he breathed. 'Not while I live.'

She held out her arms to him as he walked back to her. 'Show me.'

* * * * *

Silhouette Desire kicks off 2009 with
MAN OF THE MONTH, *a yearlong program*
featuring incredible heroes by stellar authors.

When navy SEAL Hunter Cabot returns home for
some much-needed R & R, he discovers he's a
married man. There's just one problem: he's never
met his "bride."

Enjoy this sneak peek at Maureen Child's
AN OFFICER AND A MILLIONAIRE.
Available January 2009 from Silhouette Desire.

One

Hunter Cabot, Navy SEAL, had a healing bullet wound in his side, thirty days' leave and, apparently, a wife he'd never met.

On the drive into his hometown of Springville, California, he stopped for gas at Charlie Evans's service station. That's where the trouble started.

"Hunter! Man, it's good to see you! Margie didn't tell us you were coming home."

"Margie?" Hunter leaned back against the front fender of his black pickup truck and winced as his side gave a small twinge of pain. Silently then, he watched as the man he'd known since high school filled his tank.

Charlie grinned, shook his head and pumped gas. "Guess your wife was lookin' for a little 'alone' time with you, huh?"

"My—" Hunter couldn't even say the word. *Wife?* He didn't have a wife. "Look, Charlie…"

"Don't blame her, of course," his friend said with a wink as he finished up and put the gas cap back on. "You being gone all the time with the SEALs must be hard on the ol' love life."

He'd never had any complaints, Hunter thought, frowning at the man still talking a mile a minute. "What're you—"

"Bet Margie's anxious to see you. She told us all about that R and R trip you two took to Bali." Charlie's dark brown eyebrows lifted and wiggled.

"Charlie…"

"Hey, it's okay, you don't have to say a thing, man."

What the hell could he say? Hunter shook his head, paid for his gas and as he left, told himself Charlie was just losing it. Maybe the guy had been smelling gas fumes too long.

But as it turned out, it wasn't just Charlie. Stopped at a red light on Main Street, Hunter glanced out his window to smile at Mrs. Harker, his second-grade teacher who was now at least a hundred years old. In the middle of the crosswalk, the old lady stopped and shouted, "Hunter Cabot, you've got yourself a wonderful wife. I hope you appreciate her."

Scowling now, he only nodded at the old woman—the only teacher who'd ever scared the crap out of him. What the hell was going on here? Was everyone but him nuts?

His temper beginning to boil, he put up with a few more comments about his "wife" on the drive through town before finally pulling into the wide, circular drive leading to the Cabot mansion. Hunter didn't have a clue what was going on, but he planned to get to the bottom of it. Fast.

He grabbed his duffel bag, stalked into the house and paid no attention to the housekeeper, who ran at him, fluttering both hands. "Mr. Hunter!"

"Sorry, Sophie," he called out over his shoulder as he took the stairs two at a time. "Need a shower, then we'll talk."

He marched down the long, carpeted hallway to the rooms that were always kept ready for him. In his suite, Hunter tossed the duffel down and stopped dead. The shower in his bathroom was running. His *wife?*

Anger and curiosity boiled in his gut, creating a churning mass that had him moving forward without even thinking about it. He opened the bathroom door to a wall of steam and the sound of a woman singing—off-key. Margie, no doubt.

Well, if she was his wife...Hunter walked across the room, yanked the shower door open and stared in at a curvy, naked, temptingly wet woman.

She whirled to face him, slapping her arms across her naked body while she gave a short, terrified scream.

Hunter smiled. "Hi, honey. I'm home."

* * * * *

Be sure to look for
AN OFFICER AND A MILLIONAIRE
by USA TODAY *bestselling author Maureen Child.*
Available January 2009 from Silhouette Desire.

You're invited to join our Tell Harlequin Reader Panel!

By joining our new reader panel you will:

- Receive Harlequin® books—they are FREE and yours to keep with no obligation to purchase anything!
- Participate in fun online surveys
- Exchange opinions and ideas with women just like you
- Have a say in our new book ideas and help us publish the best in women's fiction

In addition, you will have a chance to win great prizes and receive special gifts! See Web site for details. Some conditions apply. Space is limited.

To join, visit us at
www.TellHarlequin.com.

REQUEST YOUR FREE BOOKS!

Harlequin® Historical
Historical Romantic Adventure!

2 FREE NOVELS PLUS 2 FREE GIFTS!

YES! Please send me 2 FREE Harlequin® Historical novels and my 2 FREE gifts (gifts are worth about $10). After receiving them, if I don't wish to receive any more books, I can return the shipping statement marked "cancel". If I don't cancel, I will receive 6 brand-new novels every month and be billed just $4.94 per book in the U.S. or $5.49 per book in Canada, plus 25¢ shipping and handling per book and applicable taxes, if any*. That's a savings of 20% off the cover price! I understand that accepting the 2 free books and gifts places me under no obligation to buy anything. I can always return a shipment and cancel at any time. Even if I never buy another book, the two free books and gifts are mine to keep forever.

246 HDN ERUM 349 HDN ERUA

Name	(PLEASE PRINT)
Address	Apt. #
City	State/Prov.	Zip/Postal Code

Signature (if under 18, a parent or guardian must sign)

Mail to the **Harlequin Reader Service:**
IN U.S.A.: P.O. Box 1867, Buffalo, NY 14240-1867
IN CANADA: P.O. Box 609, Fort Erie, Ontario L2A 5X3

Not valid to current subscribers of Harlequin Historical books.

Want to try two free books from another line?
Call 1-800-873-8635 or visit www.morefreebooks.com.

* Terms and prices subject to change without notice. N.Y. residents add applicable sales tax. Canadian residents will be charged applicable provincial taxes and GST. Offer not valid in Quebec. This offer is limited to one order per household. All orders subject to approval. Credit or debit balances in a customer's account(s) may be offset by any other outstanding balance owed by or to the customer. Please allow 4 to 6 weeks for delivery. Offer available while quantities last.

Your Privacy: Harlequin Books is committed to protecting your privacy. Our Privacy Policy is available online at www.eHarlequin.com or upon request from the Reader Service. From time to time we make our lists of customers available to reputable third parties who may have a product or service of interest to you. If you would prefer we not share your name and address, please check here. ☐

HH08R

SPECIAL EDITION™

The Bravos meet the Jones Gang
as two of Christine Rimmer's famous
Special Edition families come together
in one very special book.

THE STRANGER
AND TESSA JONES

by

CHRISTINE RIMMER

Snowed in with an amnesiac stranger during a
freak blizzard, Tessa Jones soon finds out her
guest is none other than heartbreaker Ash Bravo.
And that's when things really heat up….

Available January 2009
wherever you buy books.

COMING NEXT MONTH FROM

HARLEQUIN®
HISTORICAL

- **TEXAS RANGER, RUNAWAY HEIRESS**
  by **Carol Finch**
  (Western)
  Texas Ranger Hudson Stone can't disobey orders. He must find
  Gabrielle Price. Hud believes her to be a spoiled, self-centered
  debutante—but discovers she's more than capable of handling
  herself in adversity! Bri enflames his desires—but the wealthy,
  forbidden beauty is strictly off-limits!

- **MARRYING THE CAPTAIN**
  by **Carla Kelly**
  (Regency)
  Oliver Worthy, a captain in the Channel Fleet, is a confirmed
  bachelor—so falling in love with Eleanor Massie is about the
  last thing he intended! Eleanor loves Oliver, too, although her
  humble past troubles her. But in the turbulence of a national
  emergency, Eleanor will fight to keep her captain safe....

- **THE VISCOUNT CLAIMS HIS BRIDE**
  by **Bronwyn Scott**
  (Regency)
  For years, Valerian Inglemoore lived a double life on the war-
  torn Continent. Now he's returned, knowing exactly what he
  wants—Philippa Stratten, the woman he gave up for the sake
  of her family.... But Philippa is not the hurt, naive debutante
  he once knew and is suspicious of his intentions....

- **HIGH SEAS STOWAWAY**
  by **Amanda McCabe**
  (Renaissance)
  Meeting Balthazar Grattiano years after their first fateful
  encounter, Bianca Simonetti finds he is no longer the spoiled,
  angry young nobleman she knew. Now he has sailed the seas,
  battled pirates and is captain of his own ship. Bianca is
  shocked to find her old infatuation has deepened to an
  irresistible sexual attraction....

HHCNMBPA1208